NO SAFE PLACE

CRAIG DAWSON

trying to get his miles in, still trying to hit the numbers with push-ups, sit-ups, pull-ups. Not a tall man, not a short man, his hair cropped short, as it always had been, ever since he realised short hair couldn't be pulled. That old life was a hard one. He'd had plenty of cause to finish conversations with his fists, usually on behalf of someone, sometimes in order to walk out of a closed room, and always because it was the only way he could get paid, and possibly stay alive, in that order of importance.

Habits die hard, but it was getting easier to not to check every room for an easy exit route, or instinctively notice which cars had been following for more than a mile. Easier, but not quite over.

That life was behind him now, after that desperate midnight race out of town,, now given way to easy days, and prosaic worries – a stone splash in a mill pond, soon settling on calm waters again. Since he had moved here, he hadn't had need to ball his fist in anger once, keen to fill a new role as the quiet man at the bottom of his garden, carrying a basket around the small convenience store in the village. He liked this life. And Eleanor did as well.

"It's too cold for the garden, Tony", she called from the kitchen window.

"Don't be soft, girl. It's just a wee bit fresh". The same old routine. It'll be this for the autumn mornings, until he can start sniggering about 'cooking eggs on the paving' when there's snow on the ground.

She was kind enough to laugh. She was always kind enough to laugh. They'd had twenty years together, and he knew, all things being equal, that twenty more would be the least he could expect. The hot days of their courtship were years ago, but they had relaxed into a steady comfort, and now, finally, a settled life.

"Do you want some toast? I'm going to nip out to get that picture framed, but I can pop some in on the way out?" Eleanor called down to him from an open window in the kitchen.

"Yes, please, love" Tony said, sloshing the last of the coffee around the bottom of the mug, playing at being barista, but really just keeping his hands busy. "Actually, I fancy another brew, so I'll come in and do it meself"

"Could get used to this, Mr. Grace" she said, a familiar wry smile on her face. Wry came easy.

"It'll do for now, Mrs. Grace", he replied playfully, and with that the window closed.

Tony pulled himself up, stamped mudless feet on the mat outside the back door, and into his kitchen, with its stone walls, and butchers block table. A world away from their old flat in the city which was all angles and spotlights. This house was the sort of place they would once have laughed at, but its safe edges and worn shelves felt comfortable and different, and emblematic of how not just their surroundings had changed.

They lived away from the small village half a mile down the road, a cluster of buildings seemingly huddled together to keep warm from the North Sea chill. Tidy gardens contrasted against wild marsh which stretched out towards sand dunes, and a sea that was heard long before it was seen.

Even so, the village just down the coast was barely that. Just a shop, a pub and one or two incongruous businesses, aimed purely at those with second or third homes, and the money to pay for fake things to make their home more authentic – a "collectables" shopfront, with horsebrasses and coal scuttles painted in pastel shades; a shed converted to a gallery of sorts, filled with posters from wartime, digging for victory. Those locals who had been here long enough wore their disdain for the newer residents like medals – a sneer so much more rewarding when shared with friends. Somehow, the Graces had never been on the wrong end of those looks, or not to their faces anyway. Maybe it was because they were subtle enough to settle in to the slow routine of the village with the correct amount of perceived respect – no roar of a sports car, no expensive remodelling of their home. Maybe it was Eleanor's easy confidence with strangers, or Tony's equally easy confidence with his hands, that led to a compiled list of odd-jobs for the locals. It seemed like both of them had been part of the village far longer than they actually had. They belonged here.

The charm of the village was hypnotic – like much of north Norfolk, it could behave like a place out of time. The long list of mental checks that both Tony and Eleanor had made second nature were being delicately eroded and washed away, like those ever-changing dunes on the long beaches. Things that they swore they could never do, became "just this once" or "no harm done", and every time no consequence was felt, and something else, some other care, was broken away to sand.

A Tuesday night, three months ago, and Tony and Eleanor were sat around a too-small table in the claustrophobic snug of the Shoggy Cut pub. White-washed stone walls, plucked upholstery on decades-old chairs, and a wall of photographs of regulars alive and dead, washed from time as the sun faded the vibrancy from the colours, and the smiles.

Their choice of drinks told their own tales – a draught lager for Tony, no surprises or changes, and a curious pale ale for Eleanor, replete with punning name, her appetite for something new undimmed. There was no reason for them to be out especially, other than that they could, and the easy demands of tomorrow meant they could spare any glances to the clock above the bar.

Tony liked looking at those pictures on the wall – that this old pub could tell a thousand tales about people either side of the bar, whilst never changing, was a huge comfort. It felt safe. If this pub could be so intransigent to the world outside, then perhaps so could Tony and Eleanor. And that wouldn't be so bad at all. Each washed-out picture of some popular barfly in a jester's hat from "Bonfire Night '88" was another brick in the wall they were building between them and every single thing that they had run from.

"Before you ask, I'm going to struggle to name all of that lot. And I've been here thirty years!" Jack had noticed Tony gazing up at that wall of faces.

"Too old or too pissed, Jack?" said Tony with a smile. Jack looked like he had walked out of central casting for this role he had – rosacea on his cheeks, unkempt sideburns and a nest of hair to top it.

"Too pissed to remember how old is too old, I reckon," Jack replied, bookended with a loud laugh, which drew a quiet laugh from Tony. Tony didn't laugh too often, but he wasn't hard. He was just happy to settle to be one of the audience, happy to not be the main player. Jack, however, was quite the opposite. Never a conversation between two people, instead a performance to those on the cheap seats.

"You know a few of these, though, right, Tony? Eleanor? Help him out, will you?"

Eleanor got to her feet, with her drink, and started leading Tony through the archaeology of the pictures. Though they had been put up randomly, the only pre-requisite for a new picture to go up was whether there was space for it. Eleanor was able to trace something of a route through, hopping from familiar faces to familiar faces, surprised at how many she knew, another testament to just how many people had found this place and decided that this would do nicely for them, never needing to leave.

"Christ, Jack – what on earth are you doing here?" Eleanor was pointing at a picture of Jack, slimmer by several stone, dressed entirely in black, and suspended from the ceiling of the pub, all whilst draped in thick ropes.

"Obvious, innit? I'm a bloody great big spider. It was

Hallowe'en, I think. Or was it the harvest festival? D'you know, it might just have been a quiet bloody Sunday!" and with that, he roared with laughter again, and now, so did the rest of the pub.

Tony didn't make friends easily. Eleanor could, but Tony preferred the safety of silence – that old line about "if someone thinks you're an idiot, don't open your mouth and remove all doubt" often bubbled up, probably planted there by some misanthrope teacher when he was young. But he liked Jack. A force of nature who bought people along with him, and any airs and graces bulldozed by weapons-grade bonhomie. Tony tired of platitudes and small-talk, but Jack deployed these like a surgeon. Whether it was the latest development with the bypass road, or why that Dutch centre-half that City had just bought was no good at corners, they all became Trojan horses for Jack. Tall tales and punch-lines that would have his audience simultaneously rolling their eyes and laughing along.

"I know! I know! You pair just hold fast for two seconds," Jack said, waving his hands, before turning on his heel, and rushing into the back. A trademark curse at his height, as Jack, yet again, clanged into the bell that hung too low from the back wall by the optics, which meant that "last orders" were often called six or seven times every evening. There was loud clattering from the back room.

Tony and Eleanor shared a look, both smiling. Jack reappeared, now holding a Polaroid camera, which looked at least forty years old.

"How about we get you pair up on that wall?"

"Oh, I don't know about that, Jack. Look at me, mate. I haven't even washed my hair." Tony was trying to say no politely, but not firmly. Firmly was a slippery slope to being too firm, and Tony had done enough of that down the years.

"Oh, please, Jack, look at the state of me." Eleanor was patting herself down, reading between the lines. She knew how careful they had to be.

"Now, look here, you two. You waltz into my beautiful little pub, in my beautiful little village" – arms were waving; Jack was holding court – "and here I am, formally offering to stamp your card, and I'm getting the cold shoulder!"

There was to-and-fro. Both sides smiling, but one side not prepared to let up. Jack was not going to let this go, and now he was loudly encouraging the rest of the pub to support his position. Tony knew that this was an atmosphere of fun, but all those eyes being on him made him feel uncomfortable, in a spotlight and centre-stage. He liked it here, and he wanted the quiet life that acceptance would offer him. Saying no, wouldn't be terminal, but the discomfort of being seen to be difficult, with these people he liked, made him relent. It's such a little thing. Where's the harm?

"Okay, okay. Just get it over with."

"Tony, are you sure?" Eleanor whispered. The rules were clear. They'd agreed on them for very specific reasons.

"We should relax. This won't hurt us. It's fine. It's fine," Tony whispered back.

"Right then, you pair. Against the wall there. Put your bloody arm around her, you miserable owd sod!" The flash went off, the camera whirred, and the photo was snatched up, and demonstrably waved around. The fog cleared, the shapes coalesced, and there they were.

"And. On. The. Wall. You go!" Jack smushed putty to the back of the photo, and then the photo to the wall, on one of the last bits of clear wall amongst that kaleidoscope of faces.

"One of us! One of us!" Jack led the chant, and the cheers, and the whole pub joined in, save the tourist couple at the back of the room, wondering to each other quite what kind of place they had wandered into that night.

And just like that, the thread tugged itself free. Often, you don't know a mistake until after it is much too late to address – the flicked cigarette butt that becomes a conflagration. Tony and Eleanor sat back down in their seats, shared a warm look with each other, a smile, and then sipped their half-empty drinks.

3

Perhaps it was symbolic, but by agreeing to join the rogues gallery on the wall of the pub, Tony and Eleanor felt that they had crossed the threshold completely, taking the final step from "resident" to "accepted" in the eyes of their neighbours. The walls didn't crumble. The sky didn't crack thunder. And, with that impromptu blessing, Jack had brought them into a community they hadn't realised they were on the outside of until it had changed.

There was a trade, though. To begin with, it just seemed that they were both receiving more friendly nods and waves from people whenever they came into the village. In short order, these waves became beckons, and Tony or Eleanor would be drawn across roads or called into shops, to politely nod along to whatever gossip was burning the tops of the hedgerows that particular week. But they were surprised at how easily they relaxed into the cosy rhythms of the village. It was easy, and oddly comforting, and they didn't put up a fight. They learnt names, decoded feuds, and then, did favours. This was the cost of membership. Tony, in particular, was called upon regularly, as his practical nature was discovered, and then exploited, with any inconvenience softened by healthy provision of tea and biscuits. Fixing a windowpane, digging out an overgrown shrub, or repointing some brickwork – Tony wouldn't say no, at first not wanting to cause any upset, and before long, because he enjoyed feeling like he was part of something. A part of a community, for the first time in years.

Early September revolved around the beer festival. It had only been running for three or four years, but felt like it had always been a solemn and auspicious tradition, demanding attendance by everyone within a ten mile radius. Jack quickly leant on Tony and Eleanor, as soon as he saw that he wouldn't be refused, using typical bombastic personality to push both the Graces to do more than either one of them would have otherwise volunteered. By a distance. Jack made an art out of it – a simple "quick favour" soon became "and before you go" and before you knew it, hours had passed, and a laundry list of tasks were being set.

They were lucky, that year. The roulette nature of September weather had spun positive, with the festival weekend bathed in warm sun, and blue skies. Tony and Eleanor, after being part of a last push to get every last triangle of bunting nailed up, and a vans worth of musical equipment heaved onto the stage, had managed to sneak away to get home to shower and change before coming back into the village. It seemed like the whole village had congregated in the beer garden of the pub. It was standing room only, with a constant churn of people around the various food stalls and the long gin and ale stands, plastic glasses and paper plates soon overflowing from the metal bins dotted around the garden.

Tony and Eleanor stood at the side of the beer garden,

and surveyed the scene, looking for somewhere to sit, or someone to talk to until they could swoop in a vacated seat.

"Don't look now," said Eleanor, smiling outwardly, maintaining a façade.

"What?" said Tony, pleased with himself that he hadn't automatically turned his head.

"It's Gill. Waving. Don't make eye contact."

Gill was the wife of the local doctor, and enjoyed gossip. A lot of gossip. Tony and Eleanor had both had numerous occasions to regret not having a better excuse prepared after running into her, with Gill oblivious to every social cue, keeping them trapped in conversation for long, long minutes. She was the quintessential "harmless but" and both of them knew that if they sat with her, they had a long afternoon ahead of them.

"My two favourite people in the world," said Jack, who had sidled up behind them, draping his arms around their shoulders.

"Oh Jack, thank god," said Eleanor.

"Don't worry," said Jack. "I've seen her. Give her a quick wave, and then come and sit down with me. Top table for you two, today."

Tony and Eleanor did as they were told, waving in Gill's direction, doing their best to make it look like they had only just noticed her. Jack steered them away, making sure to mouth "just need them for a moment" in Gill's direction.

Jack's table was to the side of the stage, with prime view of whoever was performing, but not dead centre, fully exposed to the volume. Tony and Eleanor were invited to sit, with Jack sitting down opposite them. He picked up a half-drunk pint, and then indicated to a full glass on the table in front of him.

"Tony, my man, I've had this one bought for me, so save queueing, and get stuck in."

"Only if you're sure," said Tony, too polite to refuse the offer.

"I'm going to get myself one, gentlemen. I think there's at least two or three hundred gins I haven't tried yet," said Eleanor, getting to her feet, leaving her bag with Tony, once she had removed her purse from inside it.

Jack leaned forward, as Eleanor made her way through the crowd to the gin stall. "She's a good one, your wife, isn't she?"

"I'm a lucky man," said Tony. They were both looking at Eleanor, Tony gently smiling when he saw Eleanor beam at the choice of gins on offer.

"I reckon you are. Have you been together long?" Jack took a sip of his pint.

"Oh, years," said Tony. Old habits die hard, and despite everything, he was keen to keep things vague.

"Well, she's something special, alright. Not many of us get lucky like that." Jack traced a finger on the condensation of his pint as he spoke, avoiding eye contact. Tony knew the story about Jack's wife, dead too long, and didn't want his friend to crash into a maudlin moment so early into the day.

"I know, Jack. Reckon I'm luckier than most. I mean, look at me. Like a potato dipped in fur, she says."

Jack laughed. It was a good line. Tony did self-deprecation well, and Jack was kind enough to indulge him.

"I'll remember that. Grey fur, too," Jack giggled. He stopped to smile and wave at some new arrivals into the garden.

"Yeah, alright, mate. I'm riddled with insecurity as it is, so I don't need some hairy old bugger taking the piss." Tony tried to keep a straight face as he said this, but both knew the game that was being played, and neither of them could stifle their laughter for long.

Tony took a long gulp of his pint. Suddenly, he noticed loud voices from across the garden. Voices raised, angrily, rising up out of the bubbling of nearby conversations. He turned to investigate, along with most of the others sat on the tables nearby.

On the other side of the garden, between one end of the beer tent and one of the garden exits, was a group of teenagers. Three boys, around seventeen or eighteen, with one of them obviously the dominant one. He was jabbing his finger at a blonde girl, who Tony could see was on the verge of tears. The crowd had lowered their voices to eaves-drop at this drama, and the voices carried.

"Fucking bitch. If you didn't want to come with me, just fucking say it, rather than embarrass me by making a shitty excuse then turning up anyway," the boy hissed at the girl. "I'm sorry, James, I wasn't feeling great, and now I feel a bit better," the girl managed to say between sobs, wide-eyed as she noticed that they were getting attention from the crowd.

"Don't fucking lie. You've made me look a right twat." James was not calming down.

Jack made to stand up, but Tony had seen something that made him indicate to Jack to sit down.

"It's in hand," Tony said.

Jack turned to see what Tony was looking at. Across the garden, Eleanor had put down her gin, and was striding across to the argument. People melted away from in front of her, as if she was a laser beam burning through balsa walls. James hadn't seen her yet, continuing with his tirade, but the girl had. She looked at Eleanor with pleading eyes.

"Hello, love. What's your name? Is everything okay?" Eleanor had blanked the three boys, and focused completely on the girl, turning her back on them. It was as if the three boys didn't exist.

"Cassie," said the girl, not quite brave enough to look Eleanor in the eye.

"Okay, Cassie. Can I get you a drink, love?"

"Who the fuck are you?" James had found his voice, and indignant that he was being shown up in front of the village, felt obliged to use it, or risk losing face. Eleanor ignored him, and instead, put her arm around Cassie, and set her off towards the gin stall as if she was launching a paper boat on a mill pond.

Finally, Eleanor turned to face him.

"Watch this," said Tony to Jack. Jack was transfixed, mouth half-open, as if he had been turned to stone in the act of having a drink.

Eleanor turned until she was looking up at the taller boy, James, holding his gaze. She did not blink, or move, or speak.

James tried to glare down at this odd woman who had appeared in front of him. He summoned up the most intimidating stare he could muster, then felt his cheeks redden as it petered out, like a candle in the breeze, when compared to the volcano-hot focus being blasted in his direction from Eleanor. She beckoned to him, and put a hand on his shoulder to pull him close.

Neither Tony or Jack could hear what was said. It was for the boy to hear only. He looked at his shoes, defeated.

"Whatever," he said, pathetically, before sloping off, now pygmy-sized, his two cronies sniggering to each other as they followed him. He made sure not to look at Eleanor in the eye again.

Eleanor walked over to Cassie, who had reached the gin stall, but turned back to watch what was happening.

Eleanor put her arm around Cassie, and whispered something to Cassie which made her smile.

"See? All in hand," Tony said, reaching for his pint, as conversations restarted on the tables around them.

"Bloody hell. I see what you mean," said Jack, chuckling.

Eleanor had bought Cassie a drink – a huge glass brimming with fruit, tonic, and most importantly, gin. There was laughter and smiles from everyone around the stall.

"Lucky man, aren't I?" said Tony, before draining the last of his beer.

4

_____

There are other worlds existing that share the same space. Walk down any street, and look at the people walking past, and then start to wonder about who they really are. That's the veneer – underneath the commonplace are all manner of secrets, of connections, of nods and glances. The city keeps hundreds of these matrices alive on street corners, or backrooms, or boardrooms. And, in Liverpool, like so many other cities, there's a hidden world that robs people, scares people and often, kills people.

Cold Cut lived in this hidden world. No-one knew him by any other name, not anymore. Some think he was really called Graham, others thought it was Carl, and, in any case, he wasn't telling. Then there were the stories of how he got his nickname – stories of the packs of cold meat he would gnaw on at school, too cheap for anything more wholesome? Or the fairy tale – a grisly story about how he got some cab driver to reveal where he had taken one of the street whores, when she'd begged him to escape, her location dragged from his lips after half an hour together in some forgotten cellar in a lost boarded-up house, with a knife and a grin? That story was the one Cold Cut liked to tell, which probably meant it wasn't entirely true. He was one of those people, who given the choice of the truth or the legend, especially when it was *his* legend, would always choose the latter.

Five foot five, tight t-shirt with toast-rack ribs defined; the rodent face, and pursed lips. Cold, feral eyes underneath a filthy baseball cap. He was once the kid at school who stood behind the thug, urging beatings, yet unwilling to ever put himself at the front of the pack. He had his uses, and he was tolerated, often only just, and only then because he had pulled another morsel of information from the next table in the pub, or between unknowing rivals, gossiping on street corners. In short, he *survived*, just because the one lesson he had learned was the currency of information.

No-one would claim Cold Cut as an affiliate, but he knew that when certain people called him, he should always answer, and knew who he had to drop everything for. Very occasionally, when his toxic personality meant that the constant flux of his assessment by other, far-from-patient types, saw his health, or indeed, existence, tipped into real danger, he knew he just needed to lie low, or even get out of town altogether.

Cold Cut had made the mistake of crossing Jim Stark. Stark was not a movie villain made flesh. He was not cackling or gratuitous. He didn't resort to fits of rage, and explosive tantrums. He didn't strut around in immaculate suits and mirror-shine shoes. The story went that he just lived in a quiet cul-de-sac, his CityArrow cab parked on the drive at night, outside the non-descript semi-detached house he'd lived in for a decade or two. He hid in plain sight. Those that knew, those that had dug down far enough through the layers of the Liverpool underworld, knew exactly how dangerous he was, or, at least, they thought they did.

People that knew Jim Stark well enough, and there were only a few who could truly claim this, knew how he'd held his position at the centre of the Liverpool underworld for so long. He was ruthless. Second chances were only given on the rare occasion he saw an unswervable benefit – a new unshakeable loyalty, or a marker where fear meant that whoever had been given such a chance knew how important it was to be productive for the rest of what might otherwise be a very short life. He would fill unmarked graves with sweatshop efficiency. Entire families would bleed to death in front of him, and, if the situation demanded it, he would wield the knife himself. Stark knew legends became more powerful when people were so scared they could only whisper his tales, this Scouse bogeyman, with a furtive look over their shoulder.

Cold Cut had failed him. A hundred other gangsters would show their disappointment with knuckles and bats, but Cold Cut knew that Jim Stark would show it in a far more final manner. Such a simple thing, as well. And it's not like it was his fault!

It was an insurance job. A "Jewish Stocktake", Big Joe Money told him, with a heavy arm draped around Cold Cut's shoulders, and one of those squeezes that *could* be friendly, but could *also* be threatening. It wasn't the first time. One of the pubs that kicked back to Stark, paying him for the dubious privilege of being where Stark's crews could operate from, was no longer doing the trade it once was. Where was, these days? A city with a pub on every other street corner suffers more than most when people can't afford to even pretend to drink anymore. Hiding in plain sight, moving wraps of drugs under a table, becomes impossible when there is no-one else in the pub to hide with. All it has left is the value of the stock, and the insurance policy on the pub. And so, even though Jim Stark didn't own the pub, he'd made it very clear, dripped down from lieutenant to lieutenant, all the way to those he *did* own, on the street, that he was going to receive the insurance money, when it was paid. From that, he would buy the building at a knock-down price, knowing that the hit to his cashflow was well-worth it, once he had put an apartment building on that land.

Now the pub wasn't contributing, it was time for it to become part of his portfolio, hidden in a web of bureaucracy and contract law, like all the others. The owners? Oh, they wouldn't be badly treated. Not unless... They would get their money for the shell of their pub, and maybe a brown envelope with a little something for "them and the kids", that last word delivered with implied threat, so they were in no doubt that this was, in fact, a very generous offer. And had they heard about Colin McGaskill who went missing last year, and had they heard from him at all? Had anyone?

Cold Cut was the lookout. These were his streets, after all, and he knew everyone. Maybe not by name, but his business was gossip, so his very health depended on him knowing about the new family that had moved in above the corner shop, or where those kids that pulled wheelies on the supermarket car park came from. No-one looked at him twice, as he pigeon-strutted around the estates, but they knew who he talked to, and, by association, he had his own reputation.

The job was easy. Just before closing time, a car full of men would park a street over from the pub. Perhaps they would light a quick cigarette as they slowly made their way to the back door of the pub. Cold Cut would be there, leaning against a gate to the rusting children's play park, smoking his own cigarette, rolled tight in yellowed fingers, at the nexus of five streets. The perfect position to see the flash of blue light, unlikely though it was, of a police car making the pointless decision to crawl these streets after dark. He'd done look-out jobs like this before – quietly watch, and if needed, send a text to CityArrow to order a cab to "the docks". This, once received, would prompt another call, from a burner phone to a burner phone, from the cab office to the crew, adding a few deniable layers if anyone did actually take the time to investigate. It wasn't a difficult task, but, either way, you didn't say no. Not when you knew who was asking.

Planning was everything. Nothing could be missed. The crew had a precise time to arrive, and a time to enter. Cold Cut had a time to be in position, and a time to leave, hours after the blaze was to take hold, so he could hide amongst the onlookers who would empty out of their homes to watch the drama, until he reached the specified time for him to slope off, back to his flat.

And here they were. Right on time, of course. He dragged on his cigarette, the crackle of the burning tobacco in the late evening dusk of a September night. He looked at them without looking, and saw them split up on one street, and loop around to the back of the pub via two different routes. He glanced at this phone, his *actual* phone, to check the time. 10pm. Last orders at 10.30pm – last orders that no-one was going to take advantage of tonight, even if they were unlucky enough to pick tonight for a quiet pint in that pub they never went in all that often anymore. An early exit was implicit. Only one more roll-up to smoke before he had empty pockets, a small detail that *he* had overlooked, but he knew better than to leave his position.

He had time. He knew he had time. The corner shop

was just two streets over, and was open for at least another half an hour. If he went now, he had could get some more tobacco, some skins, and spend time otherwise wasted rolling one after the other. Nothing was going to happen until at least 11pm. So he went, though still careful enough not to go faster than his standard strut, to the corner shop. A queue of people, three or four, with fourpacks of beer, and tubes of crisps, and friendly, though staccato, warm words with each other. The queue was not moving slowly, but anything less than rapid was not good enough for Cold Cut.

"A fucking birthday card? At ten'o'clock at night? Christ, love." Cold Cut gripped onto some patience, but it was slipping through his fingers.

"'scuse me, love, but just wait one minute", the woman, velour-tracksuit-clad, hissed back at him. He was frustrated, fretting at his decision to leave his post, but even so, knew better than to push his luck.

"...jesus" was the best he could hiss back, and even then, under his breath. He still had time. 10.15pm. Just five minutes away. He won't have been missed.

He grabbed the skins, pointed at the tobacco, and then, counted coins onto the pile of unsold papers sat on the counter. Despite his worry, and his pounding heart, even then, he still ensured he paid *the exact amount* and no more. Some habits he wouldn't break.

He strut-walked back to the playpark, a little quicker on the way back, though as soon as he glanced at the orange and blue lights that now lit up the darkening sky, reflected in window after window in the houses around the perimeter of the square, he had to gnaw his lip to fight the temptation to break into a run. He stared at the scene with widening eyes, unmoving, until his just-lit cigarette had burnt down until his fingers felt flame, and he dropped it with a yelp.

Outside the pub, a police car was parked, lights flashing. A policeman was talking into his radio. From his position, back at the playpark, Cold Cut could see the crew's car had moved, and by just moving across ten feet or so, he could see down a side street, to see it crashed into a parked car, with two doors wide open, as whoever was inside had made their escape. What had happened? Reptile instinct fizzed into life, and he knew he needed to pull in the threads of this story so as best to make an excuse, if he found himself having to make one –if he had, then he would be in very real trouble. More than he was currently in. At least now he had the advantage of not having been caught.

Groups had congregated, as they were supposed to do, according to the plan, but far earlier than they should have done. He turned his ear to them, and find out exactly what had happened.

"...pub was full of people"

"...they were there for Davey Bell's birthday"

"...Davey, the copper, Davey?"

"...bunch of lads, big lads, came in through the back of the pub. They didn't see Davey. They hadn't clocked who he was."

"...He stuck his nose in. Them fellas didn't like that."

"...so what happened to Davey?"

"...Davey's dead, mate. They fucking killed him."

Later, a story became *the* story. The edges shifted, but the kernel of it became the truth, as every telling repeated certain facts, hammered into the ground like a mallet and a peg. Cold Cut, over the next few hours, pulled together the buzzing from street corners and from his phone, and put colour into the picture of what happened inside the pub.

The four-man crew had come in through the back room in pairs, five minutes apart. No-one knew they were coming until they walked in, but Carol Carter, the landlady, knew who they were, and why they were there even though she'd never met them before. Not until she'd walked into the kitchen-cum-store through the curtained opening behind the bar. As she scratched at the wrapper of a packet of menthol cigarettes with shaking fingers, the other two men walked in – four men and her in the backroom. Kayleigh a part-time girl, worked the bar alone.

"No lock-in tonight. Get them out in ten minutes", one of the men said to her.

Carol managed a couple of pulls on her cigarette, then folded it into the ashtray, and took a deep breath. She pushed through the curtain, and back out into the bar. She knew who was in the bar, and was nervous. This could be bad. For her, or for someone else in her pub.

She forced a smile, but her eyes gave her away. She tried to occupy herself, look busy, tidy glasses or sweep empties, and not cause any reason for those men in the backroom to come out. She glanced at the curtain across the doorway to the kitchen, hoping she could convince the ten or so souls laughing, drinking, and singing, that they needed to go, but no, nothing was wrong.

"Time to go, you lot!" – she rang "last orders" on the bell – "not a night for hanging around!"

Groans from the patrons, only half-joking. Davey Bell, three-quarters of a pint in his hand, called from across the snug room, "Oh, come on, Carol, love, it's my birthday! We've got a couple of hours left, haven't we?"

"Oh, Pet. I'm just turned in. I'm sorry. Come on now. Don't be like that. It's just been me and Kayleigh all shift, and I'm really not feeling right. Not at all." Carol was holding a dirty half-pint glass, trying to smile, look relaxed, and stop her hand from shaking. Davey had had plenty to drink, but even so, he was a good copper, and he noticed things, even without looking for them.

He got up. Cat calls and cheers from his table – surely Davey could persuade Carol to change her mind? It was his birthday, after all. This pub was no stranger to late drinks and lock-ins, and far beyond turning a blind eye, the local coppers were often found taking advantage of this themselves.

"What's up, love?" Davey was at the bar now – Kayleigh had taken the hint, and had busied herself clearing tables – she was getting paid no matter what, and so, getting away early was a bonus for her, and not a hardship.

"Nothing, love. I'm sorry. I'm just not feeling myself. Next week, I promise. I'll even put fifty quid behind the bar for you. You're a good lad. Come on, now."

But she couldn't help herself. She couldn't look at him in the eyes, flicking her glance down to the counter top, and then across to the curtained doorway. She knew as soon as she'd done it that it was too late – like sand through her fingers, she was losing control of this, and she couldn't gather it back in again.

Davey leaned in. Cat calls still from the table, but he ignored them.

"What's going on? Someone back there?"

"I...I can't. Davey, love. You need to go." Whispering now, through clenched teeth.

"I'm a copper. You know that. Let me help you. Is someone back there?"

In the backroom there was silence. Cold iron looks. Calculations were being passed to each other with shared glances, with the four men weighing up the consequences of leaving by the back door against staying and hoping that this woman, this stupid woman, could unknot the situation, so they could still walk away having completed the task they were given. Feet edged towards the door, fists clenched and closed around knife handles.

"Just go, Davey. Take them and go. Please."

Quietly, Davey reached into his pocket and pulled out his phone, and tapped out a text. Sent, he fixed Carol with a certain look, and sipped his pint. Conversation continued on the tables behind him, but at a lower volume, and with querying tones. A minute passed, another minute passed, and he sipped. Staring at Carol, Carol staring back.

Something, just something, on the edge of hearing that became the sound of sirens. Davey knew that friends of his, colleagues of his, were planning on dropping in for a swift half once the pubs had cleared. They were near, and one text message pulled them from nearby streets to help. Paperwork could be finessed, after sirens were used, but Davey knew he had to have help, something was seriously wrong.

The men in the back were working through calculations, and quickly drawing conclusions, but everything was super-charged with adrenaline and no little fear. Those hard men, the gangsters hiding in the back room, all knew Davey – even in this day and age, he was a face known around the estate, with that easy Scouse way with words, the warm humour, and the same professional requirement to learn faces and names that also served Cold Cut so well. And they knew that if Davey made it into that backroom, and checked off the rollcall of names to the faces he would have been presented with, they were all going to find their next few weeks unbearable. Maybe not from the police, but from Stark and his many, many faceless, dangerous, hard men, who, at best, would stop them earning until they were back in good graces, however long that took, or, at worst, would cut them off completely, figuratively or literally, and become yet another conclusion to the estate fairy tales that people told about Jim Stark. Cold logic says killing a copper was the worst decision to make, but fear makes a fool of logic, and being cornered and desperate turns all sensible thoughts to dust.

Davey reached for the curtain, to pull it aside. He felt that someone was back there, despite there being no discernible noise – a pricking of his thumbs, a tingle at his nape. Perhaps that was what convinced him – the complete absence of sound. In fact, the whole pub had now gone quiet. As soon as Davey had stepped behind the bar, the regulars in the pub knew this was not normal, and that whatever they were doing, or whatever they were saying couldn't possibly be as important or as interesting as what was happening on the other side of the room. Davey reached up, tense and ready, years of experience giving him the confidence to walk through into the back room and face whatever was back there. That confidence was misplaced. He knew it once he had looked down and seen the knife now sticking out of his chest.

5

An explosion of noise shattered the silence – Davey, hissing breath and blood through his teeth, fell backwards, clutching at anything, and finding the curtain, which came down, pulled from its bindings, shattering glasses as his body fell back against the bar. The back door crashed open at the same time. The four men burst out into the night before they could be identified by anyone in the pub, as they had turned for the back door before any of the patrons had thought to shift their gaze from the sight of Davey flailing backwards, arms waving like a man falling down a lift-shaft. Shock rooted the onlookers for split-seconds that felt like hours. Again, a pause, and then a crescendo of screams, and shouts, and a clatter of furniture as stools were flipped as people rushed to help, or rushed to apprehend. The pounding of footsteps as the Stark crew fled, two back to the car, and two, panicked, fled instead on foot, into the maze of terraced streets.

They made it back to the car in seconds, starting the engine easily, with no desperate fumble despite the adrenaline and the panic. A roar, automatic lights beamed on, and a screech as the car lurched away from the kerb. At that moment, the police car arrived at the front of the pub, pulling across the junction at the end of the road, blocking their escape. The Stark men knew nothing about what had been set in motion, but feared everything. Had they eased away, smoothly, they would have been clear with no consequence and no panic. Instead, they bickered, and swore to themselves, and gripped the edge of their seats until their knuckles turned white –heightened by fear of what was happening, and what was going to happen. A three point turn, and desperate shouts between them, and then tight terror causing mistakes, and the car drove straight into a parked car, and then doors sprang open, and they were on their heels and away.

This was what had happened from what Cold Cut could glean from sifting through the gossip from those who had come out to watch the show. Cold Cut had heard enough from those there, or those who had heard from those who were there. The injustice of the position he had found himself in, cut him so deeply his eyes stung – what could he have done to change those events? How could he have stopped Davey Bell from calling that car, and fucking all of this up? How could he have warned the crew that Davey was there in the first place? Could he lie? Could he just say he saw it all happen, but couldn't dare leave his post *as instructed* to change things somehow? Sure, he could. But the job had failed. And he was involved, and now he was culpable. You don't let Jim Stark down.

Cold Cut assessed a million variables, and whilst he clung to the idea that he could weave a story well enough so he could survive this, all he was left with was pessimism. He knew the steel trap he'd unwittingly fallen into years ago – the first time he had agreed to place himself in Stark's orbit

– had him now. This city, *his* city, no longer belonged to him, and he needed to get out. He needed to escape. His life wasn't worth the risk of staying and rolling the dice on Stark's whims.

The rest of the night blurred so much, Cold Cut couldn't recall the order things happened, not exactly. Every ping of a text message stopped breath. A slammed door, or a tyre screech, made his head swim. He'd left that nest of houses, and scurried back to his flat – a shithole couple of rooms, with a too-large TV, a mattress for a bed, and piles of clothes that ranged from filthy, to less filthy, to stolen and clean. A sports bag was filled, and his nest-egg of folded notes pulled out from behind the toilet cistern and stuffed into his back pocket. All essentials quickly gathered together, not least the bag of skunk he had been working his way through, his treat to himself for some perceived achievement or job well done he had manufactured for himself to make himself feel better for just existing.

Cold Cut was in his flat for maybe fifteen minutes at best. Clearing steps on the way down, three at a time, then out into the night, into his shitty hatchback car, and then away, to the only place he could think of that might offer a familiar face who might just take him in, far enough from the city that he felt he could call it safe.

6

———

Tony and Eleanor never spoke about why they'd left Liverpool. They didn't need to. It was writ large above their lives, a monstrous stormcloud that threatened to deluge, washing them away, and their house of sand that they'd built across the country. But, as time went by, the storm hadn't come, and their knotted shoulders eased, and whilst they were never completely clear of that worry, squatting in the space behind their eyes, they learned to live with it, and then, to smile again and hope again. Every day was another stride away from that Ground Zero.

But they did think of it, during quiet times, under wide Norfolk skies, where there were more quiet times than they had ever known before. Tony often found himself out in the dark, in the quiet, walking the route from the cottage, to the village, and down to the beach, organising his thoughts, from the immediate and comfortable – I need to pull the weeds from those borders – to, inevitably, once again, how had he found himself here, away from the throb of car engines, street-corner chatter and beer bottle crash.

It was ironic – these days he was still the odd-job man, making nice with the new neighbours in the village by mending fences, and repointing brickwork. Tony always looked for the practical solution, and had developed an easy confidence when presented with the sort of task that many would turn away from, into the pages of the phonebook or the online trades directory. Even being on hand to steer quizzical, concerned faces had seen him bank plenty of goodwill. His confidence in what was required calming waters, even if his diagnosis suggested an expensive reckoning to come. Being able to give insight without the suspicion of being self-serving saw Tony in good stead, and he fast became a trusted, and respected member of the community, he was "one of them".

But back then, after they had first arrived in Liverpool from down South, he also became something of an odd-job man. But the jobs were markedly different. In the circles Tony moved in, being the sort of person who could "sort things" got him on the lips of people. He was quiet, capable and trustworthy – talents of high value. Talents that had pulled him into the orbit of Jim Stark slowly, inexorably and unknowingly, until he was so far in, there was no way out. Once you knew Stark's name, you knew well enough the currency of it, and minded that knowledge with incredible care.

Tony had started small – little favours asked for, and given. Even well into his 40s, Tony attacked fitness with passion – more so, perhaps, than in his youth, as it got harder and harder to maintain. A powerful build, broad-backed and thick-necked, but not overly so. He was no meat-head, those comical triangular men, barely able to turn their heads due to knots of muscle, impressive only to the naïve. He had made himself comfortable at the gym – a bare, basic place, full of old dumbbells, and rusting frames – the meatheads noticed him, commenting with a wordless glance. Over the weeks, two particular men inched towards conversation as their sessions intersected with Tony's. Tony was not terse or uncommunicative – he was quiet, yes, but had a gentle way with his words, an easy politeness that impressed, and before long, endeared.

The two men, named Ringo and Groucho, after some weeks had built up rapport, eventually suggested Tony join them for a fry-up and coffee. Tony waived the fry-up, but the coffee was welcome, and Ringo and Groucho were not the sort of men uncomfortable with someone watching them eat, happily shovelling beans and bread into their mouths, punctuating chewing with gulps of coffee and small talk about Brazilian midfielders, A-road repairs and fuckable popstars. It became a habit. Tony always abstemious, refusing to throw away the good work in the gym as Canute-like, his six-pack faded away with age, and Ringo and Groucho the opposite, trading off their hard hour in the gym against the huge plate of carbohydrates that immediately followed it.

They were always just Ringo and Groucho, with Tony's quiet manner meaning the story of their nicknames would only be discovered by some patient accident. Groucho, in particular, kept that shiny nugget of information pressed close to his chest, from everyone. However, if the boot was on the other foot, both Ringo and Groucho were the sort of people who would ask that sort of question within five minutes of shaking hands for the first time. Tony was very much of the mindset that if people wanted to tell him these things, then they would, and he could wait. He'd listen, of course – he always listened. The gift of the unassuming is the opportunity to take it all in, as there was more space to let that happen, rather than having to fill those silences with noise, and miss nuance and insight.

"Tone, mate, we've been wondering, like." Groucho took a slurp of coffee, and then continued. Crew-cut and stubble, with dark rings around his eyes, late 30s and lean, despite the diet. "We've got a job this Friday, it's good cash-in-hand stuff, and dead easy, and just looking at you, I reckon it's right up your street."

"Honest, pal. Dead easy." Ringo leaned in, mock-conspiratorially, broad grin on his face, as ever. Much bigger than Groucho, with a pot belly, but arms like pistons, tight sleeves on one of his extensive wardrobe of Everton tees. Always smiling, but with a mischief there, perpetually picking at rough skin around his fingernails, his fingers red and raw. "It's just standing around, to be honest."

"I dunno, lads. What sort of money, and what sort of job? Nothing sketchy is it? I can't do sketchy. Not these days." Tony only half-told the truth. He was comfortable in the hinterland between the legal and the criminal, but he was cautious. Or he hoped he was.

"Door work. Guy we know has a gaming night on above this boozer in town, and, you know, it's one of those 'invite only' things." Groucho leaned in, chipped mug of coffee in one hand.

"...and the wrong people turn up thinking they were invited," Ringo piped in.

Groucho played the dramatic, and took another gulp of cooling coffee, "Nothing scary, mate. Honest."

"It's just standing around scowling. We've seen you, buddy. You're good at that." Ringo grinned, and they all laughed. Tony was self-aware enough to know he was "blessed" with one of those faces. Eleanor called it his "workface", which had some drawbacks creating good initial impressions, but also some desirable advantages. The low brow and the set look of concentration would scare charity canvassers away on the main street, or see shopping trolleys gently wheeled out of his way in cavernous supermarkets. It was just a mask for his shyness, but he would never admit that, and instead, took the benefits as he found them.

"Okay, okay. What are we talking, then?" Groucho and Ringo elbowed each other triumphantly, because, despite Tony asking, they knew, from the smile breaking on Tony's face, that the answer was yes. The details wouldn't need much finessing.

Tony liked these two. Their easy rapport was hard to deny, and he liked their company, now that they had worn down his shyness with persistence and good humour. Over the past weeks, unconsciously, the three of them had tweaked their timings to ensure that they were all in the gym at the same time. It was a routine before they were aware it had happened, and none of them minded. The café conversations, mundane and lurid, were as much part of their schedule as the workout that preceded it. He wouldn't say he trusted them per se – Tony was slow to trust, and with good reason, given some of the places he had been, and people he'd dealt with – but he wasn't suspicious of them. He knew them well enough now that he could intuit their motivation, and felt that this job was one he could do, and should do, as the cash would be welcome, and the opportunity of more work was equally so, as, from experience, the hardest part about this sort of work was not the fear of fists and threats, but fighting the boredom of a long shift with no event worth an anecdote to tell Eleanor when he got home.

And so it was. Once a month, for an envelope of folded notes, Tony with Groucho and Ringo, or Groucho *or* Ringo, would stand tall at the top of the stairs outside a heavy wood door, on the first floor of the Dockland Pilot pub. Dark wood and faded photos of old clippers and seamen, in a pub that, by rights, should have closed years ago, judging by the lack of custom, though Tony was not naïve enough to ponder long on how it was able to continue trading – pints served were not the main purpose of this place. But Tony knew not to pry. Instead, he built up the impressions he needed by osmosis. He loathed trouble. *Loathed* it. The irony of the work he found himself doing was not lost on him, but the money that could be earned had always offset his worries. Groucho and Ringo were quite the opposite, breezing along with the easy confidence of their patter, but Tony knew asking questions was dangerous – some threads stayed pulled, and could lead to, at best, ostracism, and at worst, hard words and harder wounds; he already had too many of both.

The men who entered that particular back room were not the silent, looming criminals of petrol station DVD bins, but affable, jocular sorts, usually too fat, or too thin, completely comfortable with their loud laughing and coarse jokes. Invested with the confidence that being successful, and more particularly, successful in *this* company, gives them, they had no need for Hollywood posture. Very rarely did these men arrive with hulking minders looming protectively over them – they were so sure of themselves, and their world, that they had no need for protection from their peers, at least not at this level. That would suggest cowardice or weakness. Those that did bring anybody who even resembled a looming henchman were either subjects of derision –

an easy mark – or not wanted, and that's where Tony, Ringo and Groucho were meant to come in. The men that came alone knew to keep their minders away, but on a short leash – not needing them for decoration or status when they gathered, instead keeping them as a tool in their toolshed, to be reached for when push came to hard shove, who would stomp a hole in someone with just a point of a finger, or a raise of an eyebrow, when any insult needed an answer.

The first three or four times Tony was asked to help out, the only challenge was ticking off the minutes until it was time to go home. They were long nights – busy doors around ten, as the participants turned up, and then tedium. The door to the back room rarely swung open – it was a function room, or it used to be. It had a full bar, a toilet, and those inside had no concerns about keeping to smoking legislation.

Tony's watch said ten-thirty. Small talk was underway – whittling away at the slow minutes with bullshit and bad jokes.

"You know those Yank TV shows?" Ringo spoke up, breaking the quiet.

Groucho rolled his eyes, "Here we go."

"Mmm?" said Tony, with exaggerated weariness, indulging him nonetheless.

"So I've been wondering, right. You know when the guy walks into the bar, and he's proper fucked off about something?"

"Go on," said Tony, as Groucho grunted tiredly at Ringo's patter.

"So, the guy, right, he asks for whiskey, and he gets a glass, and then he says 'leave the bottle', you know, cos he's proper fucked off, and he's going to sit there and get wasted all on his own, like."

"Yeah, okay...and?" said Groucho, joining in being the shortest way to get to an ending.

"So, they never open a new bottle, right? They just hand over the one that they've got started, don't they?"

Groucho and Tony nodded.

"So, how does the barman work out how much to charge the guy? It's just guessing, isn't it?" Ringo leant back, reaching into his pocket for his pocket knife, never far from his hand, and almost always for nothing more sinister than digging at his fingernails, whittling off the rough skin around his fingers, leaving red raw skin, and the odd spot of blood. A bad habit, which he was too old to shake.

Silence.

Tony and Groucho shared a look and a grin, as Ringo leaned back eyes twinkling – he knows his role well, clowning, killing time, and these little conversational curveballs were far from unusual for him.

"...maybe they just charge him the full amount? Or maybe...mayyybe...they just take a chance that the guy is going to be so fucked up at the end of that bottle, they can charge what they want," Groucho said. Groucho had never heard a question that didn't deserve at least some kind of answer, no matter how preposterous.

"Doesn't seem fair, does it? And then the guy, who can walk just fine, by the way, will just throw three notes down and leave. Does my head in. Details, innit? Who can walk away after all that?" Ringo said, leaning back against the wall, his sermon over.

Snorts and sniggers broke out from all of them, not loud, as the people behind that door were paying, and you don't get told to be quiet more than once and expect to be on that door again next time. Pick, pick, pick at the fingers again.

"Thirty seconds closer to home time. Thanks Ringo, old son," Tony said, smirking. "Godsend, youth."

Now grins all round from the three men, which settled back to quiet with the diversion seemingly reaching a conclusion. Ringo reset the cogs in his head, and started searching for the next non-sequiter.

"Don't do that," Groucho broke the silence.

"What?" Ringo said, knowing full well.

"Your fingers. Pick, pick, pick."

"Just got a dead bit then it's done." Pick, pick, pick. Slicing tiny slivers of skin from around his nails with that razor-sharp knife.

"There's always 'just' another dead bit. It makes my teeth itch."

Tony enjoyed the tennis match of this. These two, like squabbling brothers or a thirty-year vaudeville act – old, repeated routines, flashes of irritation, but obvious affection.

"Fuck!" Ringo winced, caught hold of himself, and starting sucking on a finger-tip.

Groucho sniggered then waggled a scolding finger point, emphasised with a mugging expression on his face. Ringo rolled his eyes like a chastened teenager. Point taken. For now. Conversation reset, they returned to silence before another handbrake turn into a different topic.

The door at the bottom of the stairs opened, and a man poked his head through, turning to look up the stairs at the three men. He had a big toothy smile, on a jowly face, with receding, blond hair, slicked back, as if the product used was as much for keeping everything in place as it was for anything approaching style.

"Alright, there, Lads?" he called up. The grin was emphasised with a thumbs up, too. Who was this guy? Lost?

"There's a game on tonight, I gather? Up there is it?" He gestured up the stairs, a chain bracelet jangling on his wrist.

"That's right, mate. Pretty sure we've got everyone we're expecting though," said Tony, his easy, friendly manner not disguising the implicit firmness. He'd worked many doors in his time, and had long since learned that the mouth may smile, but as long as the eyes didn't, you ended up with a good deal less trouble, for everyone.

"Oh, that's okay. I'm one of those "just turn up" fellas. They won't mind, I promise." The man was at the bottom of the stairs now, hand on the banister rail. He was a large man, with a larger belly, trying hard to look successful but not hard enough to avoid looking cheap. The men who had arrived earlier in the night, walking past Tony, Groucho and Ringo into the back room, all adhered to a different dress code. Black shirts, sharp suits, and shined brogues. The rings they wore were heavy and expensive, and the cars parked outside were immaculate, fast and loud. Those men were known. Their cars did not need a slipped tenner to any passing youths so that they could "protect" them by them not putting the windows through themselves – that they would even think of parking a car like *that* in a road like *this* told its own story. This guy looked like someone who ran a wholesaler, or a bookie, or the owner of a cab firm.

"I'm sorry, pal, but we've been told. We've got who we've got, and no more." Tony scratched his nose. He held the man's stare without blinking. A few hairs pricked up on Tony's neck as a flush of indignation, however slight, washed over him. This fat man, this sweating, tubby nothing, did not turn his gaze away. He held Tony's gaze, unblinking. The smile, and light tone, like Tony's, remained, but there was an undercurrent. For both of them. Ringo inched across the space at the top of the stairs,

subtle enough to not be perceived as rude, or confronta-
tional, but not subtle enough that the message would be
missed.

"Come on, now, pal. You've been told. Let's just try again
another night, maybe, eh?" Ringo was turning the dial up a
notch. He needed this gig, and he was damn sure that this
golf club refugee wasn't going to piss on his shoes.

Palms up from the man. Eyebrows raised. Still the smile,
but still holding the stare.

"Maybe just pop your head around the door, eh? Just
double-check?"

"Look, mate. If you were meant to be in there, you'd *be in
there*, right?" Ringo said, harder this time. He'd just inched
ahead of Tony, and was now the one leading this failing
negotiation. The man though, was still staring at Tony, as if
he felt Tony was the man he needed to persuade. Tony was
uncomfortable – this was odd – and that uneasy feeling was
compounded by the quick sideways look at Groucho, who
had inched *backwards*, with mouth dropped open slightly,
and a look on his face that Tony had seen hundreds of times
before, but never from a man like Groucho. He looked
scared.

"Ringo, lad. That's enough now, eh?", said Groucho,
straightening himself, and trying to wrestle control of this
mess. For this was becoming a mess, and maybe Groucho
was the only one who realised just how much of a mess –
back to something manageable, where all parties could keep
face, and the embers that perhaps only he knew were
smouldering wouldn't catch. He put his hand on Ringo's
shoulder. He could feel it was tense – Tony knew that Ringo,
quick with his mouth, had a temper which could be just as
quick, and whilst he had seen Groucho manage him nearly
all of the time, Tony got the impression that Groucho knew

that this was an occasion where he could afford no mistakes with his combustible friend.

"It's okay, lads. That's fine. You're probably right. My mistake", the man said, palms up. It was as if the man and Groucho were the only ones who knew who all the players roles were in this little drama, and this man wasn't going to spell it out to anyone. A perverse little pleasure in letting these men unwrap that little gift themselves, now he knew that one of them had started to see the corners of this picture. He went to turn, in an exaggerated fashion, to exit his stage at the bottom of the stairs, causing Groucho to jettison all pretence of a calm, professional manner, and the other two men to turn heads. This was very much out of character for Groucho, and now the implicit was becoming explicit, in short order.

"It's...it's Mr Stark, isn't it? I think Carol Carney introduced me to you, once. At her Gail's 21st?", said Groucho, fumbling the words like a bad juggler.

"Carol? Could be, could be..." Stark said. He had the conviviality dialled right up, now. Stark had finally stopped staring at Tony, continued to ignore Ringo, and now turned to fully address Groucho. "Let me think now, son..." He made a show of pondering, with a rub of the chin. Again, this larger-than-life persona, which had Tony wondering how much of it was real, and how much of it was a performance, for their benefit.

"Wait on, now. I do know you! Yes, lad. You're Mark's brother, aren't you? Lawrence, isn't it?"

The situation was charged. All the participants knew that, especially those who had seen the power of their status rush from their grasp, and down to this portly, unassuming figure at the bottom of the stairs, but even in amongst an atmosphere like that, Tony and Ringo were not so completely off-centre as to miss that little nugget, that treasure, that had been thrown to them. There was a pause. Groucho still deferentially quiet, and Tony and Ringo now smiling – smiling with a relief that a way out of this situation that they still didn't fully understand had seemingly presented itself, but also, as their brows furrowed, mental gears clicked together. Of course, it was Ringo who filled the pregnant quiet.

"So...you're *Mark's* brother? *Marx Brother.* Groucho fucking Marx!"

Tony grinned – rare in itself, especially "at work", but he couldn't help himself – Ringo was laughing, loud, and he couldn't help but be pulled along in that slipstream. The man, Stark, at the bottom of the stairs had stuffed his hands into his pockets, rocked back on his heels, and puffed his cheeks out, eyes twinkling. Groucho too, relaxed. Somehow this situation wasn't going to be the disaster he feared it might have been. He knew who Mr Stark was.

"Mr Stark, please. Come on up. Ignore my...colleague." He gently pushed Ringo aside at the top of the stairs, with Tony following his lead and stepping aside. Mr Stark started up the stairs.

"Look, lads, no problem. No problem at all. I really don't get out much these days, and it's not like I'm anything special, eh?" Such deference. Such politeness. Stand aside for the fucking boss. Stark made his way to the top of the stairs. A slight nod to Groucho, Ringo still invisible to him, and just as he reached the heavy door, to the back room, he stopped. Turned, as if he had forgotten something, until he was facing Tony.

Another pause from Stark, turning the thumbscrews on their conversation up one final notch, especially now that his status had been made abundantly clear. He reached up, with a jangle of bracelet, and patted Tony on the cheek, twice.

"Well done, son. Do as you're told. I like that."

Tony trusted Groucho enough, or more accurately, trusted Groucho's behaviour enough, that no reaction other than a smile was appropriate. This man had scared Groucho. Groucho who knew this town, and *knew* people. He had waved in some of the more notorious names in Liverpool into back rooms, over many years, with back-slaps and comfortable words, but somehow, this non-descript man, in high street clothes, had left him unsure of himself. He could unpick that puzzle later, but for now, he wasn't going to risk any fallout by an offhand, unthinking impulsive reaction. Self-control came easy to him, and had served him well before.

And with that, he opened the door, stepped into the back room, all cigar smoke and brandy smell, and closed it behind him. The three men noticed that silence had entered the back room along with the late-comer, as Jim Stark made his presence known. There was no doubt *they* knew him. That was justification enough that the three men could feel that they had all dodged a bullet, figuratively, sure, or maybe more. Those men couldn't agree on the correct pour on a glass of brandy, or who dealt cards first, but for them to unanimously welcome this man with respectful silence told a very clear tale, and Tony, Ringo and Groucho didn't need to hear it twice.

Tony didn't see Jim Stark again for months. People just didn't see him. Little off-hand whispers, and loose words from the likes of Groucho filled in some gaps for him, but barely enough to get more than a faint outline of who he was – each conversation presented a different image of this man, this phantom. Moriarty, pulling subtle threads, controlling all of the crime in Liverpool, and slowly raising the waterline of the Mersey with the disappeared and the disappointing, with every "have you seen?" or "Missing" poster ascribed to a half-nod or a raised eyebrow in some dark backroom. Or maybe the truth was as plain as their impression of the man at the bottom of the stairs that night – an elaborate prank by men who should know better, or just some chancer with more money than sense, flattered and spoilt as part of some long con, to see those pockets empty, or his taxi-cabs filled with more than just punters, as they criss-crossed the city. But Tony was always listening – his great gift – never needing to fill a silence, but always listening for those without that same self-control.

Tony was asked to do more of those little odd jobs, competence rewarded with introductions, his comfort in that *sort* of work, and his calm manner throughout, saw him become something of a man in demand, never without at least a couple of nights that ended with an envelope full of twenties stuffed in a back pocket, or inside his jacket.

Over the next few months, Tony was, perhaps unwittingly, ticking off boxes for those who asked him to do jobs. Could he be trusted? Would he break the law? Could he fight? Did he know how to avoid being noticed? All of those things, these tests, overt or otherwise, all became examples of his quiet confidence, and admirable ability. And, despite himself, and that careful way he had, he didn't notice that he was wading in from shallow waters, into a world that he knew, but didn't know, at the same time. He wasn't from Liverpool, but he knew cities. This wasn't his town, but he knew people exactly like those who put their arm around his shoulder to ask him what he was doing next weekend, and what a "quiet, little job" might actually entail. Often it was just standing on a different door, nodding at the right people, and flat-handing others. Rarely, but still more often than he would like, the flat-hand "stop" became a clenched fist. His reticence for violence still viewed as a positive by those paying for his service, in the same way that the precise, controlled beatdown also drew silent plaudits. He might not throw the first punch, but he always seemed to throw the last one. He was being noticed, and he was being groomed.

7

"**W**as that you?" Eleanor broke the silence in the bedroom, with a ruffle of duvet, and a sharp elbow in the ribs for Tony.

"Oof! Don't be daft. It was the cat," Tony replied, with the giggle of a back-row schoolboy.

"We haven't *got* a cat, you smelly bastard!" giggled Eleanor, giving up any pretence at anger.

"...Are you covering your face?" Tony was laughing himself now, as he rolled over and tried to grab the duvet from over Eleanor's face. "Are you aware of the concept of a 'Dutch oven', my darling wife?"

"...a Dutch...oh no...!" Eleanor burst out from under the covers, like a swimmer grabbing for air.

They settled back to quiet in the dark room. But they were both awake now. And, like thousands of times previously, a new game got underway, with one trying to sleep, and the other, too awake now, repeatedly sabotaging the prospect. The flat was night-quiet now, with gentle background noises able to take centre-stage, previously drowned out by the motion and noise of daytime – the hum of the roads outside, the occasional clank or pop of the central heating, the soft frequency whine of some of the electrical goods in the other room – but singing their own song that just eased Tony towards sleep...almost...

"Tone, I need you to pick a birthday card for your mum"

Tony managed a grunt. An affirmative grunt, none-theless, an acknowledgement, but clearly a non-verbal full-stop to this conversation.

"I've bought three, so you just have to pick one, and write something inside."

Grunt.

"It's for the weekend, so don't hang about. Okay, love?"

He tried again with a grunt, softer this time, hoping the hint was going to be taken. She knew what she was doing. Perhaps she hadn't deliberately waited until Tony was just on the edge of sleep, but more likely, she was extracting a surgical revenge. If Tony could see her face in the dark, he would've expected to see a smile play across her lips, and a perverse twinkle in her eyes.

The quiet returned. Again, Eleanor let Tony drift, letting him ease away as if afloat, with her feeding the rope between her hands until he just got to the limits, before she again, yanked him back to shore.

"Are you working tomorrow night?"

He gamely stuck to his previously unsuccessful tactic of non-verbal communication. No dice.

"Is that a yes?"

"Yes, love" he sighed. "Just some arms-crossed work, I think". This was Tony's shorthand for those long nights where he had to rely on his stern expression, and his build, to dissuade those who might be minded to cause trouble, or more likely, just stumble into somewhere where they really shouldn't be. It was as much for their benefit as for those who would be dividing wages into the envelopes that he would be due to get at the end of the night.

"You've been doing a lot of that lately."

"I know. It's just easy numbers. The money is pretty good too."

"It's easy?" Eleanor rolled over to face Tony, her head on the pillow now close to him, her arm across his chest, with him on his back, still persisting with closed-eyes.

"I don't think I've had to *do* much of anything on any of these door jobs yet." The "do" was doing a lot of work in that sentence. Eleanor understood the implication of it. Tony was not in the habit of keeping things from her, certainly not intentionally, so she knew exactly what kind of things might be expected of him – if literal push came to literal shove – and was completely at peace with it. Tony was a good man, she had long since reasoned, but occasionally, he had to do things other people might describe as, maybe not "bad", but perhaps euphemistically "difficult". Or pick any other word that might politely massage the true meaning – a firm hand, or belt and collar gripped, and forced exit.

"You could do without any grief. Not much chance of trouble?" A question that already had an answer, but she wanted the conversation now.

"Come on. You know it could happen. We could do with the money, and well, they seem to think I'm doing okay. Maybe I can get in with something else before too long"

"What kind of something else? You're getting old, you know. If I see a five and a zero in the balloon sale, I'm buying them." That little stiletto knife through the ribs. Said with a smile, but the intent was clear. Slow down, old man. Don't get hurt, old man.

"It's fine, it's fine. The sort of stuff where I don't have to get my nose bent. I could get used to that."

"Like what?" she said, more seriously. They were having *a conversation*, which had crept up out of the dark like a mugger.

"God, love, I dunno! Look, you don't need me to tell you this, but they might well be as dodgy as fuck. Just trust that I know what I'm doing. I'm not too soft that I won't tell them 'no' if the time comes." He'd turned to face Eleanor now, just about keeping a tight grip on his irritability. She ran her hand over his chest, softly.

"Alright, Tone. I'm sorry. I know you know what you're doing, but we don't want to get on the wrong side of anyone. It's been nice just being quiet for a bit." Incidents from years past were being reviewed, internally, by both of them – they both knew what kind of thing they were talking about, but that familiarity meant that neither needed to break cover and give examples. "So, it's with these two lads again, is it? Groucho and Bongo?"

"Ha. Very good, very good. Yes, Groucho and *Ringo*, yeah. They're good lads. Honestly. I like them. Groucho seems to know what's what, and Ringo, well, he's a sweet lad really, but he does need an eye kept on him. God forbid if Groucho ever took a night off."

"So, the three of you tomorrow night? Where is it? Is it going to be a late one?"

"I dunno. Probably. Yeah, the three of us, and this time they want us to go down to the riverside – for some godawful reason, they've picked some factory offices or something for their game of cards."

"Just cards, you think? What do they need you three all out there for, if it's on the docks?" Eleanor knew he didn't have answers to some of these questions, but if she asked them, then she had made it abundantly clear that they deserved to be asked, and perhaps Tony, in future, would poke around just enough to answer them if only for himself. As always, she was steering him, and just making sure the right thoughts were given the right attention.

"It's probably just kudos or rep. You know what these twats are like. They'll all be there in the Audis and Bentleys, most likely. Driving cars worth thousands that no-one else is going to see."

"Take some food."

"Yeah, yeah," he smiled. "Big fucking roast dinner, I reckon."

But her breathing had changed. Another smile crept across his face – as always, she was the one who got to go to sleep on her own terms, and he was the one left staring at the ceiling. He flexed his neck, ground his shoulder blades into the mattress, and pushed his arm under the pillow, getting himself set, noticing the hums and the hisses and the clanks before he too would get to find sleep. Silence. Then one last little punctuation mark of noise to their conversation, muffled from under the duvet. Her revenge. His nostrils wrinkled, and he turned away from her, smiling to himself. The last word. Always the last word. How could someone be smug when they were fast asleep?

8

The dock road was quiet at 1am. The wan blink of roadwork lighting, reflected in the surface water from the shower a few hours earlier. A "road closed" sign, dented and peeling, that meandered up and down the road over weeks, along with the rest of the traffic furniture, leaving a road that looked no different than before they were set-up. Like islands between the forecourts and non-descript storage units, pubs punctuated the long stretch of road – some still with lights on in back rooms or flats above, some also with curtains tightly drawn front-of-house, with drinkers still inside, comfortable that this infraction was seen as far less of an issue for any passing police than whatever the clientele could be getting up to if they weren't inside. Other than the occasional constriction of flow around roadwork traffic lights – a queue of three, maybe four cars at worst – cars passed only very occasionally, a whoosh of tyre tread as they headed away from the city, and back to the suburbs, from whatever had caused them to come into town on a midweek night in the first place.

Tony walked through town – he preferred to walk, if he could. Why drive in the city, anyway? And he liked to see the shopping streets away from the daytime scrum, enjoying the disparity between day and night, seeing the city at a different rhythm. Maybe he'd have to be mindful of a staggering drunk, or a rowing couple, but this was unusual. Again, the benefit of a fixed expression and a confident walk, and headphones in his ears, volume just loud enough to hear the classical music he'd selected, but not loud enough that he couldn't hear any slurred aside or, more specifically, the tread of any footstep just behind him. He'd never had any cause to stop his stride when making a walk like this, but his habits were built on firm foundations, and he'd had plenty of cause not to doubt his instincts in other areas of his life.

Careful suited him. Don't draw attention to yourself. Perhaps it was just battling with that shyness that may well have been his reward for having two louder, older brothers. Perhaps there was some long-forgotten schoolyard trauma that just made it easier to step back into the crowd, rather than have that crowd turn and point. Little tics were second-nature to him now. At school he'd learnt to scan the pavement ahead of him for obstacles – some trash to slip in, or, worse, dog-shit to tread in, bringing laughter and shrieks, as well as everything else. To avoid hazing when using the toilet, he learnt to piss directly on the slope of the porcelain bowl, rather than directly, and loudly, into the water. Quiet, quiet, and not risk the lights being flicked off, and wet toilet paper thrown over the walls of the stall. Even now, near 50, he concentrated on projecting determination and confidence, and *don't fuck with me*, but with a steady stride, far from the cock-sure preen of the professional troublemaker.

And careful suited him in other ways – he was never

late, but also never obviously early. Happy to hang back around a street corner until just before he was due to arrive, knowing that the irritation of lateness could be equally matched by that of someone who arrives before they were wanted. This night was no different – he'd walked down Bold Street and Lord Street, from their flat at the top of town. A few bars were still open, but no-one really went out anymore – not really, not like they used to – and those that went *out*-out during the week were becoming something of an endangered species, though the thought crossed his mind that may not necessarily be a bad thing, given their usual nature. Eyes scanning ahead, but no turning of the head – look without looking – he knew exactly how long he could afford to look at someone without encouraging them for a response, acknowledgement, or often even to be noticed. Sometimes, though more than rare, he had had occasion to do something – his early life may have been all about perfecting ways to drift, if he so chose, through his world, like walking across sand without leaving footprints, but as he grew older, instances would require action – decisive action – and he'd learnt methods to manage those situations as well. A sliding scale of reaction, from the stern glare, to the confident put-down, to, at the extreme, sudden, sharp violence. As with everything, his attitude to that kind of response was a practical one – no need to strike, if a word would do, and no need for a word, if a look would do. But sometimes, nothing else *would* do. Surgical, decisive strikes, deep from muscle memory, ingrained from years of training from all manner of sources. Some formal training, hobby martial arts, a few years of boxing – a cocktail of instruction, and the hard assessment of practical use.

Then he turned away from the pedestrianised walkways, and down side streets and cut-throughs until he was alone on the dock roads, heading to the factory complex he had been told to report to at 12.45am, ready to start work, whatever that was *exactly*, at 1am.

He turned down one last street, leaving the larger A-road behind him, and even the quietness of that road was stark compared to the absolute stillness of the road he was now walking along. A grass verge, up to a featureless wooden fence along one side, and a procession of forecourts, mobile huts and security booths, dot-dashing down the other side of the road. Nonsense names, portmanteau manglings of words and surnames, and fading phone numbers on business boards, and other than the occasional kiosk light, or torch beam of a lone guard patrol, nothing to draw attention. Tony had a quick check of the watch, then the address, and then found the exact gate he was looking for. He couldn't help himself from quietly assessing what was in front of him. Tony clung to the notion that the one time he didn't take a couple of minutes to scan for alternative exits, pinch points for those who might have less than charitable intentions, would be the time that he found himself backed up against a wall with no way out. He simply was not prepared to countenance that.

He'd done more than a few of these nights amongst the list of jobs that had been asked of him since he had thrown in with Groucho and Ringo – security jobs, he called them. The venues changed frequently, ostensibly because the hosts also changed, but Tony was not naïve enough to think that there might be other reasons for these little get-togethers to not settle in one particular place. Each time he was called for, he added new shades to the picture in his mind he was drawing up, assessing the different players in the drama, and the position that they held, and then how those roles subtly, or, very occasionally, not-so-subtly changed over time. Perhaps the car they pulled in with had gotten bigger, or perhaps they were no longer being driven and were having to drive themselves. A few less rings on the fingers, or maybe a new one, heavy and gleaming, might appear. The suits might get a little sharper, or maybe, the same one was worn more than once. There was a dynamic at play here, and he knew the currency of understanding that.

The forecourt was sizeable, used to the to-and-fro of articulated lorries manoeuvring in, and loads being taken down and into warehouses, but now, other than a couple of wagons parked up at one side, the space felt empty, pregnant for the flow of trade tomorrow. On one side, adjoining, was a similar forecourt and a seemingly similarly non-descript business, advertising to the world via signage proudly stood to attention in front of the chain link fence a business only decipherable to those who would already know the business was there. On the other side, black sheep buildings and grubby sheds, where a garage had stubbornly remained despite the pinched noses from the higher-end businesses that had moved in around it, digging heels in and refusing to smarten up. At the back of those buildings, a few stacks of cars, stripped for parts, and laid out like piles of corpses, picked clean by scavengers, and left to rust, a sentinel-like small cabbed crane looming over them, as if any twitch of life was to be swatted down. A solid fence had been built to separate this yard from the newer, cleaner fore-court adjacent, but the crane cab, and a couple of the higher piles of cars still peeked out over the fence, like voyeurs. At the far side of the tarmacked square, in front of a two-storey office block slightly bigger than the new-build semi-detached houses squeezed together on the estate behind Tony, on the other side of the fence that ran along one side of the roadway, were a couple of cars. One was a typical black "prestige" car that he had grown accustomed to seeing in uniform on nights like this, and the other, incongruous next to the gleaming chrome and black finish, a CityArrow taxi. Its engine was running and lights on, grime caked around the wheel-arches, and the white and orange finish faded and chipped.

As Tony walked across the forecourt, he could see that whatever business was going on between the drivers of these two cars was concluding. The passenger window of the black car rolled down, and something was passed across to the driver in the cab. No words were exchanged, and both windows soon closed. The cab wasted no time sharing pleasantries or making conversation as it pulled away. The car passed Tony as he was walking towards the building, and he swapped a glance with the driver – a pale, tired-look-ing, thin man, with cap pulled tight onto his head, and the visor bent tightly to a D-shape. The driver had an expres-sion of irritability and lethargy on his face, scowling, tired eyes from the driver to Tony. The driver had presumably relaxed to a default after due deference was given to whoever was in the black car – Tony was an equal at best, and, at the very least, "nothing special" – after all, if this man was walking here, then he was an underling - so the driver felt comfortable enough to transmit some misan-thropy to whoever he happened to see next. Tony wasn't naïve enough to not understand how these dots were being joined-up. He'd seen enough of the taxis around when he was working to understand that they were likely used as couriers for contraband or messages, hidden in plain sight, as they criss-crossed the city.

He heard a whistle from behind him, just loud enough to have him turn his head. Groucho was half-jogging across the forecourt, having been dropped off on the main road. He wasn't late, but he was cutting it fine. Fine enough that he was relieved to see Tony, as he knew how Tony felt about punctuality. If Tony hadn't arrived yet, then Groucho couldn't possibly be in the trouble he suspected that he might have been. The politics of time-keeping on these jobs was hard for Groucho to decode – don't be too early, but always be earlier than the time you were instructed. If you were going to be late, best to just throw yourself in the Mersey, holding onto a washing machine. Despite the obvious relief – a broad smile, and an unfurrowing brow – Tony could see that Groucho was agitated.

"Tone! Alright there, lad?" Groucho said as he caught up with him. Now the concentration to, at the very least, *appear* relaxed. The stone had been thrown in the pool, and the ripples needed to subside.

"Yeah. Okay, okay. You? No Ringo tonight?"

"Well, should've been, but he's not at his house. He's going to be in deep shit over this, and I can't help him. I can't *keep* covering for him." Groucho was talking tough, but Tony knew there was an element of front in all this – Groucho indulged Ringo, and likely always would. It was just the relationship they had. Tony understood that that concept of *omerta* applied with more weight the further up through the atmospheres of this so-called criminal life. Down at the street level, handing off wraps of speed, or doling out beatings to foolishly stubborn tenants, meant there was always a certain amount of churn with the staff. The pool of available talent, down amongst the gutters, was full of failures and the lost, and by definition, these were the ones who, at best, just vanished, or at worst, were found, grey-eyed and white, stiffening under flyovers or in condemned squats, too high on their own supply. But if you had the wherewithal to ascend, then each level demanded more precision, more integrity, and more loyalty. As everywhere, the responsibility increased, but unlike the corporate labyrinth, the worst that could happen was not a walk of shame through the office clutching onto a cleared desk worth of keepsakes, but more decisive and drastic ramifications. Groucho had seen his star rise since he had introduced Tony to this world, with Ringo able to coast in their slipstream. The work had been good, reliable even. Ringo had been tolerated, even if not wholly indulged. Groucho had made Ringo abundantly aware of how to manage in this new eco-system, and Ringo, with that serious expression that nearly always melted into that shit-eating grin, was equally plain in acknowledging this. Even he couldn't be as stupid as to jeopardise what they were working towards – no grand plan, but an extra hundred here, and an extra hundred there, moving forward propelled by back-slap and quiet nod.

"We can't worry about that, mate," said Tony, knowing full well that that platitude was nothing more than a shout in a hurricane for Groucho. "We can manage this. Keep things tight, and we're golden. Honest."

"You're right. It's okay. I'll just put it out of my mind," said Groucho, almost managing to sound convincing.

"Get it together, matey. Two is more than enough for these baby-sitting jobs." Tony said. Firm words from a quiet man carried more weight. Re-assure. Re-focus. Work.

Five minutes until 1am. Perfect timing. The two men walked up to the front of the building. The window of the black car wound down again, and the driver beckoned them over. The driver looked so *expected*, as if he was in a uniform. In a way, he was – dark ruby-coloured shirt, open collar, plain, heavy jewellery, cropped hair. Tony hadn't seen him before, but it was obvious that Groucho knew him, especially by how deferential he became. No "mate" or "lad" this.

"Gentlemen. You've done this before, but indulge me. You'll stay here until the last person has left. Guests are expected from half an hour onwards, and expect a long night. There will be drinks. Associates of the guests are not to be permitted in the gaming room, which is clearly marked. Guests will be required to enter a fingerprint on this tablet in order to enter. There are no exceptions. If the tablet doesn't recognise them, refuse entry, in the most appropriate manner. I notice that there are only two of you – this is disappointing, but mostly for you, as you will not be permitted to leave your post for a shit or a piss or a smoke or anything. Do not be tempted otherwise."

Groucho and Tony shared a look at this, understanding that tonight was going to be uncomfortable for them, but Ringo hadn't completely torched their reputations.

The driver continued to give instructions.

"You will be paid off-site, at a later date. I believe you–" he gestured to Groucho " – are aware of the payment protocol. I'll leave you to get acquainted with the building. One of you is to man the front door, and the other is to man the boardroom."

The tablet was passed out and the window wound up. Tony didn't dawdle. Nothing he heard was a surprise. In a way, he respected the fastidiousness. It was a card game, by the docks, for crooks. No-one was really likely to care, and the only ones who were likely to even have a passing interest in the attendees were the police, who were either in the pocket of half of those attending, or not foolish enough to shake these particular trees. Maybe this gathering would present an opportunity for some distant rival, but, in all likelihood, who was going to challenge the men who were going to sit, and drink, and gamble, inside? But the minute complacency squats at the back of a mind, the cracks begin to show themselves, and Tony had been around people like this long enough – greedy, craven men, almost always – that a crack can become a fissure with only the slightest pressure. The vice-grip is everything, and that was something Tony could respect, and indeed, give comfort. Dealing with amateurs never worked out well, and he had the scars to prove it.

Tony felt that they had ten, maybe fifteen minutes, before they would be expected to find their positions, which he intended to use walking the perimeter of the building, then understand the layout inside. Groucho, who once would have simply found a quiet corner for "one last smoke" before duty, had found some of those same habits rubbing off on him, with him checking the inside as Tony checked the outside, and then, vice versa, so they both felt they had a good understanding of the place. It may be the same way that a child mimics an adult, marching like a soldier and saluting, but Groucho was trying, and Tony was comforted that he was at least making the effort.

The building wasn't large, with a fire exit to the rear, opening almost onto the dockside, and a second fire exit on the first floor, which led down at the back of the building on a metal fire-escape stair. The front of the building, on the ground floor, had a reception area, with a generic brushed steel table, and pleather couches, brochures fanned on the table-top. A counter was at the back of the reception area, and a coffee machine and snack vendor were pushed into one corner. Next to the counter was a door to the offices upstairs.

Upstairs was similarly generic. Open plan for the most part, with a couple of side offices, and a boardroom, separated from the main office by doors, but viewable through glass windows that stretched floor-to-ceiling. Blinds had been pulled across, and closed, but a low light behind the blinds indicated that this was the room where the guests would gather. Despite the mundane, bland setting, in an almost-laughable incongruity, three young women, exclusively East-European, were milling around, preparing food and drink, in skirts that made walking a challenge, and décolletage that was there to distract from the deadness of their eyes. A box of cigars was open, with cutter and matches and ashtrays laid out in front of it, on a separate table. Tony understood, as always, this layout was to prevent unwanted to-ing and fro-ing in and out of the boardroom by anyone other than those invited to participate in the games. If they wanted something, they got it themselves, and the conversation inside was for those select ears only.

Tony took this all in his usual stoic manner. A brief nod was all that was required for the women, and, as always, Tony took the first position – "customer contact" – on the door outside, leaving Groucho to manage inside. Surveys completed, Groucho gave Tony one solid pat on the shoulder, handed over the tablet, and they went to their positions. Groucho was chewing his bottom lip, fretting. Ringo was clearly on his mind, but Tony hoped that the monotony and deference of the night ahead would give him something to concentrate on. An inappropriate joke or remark to the women might also distract him. There was nothing to be done. Nothing that couldn't wait until they had finished.

1.20am now. Everything in place. Tony stood in the doorway of the office building, underneath the plastic canopy. Black shirted, with crisp trousers and a shine to his shoes, he knew the impression expected of him. Arms in front of him, the tablet in hand, and stern expression now locked on his face. He was a sentinel, and despite the faintly ludicrous cross-pollination of these plain surroundings and the Vegas brochure trappings upstairs, all that mattered was pleasing the right people, and getting paid.

Cars started to arrive. All black. All gleaming. Every guest driven, and not driving, with the drivers all following the same pattern as the man who had given them their instructions half an hour earlier. Tony knew who these men were, if not by name, certainly by role. These were the trusted hands, the men who were paid to be close, to be trusted, and to manage whatever whim was thrown their way. In truth, though they were more than able, they were not necessarily in their position because they were solely capable with their fists, but simply because they knew how to get not just *a* result, but the *right* result – a process of evolution in a world that saw mistakes cruelly treated, be it imprudent gossip, or inattention to detail, until only the capable held their position. These were the men who didn't handle the blade anymore – they had wiped it clean years ago, passing it down to those below them, who, nonetheless, understood that they were the ones to get their hands figuratively dirty, even if they didn't do the deed themselves, so that those who gave them the lifestyle they sought were never left in a position where their own assets were threatened, or worse, placed in any kind of peril.

But even the most careful had tells, and Tony, inscrutable as ever, was drawing up his own lists, as these men arrived. Who opened the car doors for their bosses with their left hand, and which with their right. Did he see a slight limp in one? A dead eye on another? Gauging ages, weights, gait. Who used size as intimidation, and who likely used ability in the same way? And then their bosses. It was these men, and they were all men, who displayed the variety that their underlings did not. Some tall, some short, mostly overweight. Some in immaculately tailored clothes, and others mirroring the style, but not the cut, as time and gravity were both defeating their Canute desperation, straining waistbands. Six men, six important men, too loud and too vulgar, with the usual dance of status and rivalry disguised as geniality, as they filed into the building, all pausing to apply their fingerprint to the tablet as they had done many times before.

Tony didn't flinch or change expression. Due deference given, but each guest met with a confident look, and the tablet presented to them. "Just here, Sir" was all he said, and then the affirmative nod after each positive chirp from the tablet. Most of the men barely acknowledged him, treating him as another appliance, not breaking their conversation. One of the men, a squat man, all forearms and neck hair, looked up at Tony, held his gaze just slightly longer than was polite, before grinning and pressing the tablet screen. These men and their tests! They both knew it was a demonstration of status, and that Tony had to react with due deference, but nonetheless, the game was still played. The thought of how good it would feel to truly school this little orc of a man gave Tony a moment of cold comfort. It was a long line of people who enjoyed this game of power, and his thick skin had long since hardened to it. After all, this wasn't the sort of man to worry about – empty drums make the most noise. It was the quiet ones that were *always* the most dangerous. The thinkers and the schemers.

All inside – Groucho could take over now. He'd be more comfortable with a smile, and the genuflections. They had found their roles quite easily, cleaving closely to their natural personalities. Groucho was good with people, and was easy to like, even by the sort of men currently climbing the stairs to the boardroom. Tony was happy to be forgotten, or underestimated, in position at the front doors, and let Groucho have the dubious pleasure of monkey-dancing for them. Tony would stand, quietly, unmoving, and find a trance to distract him, mentally sorting tasks and issues outstanding as the clock ticked on. Not least amongst these mental exercises was the continual stress-testing of the environment he was tasked with managing. Could the men in those cars be trusted? Was anything about their behaviour suggesting a problem he might need to be aware of? He scanned the dock road for movement. Nothing. The forecourt, away from the low hum of quiet car radios from the cars parked by the building, was similarly quiet. Cliché would suggest "too quiet" but he felt like he had the measure of this place; of this job.

An hour passed. The radios buzzed on. Faces in the cars were illuminated by the glow from their phones. Occasionally, a too-loud laugh would come from inside. He thanked Groucho, silently, for taking on that role, so he could take comfort in the quiet solitude out here. The discipline of it helped him think. Think particularly about the precariousness of the position he found himself in – he was concerned he was on a slippery slope, inching closer to situations that he neither wanted to be in, nor felt he could get away from clean. Looking impassive on a door, or being deferential to besuited idiots was a pill he could easily swallow, given the rewards, but how long until he was asked to just "look after" a package for a week, or be called to pull some ne'er-do-well down a back alley and leave him bleeding. Dirty hands take some cleaning. At what point could he comfortably say "no" to these people and not have any consequences? Had he passed that point already?

Even for someone as careful as Tony, he wondered if

he'd been pulled in by easy money and warm words. Perhaps it was time for a break after tonight. Just switch the phone off for a few days, and let them know that he wasn't solely at their beck and call.

His thinking calm was lost, too quickly, as the real world snapped back around him like a taut spring, by a car that had screeched to a halt at the gates. It was two hundred yards away from Tony, the building and the clutch of cars. Three men, all wearing caps and tracksuits, opened the car doors and leapt out, almost as one – two of them were holding baseball bats, with the third waving towards the building, before rolling his tongue in his mouth, and letting out a whistle. These new arrivals demanded attention and that was what they received. Any noise in the cars stopped. Phones were put down, windows were rolled down, or doors just slightly opened, just in case something direct was needed, without removing the option of a car pursuit, or indeed, a getaway, being removed.

Tony took a few steps forward, away from the door, so he was stood in front of the cars. Some of the cars had switched on headlights to better illuminate the forecourt, and the scene beyond, with the lights casting his shadow across the distance between him and the car, like some fearsome phantom or spectre. He was taking it all in, weighing up probabilities. Despite the shock of this, the unknowability of the motive so far, he was far from naïve, and was scanning side-to-side, along the dock road, across the forecourt, muscle memory not letting anything side-swipe him.

"Tell your man that this is one of his! He knows we don't fuck around!" said the lead man in a baseball cap, his voice a screech of too-accented Scouse which captured everyone's complete attention. Revelling in the impromptu spotlight, literal and figurative, he reached into the backseat of the hatchback car, and, with a handful of hair, pulled out a large man, pathetically hunched, arms bound behind him, eyes down but wide. Blue t-shirt under his jacket. The belly. Ringo.

Tony walked towards them, slow but determined. A couple of the drivers half-stepped out of their cars. Whatever was happening in front of them was not good – at best, their bosses would be disturbed, and taken away from this, and, at worst, would be at risk. But it had to play out in front of them. These interlopers made the gaggle of henchmen and drivers feel like they were on shifting sands, as did Tony. He needed sure footing to give him confidence, and losing it with the introduction of this new element gave him a tingle at his nape, as his mind spun with hurried assessments.

"Tony, lad. Stand back. Don't push it." Ringo said, his voice feeble.

As Tony drew closer, he could see Ringo was bleeding from a cut underneath a swollen eye.

"Fuck off, mate. Don't fucking move," the bloke holding Ringo barked. Ringo's pocket knife, was in the hand of whoever was holding him, underlining the command with a threatening jab at Tony. This character was either foolish enough to toy with suicide – given the audience he had selected for himself – or knew something that gave him the confidence he could escape this. It was the latter that was unsettling Tony. This wasn't right. It made no sense as a tactic, on any level. The world was all Dutch angles.

"Fucking hell, Tone! Back the fuck off!" Ringo was forced to a half-crouch by the hand gripping him by the hair. The knife alternated between demonstrative waves, almost orchestral conducting, and resting by Ringo's carotid artery.

Time crawled, the colour drained from the world, with only bare essential information required. How long had passed? Surely only quick minutes, but even Tony's breathing had slowed to nothing.

The leader looked beyond Tony. It was like a slow procession behind him, with the six henchmen all at different stages in this drama – a couple of them had completely stepped out of the car, one even taking a few strides towards the group. The rest had all opened their doors, some half-out of the cars. Only one played caution over posturing and still remained in the car. The first two men who had left the comfort of their expensive, black cars, now armed with baseball bats, were perpetual motion, twitchy and scowling, unsure of their roles in this performance, other than some attempt at threatening. Tony knew all of these men without knowing them. He'd dealt with people like this a million times before, and knew that behind all of their front, and their ground-teeth attitude, they would all fold, pitifully, if they ever found themselves with a wall behind them, and all exits blocked. But edgy men make bad decisions, their bosses running the risk of being embarrassed or inconvenienced in the building behind them, and there was a knife at his friend's throat.

"Yeah. Fuck off, *Tone.*" Hissed the tracksuited scally, tightening his grip on Ringo's hair. "Tell your man inside that we know who he is, and we know what he wants, and he's not. Fucking. Getting it." His knuckles whitened, and a cut appeared at the blade edge where it was held against Ringo's neck - a red wine underline beneath each word.

"...christ, man!" Ringo, between his teeth, felt the sharp edge, and his concern was near-palpable.

Tony put his hands up. There was a way out of this, but it was about finding the right key for the lock. He was still twenty yards from the men, a hundred from those behind him, and all he had, for now, were his words. The man was talking again.

"Tell your man inside. Go and tell him this is what happens. Our streets. *Our streets!*"

With that, the knife, dancing in the headlight glare, plunged down, and into Ringo's belly. Ringo gasped, a fierce tension shot through his body, and then, both too fast, and glacier slow, the dark colour of blood bloomed on Ringo's t-shirt.

Tony needed to move. The incision made the situation desperate, and tumult took over. Tony sprinted towards his friend, with three of the drivers behind him breaking into a run. The distance was too great for any retribution, though, as the three interlopers wasted no time in jumping back inside their car, engine still running, pedal down, steering cranked, and away back up the dock road they had come from. Ringo had fallen onto his side, each breath wheezing out, an accusation of failure which Tony felt acutely as he closed the distance.

"...I'm sorry. I'm sorry," was all Ringo could say as Tony finally reached him. Tony pulled up Ringo's shirt, and saw the wound, the blood, and the bubbling mess that each breath was making worse. Tony had seen wounds like this before. Indeed, he had some scars in similar places – cold comfort, but comfort nonetheless. His friend was not going to die.

There was a chaos of activity around Tony as he cradled his friend, with all present making rapid assessments on the next best step forward. Two of the drivers had broken into a sprint in a vain attempt to chase after the speeding car, with another two running back towards their cars to pursue on four wheels. Two more had switched on their engines, and were now gunning them, ready to take off in a burst of wheelspin and engine groan. But almost as soon as it began, the adrenaline of the chase was replaced by the realism of their situation – this man, bleeding, was no friend of theirs, and any concern for him was far outweighed by the vice-like obligation they had to their employers, who, as far as they knew, were all completely unaware of the drama that had just occurred. Sprints became jogs became returning walks, cars were put into neutral and then engines silenced, and the shouts and epithets gave way completely.

Within seconds, it was an inquest, with four of the six drivers standing around the wounded man, and the other two now making their way over, a brittle reassurance that there was no immediate threat to their bosses, now the car had driven off, and they had some time to get the story clear in their head before they did the unthinkable, and interrupt their employers from their games. Tony didn't know these people, and certainly wasn't prepared to let them take anything more than a passing role in the care of his friend, so felt emboldened to give instructions, sure that these men would happily defer now, given that Tony was volunteering to literally get his hands messy here – after all, who cares what happens to some foot-soldier, rungs down the ladder?

"You, get inside, and find me a towel or something," Tony said pointing at one man. "You, go and find me a water or a drink or something and you, call an ambulance."

"No ambulance. We sort this a different way," came the reply. "We can't have them here."

Tony expected that response, but had hoped for a different one nonetheless.

"Okay, okay. I need your car. He needs to get to a hospital. A fucking dead body can't be here either, right?" Hamming it up, maybe, but pressing a finger on one end of the scales weighing up options in the face gormlessly staring at him was the quickest way to move this on.

"Fine, fine." The man, a coiled spring of twitches and flexes, of muscle and scars, strode – not ran – to the car. As he walked away, Tony noticed for the first time that one of his ears had been ripped from the side of his head, leaving only a mangled mess of skin tight to the side of his head. The walk seemed like deliberate posturing - this might be a problem that needed solving, but unless the man who paid his wages was holding the whip, he wasn't going to run for anyone. Begrudging even giving the appearance that Tony was calling the shots, One Ear couldn't resist calling back to Tony. "I'll call inside. This is on you, if there's hell to pay, just so you know."

Tony's phone was soon in his hand, dug out from his pocket, and dialling, as the driver made his way to the car. The other men were lost for direction – the two nearest men had been dispatched to the building, to get the things Tony had asked for. The others had taken the chance to wander back towards the road, more to give the impression of investigation than the hope that they could actually achieve anything.

As Tony waited for the phone to connect, he turned back to Ringo. "I'm sorry, mate. I'm so sorry. Stupid. Fucking stupid."

Ringo was breathing heavy, labouring, but just the out-of-breath stress of a man who had taken too many stairs at once, rather than a gurgle of blood.

Hard to avoid sounding hackneyed in a situation like this. Tony just cooed platitudes at him, gently removing his jacket, and pressing it to the wound in Ringo's stomach. Blood was flowing, but it seemed to be slowing, Ringo's groans and moaned curses an odd kind of reassurance – the seriously hurt didn't take the time to swear or seek comfort. Tony felt his heartrate return to something approaching normal, now the immediate drama had passed, the adrenaline flushing from his limbs, taking the warmth from his fingers as it went.

"*Christ.* Okay, okay – I'm coming!" One Ear barked into his phone, and broke into a sprint, towards the building. Tony absent-mindedly wondered what was keeping the other two drivers he had sent in for help – he knew there were complimentary bottles of water on the desk in reception, so surely at least one of them should have come back by now? What was going on?

"What is it?" Tony called across the forecourt to One Ear.

Ringo sighed, a quiet whistle between his teeth.

One Ear shouted back, all pretence at posture forgotten. "Inside. Something's going on inside!"

Tony was now the one making assessment. One of the drivers, from the clutch who had moved towards the road vainly trying to make themselves look useful, seemed younger than the others, more inexperienced, and presumably, easier to manipulate. All of the drivers, with their employers in the building behind them, had all seen One Ear dash towards the building, and knew that their positions would also demand a response – a quick one – for fear of reprimand, or potentially, much worse depending on what was actually happening in the building crouched by the riverside, but Tony hoped that a firm word could possibly re-route the younger of them here.

"You! Come here."

The younger driver slowed his half-walk, half-run, and turned to see what Tony wanted. "Never mind that. Let me go and look."

The driver paused, his mouth forming the pursed lips of "But..."

Tony kept on, not giving him time to think or to challenge. Hoping that a confident tone would override any complaint.

"Sit with him. Just press this – " he nodded towards the jacket – "hard against his stomach. Do *not* let go."

There was hesitation on the face of the younger man, eyes darting to the building, and then back to Tony. He was tall, wiry even, and now, abundantly clear that there was shit spraying back from the fan, wide-eyed, with posture and poise falling away like a child's block tower collapsing on weak foundations. His head was turning from the building to Tony and back to the building. His boss was *in there* but this man, this commanding man, was *here and now*.

"Don't worry. I need to go in there. I know your boss," Tony lied. "I'll straighten it out with him, but – what's your name?"

"Max," stuttered the young man.

Tony carried on, not allowing any pause for contemplation – "this is *my* job. Just stay here for a minute and don't move him."

Ringo managed to brace himself on one elbow, leaning back, until Tony put a forceful hand on Max's shoulder, to guide him down to his knees and make him take his place looking after Ringo. There wasn't time for a debate or conversation, just action. Before Tony allowed any space for any dissent, he took off towards the building. All of those who had been left on the forecourt after the scallies had made their escape, except for Ringo and the young man, were now either in the building or soon to be.

As soon as Tony made it through the double doors, into the reception, he could hear raised voices from upstairs.

What was going on? Something was not right at all. He *hupped* the stairs three at a time and ran into chaos. The guests, and the hostesses, were all behind the glass of the boardroom, which was spiderwebbed from attempts, both from the inside and outside, to break through. The double doors to the board-room were secured with a u-shaped bicycle lock, tight around the two handles, making the door just wide enough to rattle, and perhaps fit a finger or two through, but not wide enough for anything else. One of the drivers who had gone into the building ahead of him was kicking at the glass. Others were alternately shouldering the double-doors, or smashing chairs over the door handles. Just to the right of the door, stretched out, was Groucho, eyes closed, unmoving, but, as Tony drew near, still breathing. He had been hit across the temple, at least, judging by the wound dripping blood down his cheek, and across his nose and mouth. First things first – Tony turned to assess the rest of the room, tuning out the curses and screeching from the players of this drama, as he moved towards Groucho. No-one else was here. Then he noticed that the fire exit door was open. Pieces clicked into place.

He turned Groucho onto his back, to see the extent of his injuries, before turning him onto his side, ensuring that he wouldn't choke on any blood. His breathing was strong. He was unconscious.

Wordlessly, he continued to ignore the general commotion; the pounding on doors, or the clang of metal on metal, and moved across to the fire exit, and through the door, to stand on the top of the metal stairwell which led down to the dockside outside. It was quieter out here. He scanned the area, demanding his eyes readjust to low light after the fluorescent glow of the strip lights inside the office, which were all now switched on, any concession to atmosphere long since expired. And then he heard it. Softly. So soft he had to concentrate, but he was convinced that it was there. An outboard motor, buzzing like a midge, hundreds of yards away from him, across the water. Maybe a coincidence, but almost certainly not, and once the immediate issues here had been managed, and the story came out, he was certain he knew what it would say. A heist. A *fucking* heist. On one of his jobs.

He came back inside. Still the glass held. Still the lock kept the double-doors closed. Max had now joined the group of drivers inside, all trying desperately to be the one who atoned – and atonement was most definitely uppermost in their thoughts – by freeing some of the most powerful and dangerous people in the city, taking turns to find new and inventive ways of hitting things with things.

"What are you doing here? Who is with Ringo?" Tony asked, spinning Max around by his shoulder.

"Who the fuck is Ringo?" – a pause – "oh, he was fine. I've got a fucking job to do! He told me to get in here. Said he was okay."

"*Jesus...,*" Tony hissed. He was losing control. He'd lost control. His friends were hurt. Groucho was, at least, with people, who he hoped were aware enough to keep him safe, if only for the minute or two he needed to get outside to get to Ringo.

He took the stairs in two jumps, and burst through the stairwell door, and then the reception doors. The forecourt was quiet. Tony's jacket was left on the ground, crumpled. Ringo had gone.

Tony was control. That was his constant internal mantra. Keep calm. Cold logic. No rash decisions. But hiding in the shadows was a dangerous, bubbling rage, an angry dog on a leash, pulling and scrabbling at the floor to be freed. The rage was pulling now. Building pressure. He turned on his heel, problem after problem looming up in front of him. Faces focusing in his mind's eye – Ringo, Groucho, Eleanor even – all in his orbit, and all affected by what could happen next. The rage strained on its chain a little harder. Through the double doors. Up the stairs. No hurry this time, but an electric charge across his shoulders, down his arms, clenching his fists. Through the door at the top of the stairs.

"Back," he said, firmly. Those outside the boardroom heard him, those inside intuited his meaning. All inched away from the window. His teeth were clenched. The fury was king now, all that lost adrenaline having returned, more than before. He picked up a desk, papers and folders fell to the floor, and with a grunt heaved it above his head, then, as the momentum of the weight brought the table down from the military press above his head, the legs facing outwards, he drove forwards, all legs and shoulders, and through the glass.

9

The rest of the night was a blur. Tony trying to find some surety again, but just feeling he was grabbing at smooth surfaces with oiled hands. A fight to find his equilibrium again, plates spinning, wobbling, and crashing. So many things to consider, and the path to safety unclear, with the real, crushing impression that a wrong step would lead to disaster, not just for him, but maybe for those near him – Eleanor. His reassurances, and game insouciance, a house of cards in a cross-wind.

There was an inquest. Threat was made implicit as the hierarchy of those who were left was made abundantly clear, with the bosses – these cruel men who had climbed to the top of their trees by treating embarrassment and failure as runt from a litter that needed drowning – eager to blame anyone for the inconvenience of what had happened. Everyone had gone, bar two of the guests, and their two drivers. The drivers were comfortable again, relaxing into their usual roles, hovering at the back of the darkened boardroom, detritus – food, glasses, poker chips, ashtrays – still strewn everywhere, but the clean-up could wait. Intimidation was the priority. At least, that's the game that Tony knew was about to be played. He had his role too, and maybe through whispered aside, or just the ease of punching down, the drivers and their charges found unanimity of purpose easily. They had reverted to their default of "Them and Us", and were happy to cast Tony in the role of scapegoat. They had been embarrassed – all of those important faces who had attended tonight had left it significantly worse off, both materialistically, with their money, their phones and their jewellery all taken from them in a sports duffel bag. But also their reputations and machismo at a lower ebb than just a few hours ago, when they were comfortable in their feelings of being untouchable. This embarrassment needed a release, and Tony would do.

Tony had sat in positions like this before. You didn't operate in these circles for so long without occasionally being on the receiving end of demonstrations of status such as this. That didn't make it any less concerning. Tony knew that there was always the chance of violent sanction, potentially ultimately so, and would have to navigate these waters carefully and deferentially, yet with enough confidence to create a defence of sorts. So, he sat and waited, and let them play their games of delay and pregnant pausing, before the inevitable finger-pointing and balled fists.

There were whispers in the corner between a driver and his boss – One Ear, still seething from the association with failure that this night had delivered to him, and his boss, all tan and identikit suit and shoes, mid-30s, with immaculately groomed facial hair and a single stud earring, who Tony had only ever heard of referred to as Carlo. Carlo, one of the few who had managed to keep hold of his phone, had it gripped in his hand from the moment the robbery concluded. He tapped out text after text, paranoia driving him. This attack, the *trespass*, could be part of some power-play or larger move. Carlo had been so fixated on sending messages out to all parts of his network – presumably calls to arms, and offers of retribution or reward in exchange for information or otherwise – that it jarred when, suddenly, the phone was slipped inside his jacket pocket. Carlo looked up, and outside the boardroom, before gesturing for someone outside to enter with a cursory *hither* of fingers.

The person who walked in was someone Tony had not seen before. He would have remembered this person, for sure. A Bond villain in height and build, well above six feet tall, broad shouldered and thick-legged – his black t-shirt and tailored trousers tight against knotted muscle beneath – with a bleached crop of short hair sharp contrast against his clothing, and the dark of the main office he'd emerged from. A tic-tac-toe cross was scarred into one side of his forehead, like an asterix above his eyes and into his hairline. His eyes were dark, unblinking, and staring directly at Tony. His smile was broad and friendly, but the cold stare of his eyes made that grin a lie. Tony understood the theatre of this intimately – the boss, the subordinate, and the summoned "specialist" – but, still, there was something about this man that unnerved him. He'd met people like this before – the men (and they were always men, other than a frankly terrifying woman he'd met ten years prior, who he heard had unpeeled someone's face with a craft knife, all over a missing hundred pounds) who were *summoned*, who entered problem scenarios not necessarily to always find answers, but usually to dole out pain and threats even if only to make the taskmasters feel better. Tony was careful to have rarely been the one on the end of the intense spotlight of suspicion or retribution. But even with the relative comfort of repetition and expectation, some lower, primal feeling, on seeing this man, gave him cause for concern. The ones to worry about were the sadists. There was usually a practicality to the punishment role – a clear and defined role in every organisation that Tony had come across. Results were key, but Tony had also encountered, thankfully from a distance, those punishers who made it abundantly clear they enjoyed their work all too well.

"Don't get up, son," this big man said in a soft voice, honeyed by the local accent. "I'm just here to ask a few questions. And we'll see how we go from there."

Tony gripped his calm. This was everything now. He had his own role to play. "No problem. Ask away."

The grin widened. He nodded at Carlo who presumably had summoned him here, then swung his leg over the back of a chair, sitting reversed on it, crossing arms on the back-rest leaning forward.

"You're a lucky man. Auspicious this. I don't get out much, so it's nice to meet new people." He leaned forward, from his position opposite Tony, who was holding hard sat in a relaxed position, legs crossed, arms folded. The man grinned again, wide this time. "They call me the Red Pope. I'll tell you why sometime."

He was hard to age, but Tony pegged him for maybe thirty? The voice had a warmth to it, a softness, that uneased him. He was used to these enforcer-types being older, proven and worn, desperate men who had lost their morals years ago, and were left with just cold hearts and angry eyes.

"The Red Pope," repeated Tony. A ridiculousness inherent, but there was a time and place. Fools still made dangerous men, and he couldn't be sure that this man was a fool for sure.

The Red Pope gave a shrug and a laugh. But the eyes

glinted, and he revelled in his notoriety, however he had earned it.

Tony tried to meet the smile, but it was forced. He'd wrenched a muscle in his shoulder when he put through the glass, and now he'd found his control again, was angry with himself for losing it in the first place.

The Red Pope interlaced his fingers, and leaned forward.

"It's Tony, right? Okay, Tone. Let's go through tonight. Nice and slow. Don't worry, though," he said grinning. "I just want to get it all straight in my own head."

Tony made sure to meet his eyes. Not aggressively, but not passively either. This was powerplay, and it needed careful management.

"Who gave out the job, tonight?"

"Groucho." A raised eyebrow from the Red Pope. Tony waved to the space where Groucho had been knocked out. It was empty now, one of the drivers, presumably – hopefully – had taken him away for care and attention. No doubt he would be sat in a chair like this, across from a man like this, in due course. "I don't know his full name but he's..."

"...Mark's brother, yeah, I've heard that. It's a funny joke, isn't it?" The geniality that was being projected was nothing more than a stiletto knife hidden up a sleeve. The conversation of whispers in the corner of the room had stopped. Tony started to heat under the scrutiny from all three of the men in the room, like a boiling frog.

"And you've been doing a bit of work with him, and the other lad, right?"

"On and off. Once a week, maybe? Nothing special. Door work, really."

"Bit of pocket money, like?" the Red Pope said. Pompous and inflated a name, but beware those with a reputation to maintain.

"Yup. That's it. It's straightforward enough."

"Is it? Not always." He tilted his head, indicating the mess in this room, and the next.

"Okay, okay. Fair enough. You're right. We were let down. There should have been three of us working tonight." Tony felt bad bringing Ringo into this, but it needed to be a truth. He needed to offer them something, and he had plenty on the table to lose, not least Eleanor. She wouldn't be worried, yet, but the sun would be up soon, and he would need to be home, or at the very least, in touch, so she could relax before she started her day.

"And that's the guy who got himself in a spot of bother? What's his name?"

"I only know him as Ringo. God knows why."

"And how did you meet him? Who brought him?" He imagined the Red Pope reordering the playing cards hands in a hand of poker. Here we go.

"Groucho. I know him through Groucho."

"How?"

"Gym, first. Just got talking."

A pause. The Red Pope wanted to make him sweat. Easy. This was basic stuff, but Tony knew better than to call them on this. Let it play out. He needed to get out of here clean. Scared men, angry men, make quick decisions, and he didn't want to worry if he left town about every rev of car engine, or angry footsteps, behind him for weeks into his future. He knew what they wanted – they wanted him to break, to speak first, to show weakness. That's fine. He could swallow that. Let them think they held all the cards.

"We did okay. No problems before tonight. Clearly. Or we wouldn't have got this one." *Clearly*. He was going to regret that.

"Clearly. Yeah. Got you." The Red Pope sat back, put his

hands behind his head, looked up to the ceiling and exhaled, loudly. A little look to his left, at the One Ear and Carlos, still silent, still watching, then back forwards in his seat focusing on Tony.

"So. Tony. How much did you know?" Those imaginary poker cards were being laid face down. Want to call?

"Nothing. Ask them." Tony's turn to gesture to the audience.

"I have. Now I'm asking you." The Red Pope's eyes weren't so friendly now.

"Look, mate. I came when I was asked. I did what I was told. I've never had any complaints. None. I didn't fuck up tonight. We needed three men, and had to make do with two."

"Your mate fucked up. Your mate." His teeth bared a little bit, but he still retained the pull of a smile at the side of his mouth. The impression, as always with men like this, is that they really wanted things to go badly, so they could prove their worth in a completely different way. A sharp way.

"Not my mate." There. Said. He knew what it would mean for Ringo, but he also knew what had happened tonight. Ringo had put himself in this position – he must have – and by doing that he had put chains around the ankles of Tony, of Groucho, of Eleanor and there was nothing Tony wouldn't do to get free of this. He was angry that, yet again, he'd slipped down the slope to be in a position like this, after all those promises to Eleanor before, when they had been forced to escape their home in a different city before. But it's insidious. Tiny increments and before you know the walls have closed in so tightly the breath has been pushed out from you.

"Just someone you knew. What's - what's the word? An acquaintance."

"Whatever you like." Tony put hands on his knees and exhaled and regrouped. "Look. You lot aren't bush league,"

"Bush...?" The Red Pope said, clearly missing the reference.

"...Aren't amateurs, right? Okay. So, I guess we've all been checked out? Maybe not on the first job, but for a gig like this? With these fellas? You'll have checked?"

The Red Pope shrugged, friendlier, but seeing where this was going. "Sure. Sure, we would."

"So, you know my work. It's been good? Look. We even met Mr Stark and he seemed to..."

It came so quickly Tony couldn't brace himself. He barely saw it. But the Red Pope had launched himself from his chair, and thrown a slap so quickly, so powerfully, that Tony's eyes watered and he rocked back in his seat.

"You don't get to say his name, son." The Red Pope loomed over Tony, then allowed himself to regain his composure, and slowly retook his seat. He waited for Tony to find his seat again. A long minute passed. Tony was angry at himself. He was playing this well, but only up to a point. He'd found that point.

"Look, sorry. Okay. My mistake," Tony said rubbing his jaw. It stung. It had been a good shot. This man knew how to hit people. Something to file away for a later use he hoped he'd never need to call on. "Think about it from my point of view. If I knew anything, why would I stick around? You fellas would have me chopped and fed to the fish in short order. He's fucked me over too, you know. If that's what's really happened here. But either way, I did what I could. You can see that."

Tony chanced a sideways look again to the men in the shadows. Tony had made sure he kept an eye on them too, either peripherally, or just by looking at the reflection in the glass. It was dark, but he could make out when they were listening, when they were whispering, when they were looking out into the main office. Like now. Carlo looked from the Red Pope out into the office. Carlo stared, looking at something, or someone, intently, then a nod. Someone else was here? Tony couldn't see clearly enough, not without turning his head, and he wasn't going to turn away from the man sat across from him.

"Enough." The first word Carlo had said loud enough that Tony could make out, during this whole back-and-forth. "We're good."

A grin again from the Red Pope, not able to resist mugging with a puff of his cheeks. "Whew!" the Red Pope raised his eyebrows, and flung his arms wide, and stood up. "We're done, then."

"Pope." Carlo said the name like a command. Tony knew what happened now. Time to take it.

Again, faster than he anticipated, Pope hit him – a balled fist this time, into the stomach, and even though he had tensed as best he could, being sure to breathe out, the punch surprised him. A rib cracked – he felt it go. But he knew, this was just an underlining – *you're clear this time, but this was a mess and no-one gets out of here easy.*

"Ok, son. That's your lot. Fuck off out." the Red Pope said, putting his arm around Tony, as Tony fought to stand up straight. His guts churned, his rib aching. Tony was shown to the door. That was something at least. He'd passed their test. Or he hoped he had. Whatever, he could go, and he could prepare for whatever might happen next.

As Tony left the boardroom behind him, and made his away across the darkened office, to the stairs down to the main reception, he heard a dull clank from the other side of the room. The fire exit door had closed itself. Someone had just left. Whoever it was who had given some kind of prompt or command to Carlo from through the glass. Someone who was more important than anyone else in the building. The person who had given him the pass. Tony had an idea who it was. He wanted to know more about them, but knew any questions might come back to hit him harder than any sucker-punch to the gut. He was in the spotlight now, even if only for a little while. He didn't like it. Not one bit.

10

C old Cut sat in his car, breathing heavily, glove compartment open, and the detritus inside exploded across the passenger seat, after a desperate search for cigarettes, for tobacco, for *anything* to steady his hands. He felt safer in his car, doors locked, engine rumbling as asthmatically as his own rattling chest. The lights were on, and it just needed setting into gear to leave. But he couldn't leave just yet. His rat brain was all about the balance of probabilities, and the fierce and single-minded search for self-preservation, and so, even now, the Sword of Damocles above him, he was working angles and weighing options. Banal calculations about safest routes out of the city, or how far his quarter-tank of petrol could take him, collided with grander schemes of how to re-ingratiate himself with those who he feared would want him sanctioned, punished and disappeared. The tales of Jim Stark were legion, and he knew so many stories simply in the category of "faces no longer seen" to believe the truth of them – faces with names that had their own legends following them, all of whom seemed to just vanish from one night to the next, leaving only gossip and whispers behind them, like smoke after a magician's trick.

How could he make good? He had wronged these people, he knew that. Just by failing to follow those simple instructions he was complicit in a mistake, which would, at best, cost someone money. But even that "at best" was unacceptable – as he sat in his car, the heaters fighting hard to pump warmer air around the car, the wizened optimism of his mind wondered whether he could talk his way back into good graces, but it was soon dwarfed by aggressive realism that suggested that if he was ever in a situation to make his case, he ran the very real risk of finishing the conversation with his hands bound, and a bag over his head.

There was nothing more to it. He had to leave. *Had to.* He stuffed a handful of pork slices from the vac-sealed pack he had grabbed from his fridge into his mouth, wiping saliva from the corner of his lips with a dirty, stained hand, before gripping the wheel with set determination, ready to drive away, away from this city – *his city.*

In gear, and ready to move, his phone chirped. The screen lit up, and then chirped again before the light could fade. One message. Two. Now three.

"Fuck," he hissed. He was angry, frustrated. His mind had been made up to go – he was a kid on a diving board who'd finally built up the confidence to jump, only to be called back at the last minute. But he couldn't risk missing something important – knowledge is power, and he needed every last scrap of it he could dare find.

He put the car into neutral, pulled the handbrake, and reached across to grab his phone from the passenger seat, where he'd thrown it when he burst into his car, panicked and scared. More messages were coming in. What was happening that had generated so much interest at - what was it? – 3am in the morning? Was this it? Was he being told that the hunt was on? That he was being called in for a "quiet word"? His hands started shaking again. No. This seemed different. Group chat. All the street corner boys were talking.

Acer - "U LOT HEARD? ITS GONE TO SHIT AT DOCKS"

Acer - "BIG FUCK UP. STARK LOT TURNED OVER"

Belly - "FUCK OFF!"

Acer – "TRUTH. BILLY MAC TEXT ME"

Belly – "WOT HE KNOW?"

Acer – "PARKLAND LADS DID IT HE SAYS. INSIDE JOB"

Belly – "FUCK. INSIDE JOB?"

Acer – "HE RECKONS THEY CHATTING SHIT. INSTA POST WAVING NOTES"

Belly – "FUCKING TWATS. THEY DEAD"

Acer – "IKR. THEY DEAD OR THEY RUN"

Cosmo – "THEY DEFO DEAD"

Belly – <LAUGHING EMOJI>

Acer - <LAUGHING EMOJI>

Cosmo – "WHAT THEY SAYING?"

Acer – "DON'T KNOW MUCH. HEARD INSIDE JOB. STARK POKER PARTY."

Belly – "UNLUCKY STARK! LOL!"

Cosmo - <LAUGHING EMOJI>

Cosmo – "WHO TURNED?"

Belly – "DEATH WISH"

Acer – "LOL"

Acer – "SOME DUDE RINGO"

Cold Cut hadn't blinked in minutes, hadn't breathed. Staring at the phone. Perhaps this was why he hadn't been found yet, called yet. Something else had happened tonight. Something worse.

Belly – "DUNT KNO HIM"

Acer – "DOOR GUY. A BLUE. FAT LAD."

Cosmo – "LOL"

Belly – "KNO HIM NOW. WITH TWO OTHER GUYS"

Acer – "YEH. THREE ON THE DOORS. TWO SCOUSE AND ONE NOT. NEW GUY"

Cosmo – "NEW GUY???"

Belly – "SEEN HIM AROUND FOR FEW MONTHS"

Acer – "DOOR WORK GUY. OLD MAN"

Cold Cut – "I KNOW HIM. NAME IS GRACE. WHAT GOING ON?"

Acer – "YEH GRACE. THAT HIM. PARKLAND LADS ROBBED STARK WITH RINGO. RINGO GONE."

Cold Cut – "OTHERS IN ON IT? NEW LAD GRACE?"

Acer – "DNT KNO"

Pause. No new messages.

Then...

Acer – "GOT TEXT. SAYING REWARD FOR RINGO. POPE LOOKING"

Christ. Red Pope. Serious shit.

He put the phone down, and pinched the bridge of his nose. Could he find a way back into favour? It was possible – maybe they hadn't even heard about the mess earlier in the night? Not yet, maybe. And maybe they hadn't heard about his role in it, or lack of it. If he came to them with something positive, would it make that negative – that small, trifling negative – be forgotten, brushed over with a warm word and a little something as thanks?

No. This was Stark. The stories didn't become stories without truth. No forgiveness. Ever. There were no warm words to be had, so perhaps the best he could hope for was a stay of execution, and starting out at the bottom of the ladder again. He could live with that. He could live with *living*. He knew he still had to get out of the city, but he figured he still had time for a few stops before any spotlight was cast in his direction – maybe, just maybe, he could find something he could throw their way that might mean, at the very least, he could go back to his squalid little rooms, and close his eyes with the comfort that he wouldn't open them again with a knife at his throat. He put the car into gear again, released the handbrake, and pulled out. The roads were quiet, and the only people on the pavements were those who didn't know any better. He absent-mindedly patted the inside pocket of his jacket, comforted by the shape of the package he'd squeezed into it. One more text to send to the group chat.

Cold Cut – "MEET ME IN 30 MIN AT GARAGE"

11

H e took a circuitous route to the garage, all bright lights on the dual-carriageway that led from the suburbs into the city centre. He needed to kill a bit of time, to allow that rabble to pull themselves out of whatever dark hole they had set themselves in, and he was too on edge to even think about spending time waiting anywhere near his flat. He used to think that this was his city, with the rhythms and reasons behind every door or on every corner no stranger to him, but as he drove around those streets again, in the early hours of the morning, he realised that he was but nothing in the scheme of the city – a parasite that lived off scraps. The kings of this city were mighty and truly in every corner, and if they so chose to scour the streets of him, he would be lost. The realisation was crushing. Terrifying. Like being in a pool and not knowing how deep to go to find the bottom, so he could push away and back up to the light. But he could hope, just. Hope that somehow he would touch a solid surface, and swim back to the light, and to safety, and the quest for something better, whatever that might be.

As he drove, he scanned the streets. Maybe a lifetime of shitty luck, and unfair circumstance would finally tip back to an outrageous fortune that he truly must deserve – one offhand glance might see him tie this Ringo to a location, and then, he could call in his reward, even if that reward was nothing more than survival. A passenger in a car, or a man in a kebab shop queue – it could be any one of those people, and he couldn't afford to not look.

Nothing. No long shot for him tonight, so he sighed, and took a few turns, onto the main road, and to the petrol station.

He was five minutes late. A tiny flash of importance fired in him when he saw the others waiting for him. He had status, hard-earned and hard-fought, and was comforted to see that he still had some sway. Or was it something else? A fog of pessimism stung his eyes – these were his people, but they didn't belong to him. They were just like him. Information was everything, and he realised they were early simply because they couldn't afford to not hear what he had to say – there was no respect, no affection towards any kind of perceived rank, it was simply the currency of words, and nothing more. But fuck them. This is how you rise in his world. By scratching and fighting and standing on the shoulders of those beneath, pushing them down into the mud as you clamber towards better things. There is no love in this world, only bodies to stand on.

They had congregated away from the bright lights of the kiosk window, but still underneath the canopy of the petrol station. He pulled up in one of the parking spaces, instinctively sharing a look with the sales assistant behind the reinforced glass. Dismissive from Cold Cut, resigned from the assistant – not worth raising a fuss, and certainly not worth leaving the warmth and light of inside.

Cold Cut got out of the car. All worries and fear wiped from his expression like nerves from an actor walking onstage. This was its own performance, as it always was, and he couldn't spare the slightest doubts with any of these.

Acer, Belly and Cosmo – the ABC of street-corner tattle. All in an approximation of uniform – all tracky and trainer, stolen or bartered for. All three of their outfits had lost all their high street sharpness, as if the clothes had faded and crumpled simply by being in contact with them. All three boys were in their late 20s, all rake-thin, and all with voices like dying gulls, thick Scouse accents hoarse and shrill at the same time. Acer was wreathed in smoke, a vape glow as he inhaled, and the odd sight of too much smoke breathed out.

"Cut, Lad. What's on?" Belly was first to speak. The others ready to chirp in, heads pecking forward like a chorus of crows on a line.

"Right, youse. Right. Important this," Cold Cut said, as he closed the car door and sat himself on the bonnet, performing insouciance as best he could.

The three heads inched forward haloed by vape glow and smoke.

"Seems to me we've got a real chance at something here. We know these Parkland lads, right?" Cold Cut said, holding court.

The lads nodded.

"Reckon we know where they might hang about, and we might be able to get there first. You know, give Stark's lot a heads up. Could be...," he rubbed his forefingers and thumb together, and raised his eyebrows. All three of them knew what that meant, a reward.

"They'll have got them already, daft twats," Acer said. He was happy to get a reward, but happier to do nothing.

"Maybe, maybe. Can't hurt, though, right? And I tell you

what, lad," Cold Cut leaned forward, all four heads closing together. "If we find them, we might find this Ringo. And if we find this Ringo, then we proper coin it."

Cold Cut saw the thought process dig its heels in, across all three faces. The Parkland Lads were doomed, they all knew that. If they were stupid enough to brag about what they had done to even one person in this city, they were as good as dead, but being so loud, so soon, and they might not even make it until the morning. If you earned money from Stark, even if just doing menial door work, or cash handling, or street corner work, then you had to have some idea about the consequences of fucking with Stark. By definition, you also had to either have a cast-iron escape plan, or were so desperate you were willing to lay on the longest of odds. Ringo was the trophy here. Find him, and sell the information, and he had his way out. It had to be.

"So I know what you fuckers are like. We'll just tell Stark ourselves if we find him. So, I've got an offer for you." Cold Cut reached inside his jacket and pulled out a tightly-wrapped package; a palm-sized brick of something. Something valuable.

"Third of a kilo. Argentinian, from the Olympic drop." They knew what that meant. The summer of 2012 saw the best coke the city had ever seen come into town – a sweetener from an overseas gang looking to make their own impression on the city. Needless to say, Stark had moved on them, and those foreign boys soon learnt that the backwards hicks in this town weren't quite as unprepared as they anticipated. That coke was swept up, and resold on, down in London for twice what it could have got up here, gone in a heartbeat, and left only as a fairy tale of "what could have been" for the local estate agents and recruitment consultants. Stories of stashes were told of like the loot of Edward

Teach, buried under a metaphorical cross somewhere. And here was Cold Cut, waving a block of white, saying he had some of this mythical treasure.

"Find Ringo, tell me first, and this is yours." Cold Cut couldn't help but inch backwards, just in case temptation got the better of any of the three men opposite him. He was angry at that minor show of weakness, of fear, but he tightened his neck, and gathered himself.

"That's a fuck lot of money, Cut lad," Cosmo said. "A fuck lot. Don't believe you, mate. No-one gives away that much nose."

Cold Cut nodded, bottom lip out. "Good point. Bright lad, you. What do you reckon we have here? Eight grand? Ten? Maybe. But you have to sell it slow, so you don't get the wrong kind of attention, right? I ain't got time for slow. Looking to go up in the world, aren't I? I reckon this Ringo fucker might just get me there. And it's not like you lot want any more grief by being further up the chain, is it? So win-win, right?"

The three lads furrowed their brows and gave each other sideways glances. They didn't want to put their heads above the parapet, even if there might be rewards at the end of it. They'd heard too many tales about those who flew too close to the sun, never to be heard of again, and they were happy swimming in their own shallow pool. They knew this world, and were content to stay in it.

"Reckon. Reckon," Acer puffed out.

"So, I'm out of town for a bit, so you chew on what I've said. But don't fuck about. He needs finding before anyone else gets to him. And," he reached into a trouser pocket, "three for you, good faith, like." Three tiny wraps of white, one each. Sweeteners. What you could win, contestant.

Cold Cut paused to reiterate, "Don't fuck about." As he

eased back into the car, leaving the three boys to their gossip and whispers, he was convinced his performance was good enough to persuade them to do the work for him. They had smarts, but they weren't clever. He tolerated them because of what they brought him – street-corner headlines, but also no desire or will to coalesce any original thought. Controllable and predictable. Useful.

Cold Cut gave them a showy nod as he drove past, and threw a scowl at the assistant still daring the odd glance out of the window. Then he was back onto the main road and away, waiting a few hundred yards before he let his grip loosen on the wheel. He let his hands shake again, hoping that he had done enough so this wasn't to be the last night in his beloved city.

12

————

It was 6am when Eleanor heard Tony turn his key in the door of the apartment, smiling to herself as he carefully opened the heavy, self-close door, taking care to close it as softly as possible; maybe this time would be the time that he could sneak in without waking her, but, wryness on her face, once again she was awake to enjoy this performance. Now, she thought, he was probably desperately trying to turn cogs to come up with a story convincing enough to ease any concerns or deflect enquiry. He hadn't managed it yet, in all these years, but he continued to cling to the forlorn hope that maybe this would be the one time to change all that.

In truth, he was later than she anticipated, but though she had just strayed into concern, she had had too many nights like this for it to be a committed worry. She trusted him. She trusted him to navigate dark nights and the people that move in that monochrome world – he'd never given her any reason to suspect he was holding anything back, and, on rare occasions, she'd seen how he could handle himself if backed into a corner, literal or otherwise.

They always talked. No secrets – an offhand promise that became a mantra – which had served them well over the years. Eleanor had seen Tony exist in that world, but had never tried to dissuade him from it, because she knew there was an end planned. Every late night, or phone call summons, or bruised knuckle, was a step towards a better life, and whilst there was occasionally some debate about how much further along the road they still had to walk to get that life, there was never any doubt that both of them were determined to find it. Money had been stashed away, sometimes literally, sometimes in a network of bank accounts, assets accumulated, so that one day, after perhaps a handful of phone calls, they could leave their life again, as they had before, but this time, for good, jumping the tracks to finally settle in a world where they could set their own pace, taking comfort in the obscurity they craved. It was persuasive, though, this life. Living off the books, from bags of cash, to envelopes of notes, or instant deposits in off-shore accounts, suggested a freedom from the chains that normal people seemed to rail against. This was the big lie they had told themselves, though, and over the years, tough lessons had been learned. Chains did still exist for them, and they were weightier, and harder to get free from than any mortgage or credit card debt. These chains came with sharper edges, and took an awful lot more escaping, especially if you planned on getting away clean.

Eleanor was in bed, but could see Tony through a gap in the bedroom door to the corridor outside. The dim landing light was on, silhouetting him, and she could see that he'd paused, as he often did, at the cluster of photographs and memorabilia on the sideboard in the corridor. Here he was taking a breath before he came in, usually to crawl into bed next to her, for an embrace and an easy five minutes to sigh and unclench the duty from his muscles, but also, to maybe remind himself of other, less complicated times. She knew how proud he was of those photographs, and those mementos – pictures of army platoons, of camaraderie and commitment, regimental standards and awards, framed and arranged, as a testament to an earlier life. She was sentimental in her own way, but maybe not as demonstratively as him – if she had her way, those keepsakes would just be kept in a box somewhere; happy they were safe, but not on display. But this was not important enough to fight about – he took comfort from them, so that was enough for her.

This was their life. A life of happy compromise. They didn't argue any harder than the occasional bicker. The trust they had in each other was total, and whilst Eleanor yearned for their prized destination, she was in no hurry to get there, as they both understood that hurrying led to carelessness, which was a characteristic that neither of them had much time for. Perhaps this was why they meshed so well, having that rare gift of patience and detachment when it came to matters personal. They would get there. But it would take time. Even slow progress is progress, and considered pace meant that all angles could be assessed as they readied themselves for that final escape to a life free of threat and worry.

The bedroom door opened and Tony eased into the bedroom, as quietly as he could. Normally, Eleanor wouldn't move, so she could enjoy watching him navigate across the room in his vain attempt to not wake her, but on this occasion, she saw that he was not walking easily, and every odd step was accompanied by a hiss of pained breath. He was hurt, a fact confirmed by the hand braced across his ribs.

"What have you done?" she said, sitting upright. The

room was dim, but brightening by the second as dawn was trying to break outside.

"It's been a night," Tony managed to say, not raising his voice above much of a whisper, as if the early hour demanded a softer tone, even with Eleanor awake. He sat down on the edge of the bed, back to Eleanor, with a sigh.

"What's happened?" Eleanor said, as she slid across the bed until she was sat next to Tony. She put her arm around his shoulder, inspecting his face for injuries with her other hand. His face was unmarked, but the frown said enough.

And so he told her. Ringo. Groucho. The Red Pope. The whole sorry mess. And after the bare facts, the conjecture, prompted by her, as always. What did this mean for them? How would this affect them? What was the worst that could happen, and how could they prepare for it?

But that could wait, even if only for a little while. She had an hour before she needed to be out, and away to that no-mark job, in that no-mark office, lost amongst the pods and the "collaborative spaces", and he was clearly in need of the quiet security of his home. So she eased him back onto the bed, pulling his legs up, shoes be damned, and nuzzled into his chest. Just a few stolen moments of quiet, of *them*, adrift, before they would consider letting reality crash in around them once more.

ELEANOR HAD FALLEN BACK ASLEEP, but Tony hadn't. He stayed recumbent, with her draped across him, but despite his best intentions, he couldn't slow his mind to join her in dozing. She could always compartmentalise, putting her worries on shelves for later, but he could never settle when there was a conundrum that needed solving.

The relief he felt from being waved out of that room

mere hours before seemed like it had happened to someone else. He knew that he was going to face the sort of scrutiny that anyone, let alone him, so eager to find the quiet calm of the shadows, would rail against. He always knew the organisation he had tied himself to was one that hid secrets and crimes in equal measure. But he'd managed to convince himself that he could stay above the murk and the mystery that surely must be stock in trade at the higher echelons of the business – clearly, he had been wrong. He would add his own recriminations to any that might follow from anyone else. He had been in positions like this on, thankfully rare, occasions before. This was the worst part. That there were wheels turning he had no doubt, but he couldn't see them or discern them in any way, which meant he and Eleanor were exposed. All possibilities had to be considered – logic might suggest that he had passed some test earlier tonight. But he couldn't rule out that he was now being tracked, still under the glare of suspicion, with patient, calculating eyes instead just biding their time, watching their movements, examining everything they did to make connections and draw conclusions that Tony and Eleanor themselves hadn't considered. Maybe Tony was in on this somehow. Maybe, even, the simple *possibility* that he was would be enough for action to be taken. He and Eleanor were careful and analytical – they had to be – but they learned at an early stage that so were other people, but also, often with a fuel of emotion that meant that the threat of drastic sanction was scarily real.

But what could be done? They couldn't run. Not yet. There was too much to put in place, and the fear of some kind of close surveillance meant that a clean escape was too risky, especially given that escape would be an admission of guilt, even if it was not truth. So, they both had to accept that the next few hours, days, weeks, were going to be a time of testing. If those charged with handling this problem behaved as Tony expected, then they would be thorough and diligent, then potentially decisive and comprehensive, should they draw certain conclusions. Tony and Eleanor would have no choice but to attempt to behave within those boundaries as "normally" as possible, and steer their course through whatever suspicion was aimed in their direction as carefully as they could.

As he lay there, with Eleanor, Tony decided to at least try and do something constructive – he would try and find Groucho. Maybe he would get some answers. Maybe he would make things worse by talking to him. But it was the only thing he could think of to do that wouldn't make him feel like he was in stasis, and even with the myriad threats and fears bubbling in his mind, it was also the right thing to do. But later. Now sleep.

13

E leanor left Tony to drift from a doze to a deep sleep, which she discerned almost like a car changing gears. His breathing changed, after a long sigh, then cat-like, muscle memory stretching out his limbs, unconsciously grimacing as his body remembered the pain in his bones. Finally, stillness and peace in the dark, curtains pulled tightly against a bright, brisk spring morning outside. She was concerned, chiefly because Tony was concerned – he'd been in tight spots before, places where what they disparagingly called "civilians" would fret, wail and worry - but for him to have been so unsettled was unusual, and worrying. They talked about how to manage problems in the past before, but after hearing Tony talk about what had happened that night, and with context from his impressions of the wider environment he'd been operating in these past months, it felt like there was concern suddenly around every corner, unfocused and unknowable.

Eleanor found comfort in routine, like an anchor to cling to. So she boiled the kettle, dug out the coffee grounds, and added a new filter to the coffee pot. The performance of coffee prep gave her something to concentrate on, and kick the can of their bigger problem further down the road. Maybe this pause would let her grasp something like certainty in the next step forward? Maybe. For now, she'd make do with coffee.

Routine also meant that she couldn't, or wouldn't, find an excuse to not go to work. She wasn't particularly taken with her job, organising appointments and managing procurement for the marketing company that she worked for. She felt incongruous in that office, surrounded by immaculately presented men and women, all in their 20s, in either flowing dresses or too-tight jeans and no socks, hair-styles all angles and product. But she took comfort in the plan. Their plan. A clock was ticking, and each day in that maze of free-standing pod-walls was one more day closer to them vanishing from a city again, this time away from concrete and neon forever, and to their dream of peace, quiet and solitude. They were going to go somewhere where the horizon came to meet you, and the sky was painted in more colours than grey. She walked out the door, her face set in the furrow of deep thought, but without being able to find the edges of the problem, she couldn't even begin to wrestle with it. All she knew is that they would survive it. This was nothing but a hurdle to jump, and after all these years, they were still together, still strong and still completely committed to their shared future.

Little victories were peppered into her daily routine. Instead of the lift, she insisted on taking the stairs. Instead of a cab, or a bus, she walked the couple of miles into work, irrespective of the weather. Fortunately, today was her ideal, with bright, cold sunshine filling the streets with an optimism she revelled in. Though under it she couldn't help but notice the sobering steel of the chill.

The city was awake. 8am. Cars and buses stop-starting along crowded streets, and pedestrians foregoing any pretence of calm procession, darting in-between the traffic whenever the opportunity presented itself. The polite waver, the head-nodder, and the forced ignorer, all making the way in-front of increasingly impatient drivers, all of them finding their own routes along their own routines, on their way to, no doubt, similar offices and similar office politics. Hundreds and thousands of people whose morning highlight would be some whispered gossip about a drunken embarrassment in a pub the night before, or an ALL-CAPS email about piles of washing-up in the communal kitchen. Just the decision to leave, even if there was no definitive date to countdown to, was freeing, and Eleanor wrapped herself up in some smugness knowing that whilst those around her were likely to be trapped in this Sisyphean sameness for years, or decades even, she could see the summit, and her grip was fierce.

That distraction made her walk pass quickly. The same route to work every day, though, oddly, a different route home each night, with the freedom of day-end allowing her to explore the city in an easier manner, enjoying finding new secrets and discoveries around street corners. As she walked, she thought about the Polish deli that she'd walked past the night before, looking forward to exploring the strip-lit aisles for new spices or luridly boxed crackers in the evening, where, god willing, some prosaic explanation or solution had been found to make the drama of the dark early morning, which even now felt dream-like given the distance from the bright sunshine of the day, fade away permanently.

Some habits die hard, though. Despite the drift of her thoughts, she still had some tether to what was happening around her, and suddenly, a realisation tugged at that tether, and she pulled herself back to the here-and-now. She was being followed.

It was hard at first to appreciate that someone was shadowing her, especially amongst the crowds of people, clutching coffee and shoulder-bags, many aiming at the exact same clusters of buildings as her, but with each pace, she confirmed to herself that there was someone, a few hundred yards back, who was trying hard enough to keep her in eyeline, but taking too much effort ensuring that they were at the periphery of what could be considered noticeable by inverted comma normal people. But Eleanor tried hard to never settle for whatever it meant to be normal. She made a point of being active in her relationship with Tony – she wasn't a helpless soul to be steered and guided by a strong, dominant man. Theirs was a relationship built on parity, which was no platitude. The presumption, fairly ascribed or not, that she wouldn't notice someone following her due to some weakness of awareness, or even some gender stereotype, was enough to snap her back to absolute concentration, to such a degree that her anger at that presumption bypassed any concerns about her safety. How fucking dare they?

Now that she was certain she was being followed, she allowed herself the luxury of making absolutely sure. She took detours, and doubled-back on herself with demonstratively broad gestures because she had "forgotten something" or "had a call to take". Each pause or detour saw the figure, a few hundred yards behind her on the street take similar pauses, suddenly finding an item of interest in a shop window, or attending to a stray shoelace. She used the city as her accomplice, scanning glass storefronts for reflections, allowing her to put a firmer shape to the figure, and better understand who this could be.

The man seemed maybe somewhat incongruous against the rank and file of the morning foot-traffic, but he wasn't so incongruous that he would draw anything more than a passing glance – he wasn't dressed for the office, but this was the city, and it wasn't unusual for someone dressed in smart shoes, dress trousers and sharp, black shirt, his outfit screaming its price tags and its labels, to walk the streets at 8am on a weekday – he looked like he had just left a casino or strip club. However, this did make him easier to track, without being too obvious and risk either scaring him away, or worse, to scale up his intentions. Eleanor knew what to do – establish patterns, and draw conclusions. Did he have anything about him that would help identify him at a later date? Anything that Tony could use to draw intentions from any of the personalities that he might have encountered during their time in Liverpool? Police? The opposite? What was this man's objective? Merely to follow her, to draw patterns for their own future use, or worse, to identify weaknesses. Some side-alley walked past every day, or a regular time smoking a pre-work cigarette, that could be exploited somehow for an attack, or an abduction, designed to punish Tony for an as-yet undecided infraction.

Be cold, be detached, and get information. Tony insisted on this. Eleanor knew the benefits. You can't act fully without knowing as much as you possibly could. For a mile or so, Eleanor ran that mantra over and over in her head, analysing every tic and movement from a hundred yards distance, putting in order in her head for some imagined debrief when she next saw Tony.

Fuck that.

The bubbling indignation just underneath was never far

away. Usually a flash of it at some impoliteness like when she held a door and didn't receive thanks. She couldn't help it, instead of a tut, or an eye-roll, more often than not, Eleanor would say something. She just had to. Tony, however, often took the sensible option of a step back, rather than dare risk anything intended to be a calming word, or worse, a hand on the arm, and collateral damage. So, despite one side of her brain working overtime to order facts and observations, the other side was becoming more and more exercised with fury. She knew Tony would never do anything to jeopardise what they had built together, irrespective of who he was working for, and knew that whatever had happened hours before, he wouldn't have risked so much for just some tawdry heist, and how dare anyone even think they were involved in anything like that. And worse, how dare anyone have the audacity to think they could intimidate her by following her, and worse yet, by doing it in such a way that she had noticed them.

She stopped. The performance dropped. Stood stock still for a few seconds, then dropping her shoulders, gathering that rage tight, she turned on her heel. She fixed that man with a gaze that could sharpen diamonds, and walked directly for him.

For the first fifty yards, the man maintained his own performance, avoiding eye contact, and taking odd interest in anything but the scowling woman kept heading straight for him. He gave odd glances in her direction until her steady stride, and even steadier glare, became impossible to ignore. When she had closed the distance to fifty yards, all pretence was dropped. He couldn't avoid looking at her directly any longer. Everyone else on that street faded into grey as they both locked eyes on each other. He stood still, and Eleanor paced towards him.

Then, suddenly, there was someone else on her shoulder. A big figure manifested in her peripheral vision, an iceberg bursting through Arctic fog to crash against a ship's hull, huge and unavoidable. A large hand closed around her upper arm, obvious to her, and maybe obvious to one or two of the other pedestrians close to them, but they certainly weren't going to get involved with this huge man, and this fierce-looking woman. Yet another morning drama on the streets of Liverpool, and only good as entertainment from a safe remove, and no more. And, in any event, there'll be another one around the corner if this one doesn't combust in an entertaining manner – best to let it simmer quietly, and keep walking to work.

His grip on her arm was firm, as she turned to give him her full attention. Her face full of shock, then fear, she still had the wherewithal to check off the characteristics of the man who had inserted himself into this little drama she was playing. The hair, the eyes, the build, and then, crucially, the forehead scar, all perfectly matching the description of the man from her conversation with Tony earlier – this was the Red Pope, a name that, from a distance, seemed ludicrous, laughable even, until the sobering reality of that iron grip, and the unblinking eyes, and worst of all, the bare-teeth grin.

"Let's not get too excited, shall we?" His voice was like stone scraped together, quiet but clear. His hand moved from her upper arm, and instead, rested on the back of her neck, attempting the pretence of affection for any audience that had half an eye on them, but the firmness in his fingers assuring Eleanor that affection was very much not on the agenda. It also let him subtly steer her, away from the main drag, and into a non-descript alley, all box bins on wheels, and piles of refuse bags, ready for the garbage pick-up, whenever that was. She wasn't certain what would happen if she had tried to break free from the promise of that grip, but it was daylight, and the streets were full, and what was the worst thing that could happen? The other man – the one who had made himself obvious with his hamfisted tail – had closed the distance as well, and the three of them went into the alley, the first man patrolling the threshold between alley and pavement, and the Red Pope manoeuvring her just out of obvious eyelines behind one of the large plastic box bins.

Again, the Red Pope spoke, close to her ear - "Don't be scared. Just a quick word, my love."

She wasn't scared. She was here to learn.

14

"It was definitely him?" Tony cupped his mug of tea, sipping a mouthful despite it being freshly boiled, asbestos guts at work.

Across the table, Eleanor cupped her own mug, enjoying the warmth in her fingers after her walk home from work on a bitter night, clear skies giving free rein to a blast of cold air, skipping off the Mersey and through the city.

"I'm going to let you have a little think about how daft you sound. How many six-foot, blond knuckleheads with scarred foreheads do you think wander around the town of a morning?"

Tony took another sip of tea. "Yeah, okay. Point taken. What was said?"

Tony loved her. There were many reasons. More and more, as they grew older together, but one of the first he had found was how impressive she was; how fearless and aware. People might throw an offhand backhanded compliment about someone as being "not to be fucked with" but Eleanor was *not to be fucked with*. Tony took a wry joy when someone tried to, and he got to watch the slow realisation as they reached the same conclusion.

"So it was pretty standard, to be honest. Minor monkey doing crowd control, just in case someone happened to think about putting the nose in. You know how it is. And then major monkey doing the muscle routine," Eleanor shrugged.

"Just a grip, and scare the little woman, sort of thing?"

"Exactly. Boring. Everything exactly as you'd imagine it."

"'We know where you live, and we'll be watching' blah, blah, blah?"

"Course. I shouldn't have been surprised really. Though maybe a little given they got their arses in gear so quickly after last night, probably because–"

"–They figure if we really are that stupid, we might be stupid enough to make some kind of move early doors. Whilst it's all fresh." Tony had another slurp of tea.

"Probably with us being from out of town. They might think if we could move from one town, just like that, then we could get away from this one dead quick as well." Eleanor took a sip of tea now it had cooled.

"Makes sense, I suppose. Honestly, though. Their faces when you clocked them! They must've been a picture!"

They both grinned. Eleanor thought back to her performance from earlier today, Tony picturing himself as one of the passing pedestrians, enjoying the scene.

"The little one. He was amazing. I couldn't help myself, Tone. I just had to stare him down. He went from nought to shitting it in record time. Does not compute! Does not compute!"

"And then with this Pope character? Little lady in peril?"

"Oh, yes. He liked that. I wish the villains this sort watched in their films were more like Alan Rickman. At least I'd get a laugh then. All sinister hissing and whispers in the ear. Shit scouse panto."

Tony snorted at this. His beautiful wife. Too good for him. Too capable. Too together. Lucky sod. He imagined her whole performance – wide-eyed with terror on her face, perhaps even a shiver or recoil as this Red Pope put his hands on her, nodding along and 'please don't hurt me,' avoiding eye contact and forced dry mouth. Those mooks would lap all that up. And whilst they were doing that, Eleanor would have been taking it all in, the same little details that Tony looked for – little clues and pointers that, who knows, at some point in the future might come in handy. Worth filing away. Information is everything. Knowledge is power. And on and on.

"So. He's right-handed? He hit me with a right."

"Seems that way", said Eleanor. "He grabbed me with his right as well."

"Anything else?"

"I don't know, but I think he might have a bit of a limp on his left side. Could be something, could be nothing, but he's going to struggle to move around if it's anything more than a pull. Mind you, it could be one of those stupid swaggers these kids have these days. But I don't think so."

"He hit me well. Really well. He's had practice. Probably some boxing."

"Can't help you with that. I had to be the pearl-clutcher, so he wasn't for hitting me. Stinks though, did you notice that?"

"The aftershave? I smelt something. Wasn't ruling out my own kecks, though..."

Eleanor smiled. He could still joke. That was something, especially given how he could retreat to brooding when backed into a corner.

"Fairly expensive, but nothing special, I don't think. Just couldn't shake it, he'd layered it on so strong. The sort of aftershave that is expensive in a department store, but not the sort of thing you get in a boutique with the little lolly-sticks."

"Try hard."

"Exactly. Same goes for his shoes."

They paused as they went back over what conclusions they'd drawn from their respective tusslings with this Red Pope.

"What do you make of him? Dangerous? Clearly this crowd rate him, because I imagine this whole mess is their priority number one at the moment. Especially given they pushed this on us so soon after it happened," Eleanor said.

"I think so. I think he could be *very* dangerous. Because he seems like a keen amateur. The name certainly suggests it."

"Oh. One of *those*," Eleanor said, rolling her eyes.

They both knew what that meant. If the Red Pope was any good – really good – then he wouldn't have let himself be surrounded by incompetents that meant that he had to make himself known, stepping out of the shadows and placing himself at risk, simply through exposure. He would've done what he had originally set out to do, which would've been to tail Eleanor and take his own learnings. Her routine, her route, maybe even some friends who could also be brought into this, should the need arise. Do that for a few days, and be certain of the reliability of that routine, and then, when the routine changed, for whatever reason, then react to it as an indicator of a change of behaviour that might need to be acted upon. The keen amateur was worse because they had just a faint grasp of what it took to be to be a specialist, but didn't realise how much more they had to learn, so tended to cover up this shortfall with an enthusiasm for drama. The punch in the ribs was evidence of that. It was childish. But it was also worrying. Because the keen amateur couldn't always be predicted, and when pushed into their own corner, would flail and tantrum, which, when six foot plus, and proudly physical, added to a keenness to impress, became dangerous. Empty drums make the most noise, and whilst they might not last in this world, they could cause a lot of trouble before they took that final way out. They needed to be careful, as they could expect more of this sort of behaviour before this episode was all over.

"I get the feeling he loves the sound of his own voice a little too much. He was like that with me last night. One of these sorts who bang on about 'respect' and so on, just before they beat the shit out of some scruff for spilling their gin and tonic."

Eleanor mmm'd as she took a sip of the just-about-hot-enough tea. "Oh, for sure. I wondered if most of today wasn't for the little squat lad's benefit. These ones always need to have an audience, don't they? Exhibit number one - *the stupid fucking name.*"

"Mmm. Scare the little woman, wink at the bloke three-to-one down in a closed room, that sort of knobhead." Tony might have his measure, but this Red Pope fool still irritated him. Mainly because he figured, if everything went as they wanted, he wouldn't get the chance to take him down a peg or two. Taking comfort in having "won" is all well and good, but it's that much sweeter when you can crow about it. Even Tony, careful and thoughtful though he tried to be, wasn't above having that little triumphalist urge bouncing up and down at the very back of his mind.

"One thing we know," Eleanor said, after a pause, "is that this clown is going to show up again at some point. I think it tells us something that he is either the best they've got or the most...willing."

"It's a fair bet. Confidence goes a long way around here. If this fella is the one who gets his hands dirty, then that's probably enough for them."

"So what do we do? Do we need to think about going? I'd really rather not, all things considered, Tone."

"Not yet. We're not there yet. I'm going to try and find Groucho. And Ringo, for that matter. Stupid twat. Other than that, I'm just going to keep my face in amongst this lot. Guilty man wouldn't be that stupid, so that should calm them down a little."

"Is that wise?"

"Which bit?"

"The Ringo bit. Won't they be looking for him as well?"

"True, but I can just say I'm pissed off with him, if I get pulled up for it. Which, come to mention it, I *am.*"

"Makes sense, I guess. Do you want me to put together a 'Go Bag' ready, just in case?"

"I've still got the old one packed away. But, yeah, have a look. It's under the sink."

"The one behind the kickboard? You lazy sod. That *really* needs a look, that one. Passports are probably in black and white."

More laughing from both of them. Tony felt uncomfortable in the glare of the inevitable scrutiny of the upcoming days, but knowing that, at the very least, he had Eleanor with him, checking her own angles against his, talking through expectations and likelihoods, both of them preparing each other for whatever came their way. They had been here before, admittedly, and whilst every occasion was one too many, they had long since resigned themselves that this life, and these rewards, risked things like this happening to them.

The "Go Bag" was exactly that. A bag to grab when, for whatever reason, they just had to go. They'd never needed one, but an old friend of theirs had, and when he'd managed to get away from the police, him being able to get hold of cash, passports, and a weapon, in seconds, made all the difference between being able to send wry postcards from Mauritius to Tony and Eleanor's PO Box in London, and sending all caps platitudes on HMP notepaper from prison. Since then, they'd followed the same precautions. A small rucksack with thirty grand in cash, a couple of bankcards for their offshore savings account, and their passports. There was a gun in there as well. Tony had never fired one in anger, but he would, if he had to. He hoped it would never come to that. Eleanor had a bag of her own, with her own essentials, stashed under the kitchen counter next to the one that hid Tony's – her being her, he was pretty sure she checked it every week.

"So, you're okay, love?" Tony had finished his tea.

"Fine. Embarrassed, really. For them. What a shambles." Beautiful woman. Who else did he know who could appraise some local toughs in a situation like this?

"Still. Let's not wind them up any. Maybe we can still come out the other side of this, and get back to earning. Exit plan still might hold up."

"Maybe. Be careful, Tone. And yes, I'll be careful too." She was up, the clock read 10pm, but she always did like her bed and her book, and Tony knew she would need to decompress in her own way after the soap opera of the last 24 hours. She walked around the breakfast bar, where they'd been sitting, with her cup in her hand, reaching over Tony's shoulder to pick up his empty mug, before planting a kiss on the top of his head. She put the cups in the sink, and walked into the dark of the bedroom, calling back a "night, love" before the hum of the extractor fan kicked in as she switched on the light in the ensuite.

He got up, filled a glass with chilled water from the fridge, and moved across to the living room space, to a chair next to the wide bay window, to sit in darkness to watch the city lights outside. What was that saying? "There are eight million stories in the naked city"? Maybe. It was a nice thought. Theirs was just one. But he was damn sure it was going to be a good one.

15

I t's like a hangover, the days after something like this. A crush of emotion, of endorphins and no little tension, and then, after a day or two with no obvious develop-ments, nothing is left but directionless wanderings and headaches.

Eleanor didn't miss a minute at work. Tony found himself caged in their flat for a day or two, not because of fear or anything like that, but just to take comfort in the safe, familiar surroundings of home, and not confident of being outside in the bustle of the city with his ribs as sore as they were. It let him assess every angle of their situation, as if it was a conundrum to be solved, or a treasure map to be decoded. In the end, it was the chirp of his phone that gave him new impetus, to at least do *something*.

Text message. Finally, he had the reply he had been waiting for.

Ringo – "IS GROUCHO OK?"

Ringo. Three days since he'd seen him, bleeding from his gut, with his nail-picking fruit knife sticking him deep on that bare forecourt. Calls and texts unanswered until now – not a surprise, but still Tony had to try and get hold of him. He knew the truth of what had happened, but if there was a chance he was wrong, and Ringo wasn't involved in this foolishness, then he owed it to him, and Groucho, to help him get out from under it, either by putting his story out there, or even, if there was a way, to get him out and safe, and let the scurrying Stark boys find someone else to string up as an offering to their boss.

Tony – "WHERE ARE YOU?"

Ringo – "IS HE OK?"

Tony – "DON'T KNOW. NOT HEARD FROM HIM."

Ringo – "WASN'T MY IDEA"

Tony – "WHOSE WAS IT?"

Ringo – "STUPID. THEY KNEW ABOUT THE GAME ALREADY. SAID I COULD GET A SPLIT IF I PLAYED ALONG"

Tony – "YOU ARE FUCKED, MATE. WHERE ARE YOU?"

Ringo – "CAN'T TELL YOU"

Tony – "ARE YOU SAFE?"

Ringo – "I DON'T KNOW. THEY'RE LOOKING FOR ME."

Tony – "THEY THINK I'M IN ON IT"

Ringo – "WHY WOULD THEY THINK THAT??"

Tony – "WHY WOULDN'T THEY? THEY DON'T KNOW ME"

Ringo – "SORRY"

Tony – "YOU NEED TO SORT THIS"

Ringo – "WHAT CAN I DO? I NEED TO GET OUT"

Tony – "YOU DO. WHEN IT'S QUIET."

Ringo –"I NEED MONEY"

Tony – "FUCK OFF!!!"

Ringo – "NO NOT FROM YOU. I HAVE MONEY. A BIT SAVED UP. GROUCHO HAS IT."

Tony – "SO?"

Ringo – "GET IT FOR ME. GO SEE HIM."

Tony – "I DON'T KNOW WHERE HE IS. THEY TOOK HIM AWAY AFTERWARDS."

Ringo – "IF HE COULD, HE'D GO TO HIS MUMS. TRY THERE."

There was a pause. Something was typed, deleted and then retyped. Ringo was clearly weighing up whether to let Tony in on something.

Ringo – "THERE'S A BOX AT HIS MUMS. HE KEEPS ALL HIS IMPORTANT STUFF THERE. THERE'S A BAG OF MINE IN THE BOX."

Tony – "YOU WANT ME TO GO TO HIS MUMS AND PERSUADE HER TO GIVE ME A BAG? I'VE NEVER MET HER"

Ringo – "JUST SAY THAT IT'S FOR RICHARD. THAT'S MY NAME. ONLY FRIENDS KNOW THAT."

Tony – "RICHARD AS IN RINGO?"

Ringo – "RINGO COS I'M BAD AT KEEPING TIME"

Tony – "ADDRESS?"

Ringo sent the address. At least now he had options. Something to do. But the way ahead that had been presented to him couldn't not complicate things for him, and he was very aware that he would have more dancing to do on the high-wire if he was going to keep as many options on the table as possible. Yin and yang. Positive and negative. He could do exactly what Ringo asked of him, and try and charm his way to getting hold of his escape route, and somehow find a way of getting it to him, unobserved, and chalk all this up to a foolish indiscretion, and get him on his way. Groucho could recover, time could pass, and before too long, all would be back to how it was, at least for Tony and Groucho. Or he could just tell Stark, get himself a pass, and let them stake out Groucho's mum's place, or worse (better?) bring them to Ringo, him lured out of whatever hole he was hiding in by the promise of his cash, and he could walk away with Ringo traded in for a clean slate and credit in the bank with Stark. But that sort of thing wasn't him. Even with Eleanor also in the spotlight, he couldn't forget the unswerving direction of that code he tried to live by, either for his sake, Eleanor's sake, or even Groucho's. There had to be a way for all sides to reset. And a bad option could be kept in play, if only to convince himself that he had choices.

He flung the phone across the living room, into the nest of cushions on the sofa. A bubbling anger was building in him, narrowing his vision, and raising his temperature. Involuntarily, his fists clenched, his veins bulged, and his shoulders stiffened. A growl rose in his throat, and he drew back an arm, to smash out, to burst this pressure, and break something. And then, like one of the gusts blasting in from the Mersey, it passed, and he felt smaller, and quieter, finding himself facing the bank of photos and memorabilia arranged on the wall of Army days, and Army nights. The past sobered him – purer, simpler, more ordered times with Eleanor. Reminded him of how far they had come, and also, how far they still had to go.

He would go to see Groucho's mum. Maybe she had Groucho. Maybe she knew where he was. And maybe, just maybe, he'd do as Ringo asked. But he didn't have to decide that until he was there. And kicking the can down the road was just fine, for now, as at least it gave the impression of a destination.

16

He didn't go immediately, but gave it a couple of days. He spent those days returning to a routine of sorts. He was fairly certain that the flat would've been watched for at least a period of time over those days, so it was important that he played his role to perfection, to put any suspicions out of the heads of anyone watching. A bit of time to lick wounds, to keep his head down, and then to get himself back out around town, run a few errands, and to absolutely quash any idea that he had something to hide, or something to be fearful about, over and above the "scare" that he got from his little sit-down back by the river. Go and get some groceries from the corner shop. Stroll down to the dock and sit with a pint for an hour or so. Not too obvious, but obvious enough that anyone following him would miss him. He half-expected some kind of intervention or powerplay again. But as he rolled through his thoughts in the pub, idly launching peanuts into his mouth, he suspected that Eleanor – beautiful, strident Eleanor – had popped that balloon by moving things on when she called her observers out on the street. Let them look, then. One thing he could do was wait.

Groucho's mum lived in one of the estates that clustered around the city centre like they were keeping warm. A council estate, once upon a time, hard grey walls, with the rough rendered finish, and hard angles and overhangs making the row of houses look fierce and bad-tempered. Every third house seemed to have a grab-rail and low step, as many of those who lived in these houses entered them when they were new and full of optimism, but never left, and as the paint chipped and darkened, so did their appetite to leave. One day became the next and months became years until it was too late to do any more than change the sofa suite every ten years or so. What this did mean was that the neighbourhood told its stories to anyone who would listen. When the rain stopped, it seemed like every street corner or garden fence was a soap opera, with tales of that lad in the next street, or the couple heard rowing on the green on Saturday night and didn't he leave her already? And didn't she move to Germany? And wasn't he in prison for holding all that dope in his car boot?

Tony couldn't not feel comfortable in an estate like this. He grew up on one like this, hundreds of miles away, but so similar he couldn't help dwell on his own memories. Much more comfortable than in more rarefied surroundings – he was happy drinking tea from a chipped mug in a greasy spoon café as he was pulling on a moth-eaten, decades-old sweater; as happy there as uncomfortable he was in places where smart shoes were required, unable to shake the suspicion that a genuflecting waiter was slipping in some undetectable sarcasm into his normal patter.

The house was hard to find. Council planners had tied themselves in knots when they put this estate together, with house numbers leaping from one side of the road to the other, then breaking as the road inexplicably bent off into a cul-de-sac, with the main artery road changing name to something else entirely. He walked the streets a few times, occasionally stopping to pull up a map on his phone to try and make sense of it. Four hundred yards from destination. He was always four hundred yards from destination, no matter where he walked. He stopped again, and spotted a little alleyway, a car-width or so wide, partly obscured by a fly-tipped sofa that had been dropped off in front of the road sign that signified this afterthought of local planning even existed. High leylandii hedges, unkempt and oppressive, leaned over the tarmac, isolating the houses that squatted behind them, as if they were ashamed to show their faces to the rest of the estate. A few wheelie-bins huddled together underneath a streetlight, jaunty, incongruous decoration daubed on them to passive-aggressively show ownership. It was early afternoon. Not dark yet, but thinking about it.

Now he'd found the house, he turned away, and took five more minutes to walk a loop around the side-streets, to get his head straight, preparing himself for dealing with whoever he found behind that door, be it Groucho's mum, or maybe even Groucho himself. He'd been trying to contact Groucho since that fucked-up night, but he'd had no reply at all. Perhaps he was in hospital. It was more than likely he'd had a bad knock, but if that was the case, and he wasn't here, then that threw up a clutch of other angles that would need assessing. If Groucho was still in hospital, then the injury was serious, worryingly so. Not here and not in hospital, and his situation would be a good deal worse. He'd either be hiding, like Ringo, or maybe even in some cold, bare room with a bag on his head and hands tied. Stark and his crew knew Tony was a new face, but Groucho and Ringo had been inseparable for as long as anyone knew, and guilt of one would very easily become the guilt of both of them, even if that was a falsehood.

Deep breath. Speculation was a waste of time and energy. Deal with what you know. And whatever the situation was currently, inertia would only lead to surprise, and the possibility of mistakes, so moving forward would at least take some possibilities off the table. It might add some new ones too.

Tony walked across the road, into the shadows cast by the hedgerows, and down to the end of the road-cum-driveway, a tall fence creating a border between the path and the embankment down to the old, disused and overgrown railway cutting behind it. The house he was looking for was the last on the right, similarly grey, as per the others on the estate, with ornamental butterflies vainly attempting to brighten the imposing aspect of the house front. The front garden was part-grassed and part-stone chips, both parts needing maintenance, with the grass overgrown, and the weeds pushing through between the stones. A few plastic planters were arranged around the perimeter of the lawn, but good intentions had long since died, along with the plants themselves, old stems: sad, skeletal reminders of life.

He tried to compose himself, in as short a time as possible so he didn't appear sinister or threatening, making the effort to relax his usual stoic expression into friendliness as he stood on the front step of the house. He was abundantly aware of the likelihood that there would be an elderly woman who could see him through the frosted glass of the porch door window. He tried to prepare some kind of script or approach that would see him as "friend" and not some kind of terrifying figure come to monster her, or her son, especially given who else might have knocked on this door in the past few days.

He rang the doorbell, and all of that prepared script emptied out of his head, almost as soon as he saw movement inside. At once, he had hoped someone would be in, but at the same time hoped that no-one would be, so he could walk away without having to have this encounter, and continue making excuses to himself to not head down this path again.

Through the frosted glass, he saw movement, and a darkening of the glass as someone slowly walked into the porch and to the door. A face came into slight focus as it squinted through the glass, trying to ascertain who might be on the other side, ringing the doorbell, and, if this estate was anything like the others he had been on, callers would be rare, and to be greeted with suspicion. A light came on in the porch, and the key turned in the lock, followed by the door opening a touch. A beady eye peered around the door to gauge the visitor.

"Yes? Who are you?" A gentle scouse accent called through, ostensibly friendly, but some wariness there underneath, nevertheless. The hand was gripped on the handle, ready to slam shut and lock, even though both sides knew if Tony wanted to force himself in, there was very little to stop him.

"I'm Tony. I'm one of...erm," he paused, steering his train of thought away from Groucho as *Groucho* and instead to his proper name – a name he filed away as soon as he heard it, but struggled to remember exactly where he put that piece of information. "...of Lawrence's friends. From work."

"I don't know you, son," she said, suspicion darkening her tone. Probably with merit.

"I'm sorry about that. But I work with Lawrence. We are friends from the gym. With Richard?"

"Don't know a Richard either." The door inched shut a little.

"We all meet at the gym together. Have breakfast together. Lawrence always has a big fry-up. At Coopers? The cafe opposite?" Tony was throwing darts left and right, trying to find something that might stick.

"Do you mean fat Richard? Always picking at his...at his...?" A chink of light in the conversation.

"...his fingers, yes. With that bloody knife of his!" Tony smiled, and a little chuckle. Forced, maybe, but convincing enough.

The door opened a little more. Conversational convention would have required the lady to have met his chuckle with her own, but she didn't give him even a millimetre of a smile. But he'd done enough to convince her to let her defences down a little, even if the door didn't open any further, only remaining ajar enough for Tony to see just half of her face.

She was the sort of woman who, even on her death-bed, would need to have make-up on, and her hair correct. But despite her best intentions, she couldn't mask the tiredness in her eyes, and the redness of them. Rouge couldn't hide the drawn cheeks, and her body seemed heavy.

"Is Lawrence here? Do you know where he is? I'm just checking up on him as...I haven't seen him for a while." Tony kept it vague. He had no idea what had happened after he had last seen him prostrate on the floor. Nor did he know what story Groucho had spun his mother. "Perhaps I can come in?"

"Lawrence is..." Her soft voice tailed off, Tony concentrating hard to ensure he caught every word. "Lawrence is..."

"Yes? Is he in?"

"Lawrence is dead, son. Dead."

Softness evaporated like fog clearing, revealing hard surfaces and rocky dangers ahead. She may have been a gentle soul, or perhaps just beaten down by the grief of it all, but she had found her steel now, and saying that word, voicing her pain at that stark reality, made her fierce, and determined, losing all inclination to be accommodating to whoever this was on her doorstep. The door closed, then locked, followed by the porch darkening and the door inside closing behind her as she retreated back to the sanctuary of her back kitchen. Tony, incapacitated by the shock of what he'd just heard, had no response quick enough to stop her closing the door, and now it had closed, he didn't have the energy or wit to think of a way to convince her to open it again. Everything else be damned. Errand be damned. Ringo be damned. He can sort his own mess out, and Tony needed to get away from here and think.

17

The walk home was a series of foggy images, as his concentration dipped in and out of sharp focus. If anyone had asked him his route home, he would've struggled to recall where he had walked, letting his feet take him where they willed. He lost himself in thought. Occasionally, he would find his focus, realise where he was, and then re-orientate himself back in the general direction of the city centre, and home. His brow furrowed, his teeth clacked and rattled as he beat out an internal drumbeat, staccato and insistent, as if it would help organise his mind into workable plans, and chase away the gloom that had crushed it.

Dead. Dead. Dead. He heard that word, in that soft voice, over and over again, like a timpani soundtrack. Ricochet thoughts bounced around, either replaying the incident over and over, punishing himself with ways, however improbable, that could have prevented something – anything! – or just torturing himself with how, in retrospect, he could've intuited things differently. Then his mind span off, racing forwards and backwards from that pinch point –

how had he got to this position? What would happen now? How safe were they? *What happens now?*

He got home, minutes later in his head, but hours later in reality, the door shutting behind him snapping him out of his reverie, safe again in the handful of rooms that were his. And at the centre of his safe place – his home – Eleanor sat at the kitchen table, illuminated by a single spotlight, like a lighthouse in all this turmoil. She looked up, dropped her fork into the mostly-empty food bowl she had been sparring with, not needing to say anything with the expression on her face just asking for conversation.

So, he sat down opposite her, and reached across to take a sip from her wine glass, cleared his throat, and told her.

"How?" Her tone was one of shock, and humanity, with any worry in check for now. Get the facts, then deal with the knowables.

"I don't know. I didn't think straight enough to ask her. It's true, though. She wasn't lying."

"Christ." Her voice was soft, and empty. She repeated "Christ." again, as if she needed to say something to ward off more bad news that might come to fill any silence.

But silence came nonetheless. Tony was comfortable dropping into those thoughts again, lost for any direction out, but Eleanor was always one to fight against that tide, and when he had the wherewithal to look up, and look at her, he could see her brow furrowing, not only with the weight of this tragedy, but, ever the pragmatist, running equations and probabilities. He knew Eleanor, she was trying to come up with some kind of direction or next step, even if it was a flawed one, until a better option came along.

"Do nothing." She said it softly at first, as if she was verifying with herself that this was the right course of action. Then, more certain, she said it again, a mantra for confidence. "Do nothing. What *can* you do, anyway?" The darkness of the flat, and the soft light above the table, demanded soft voices.

"What do you think Stark's lot are thinking? They must know he's dead." Tony always valued her opinion, and was never afraid to ask. Her practical nature was his tether, on those occasions where he found himself lost.

"No doubt. They'll be watching. They'll *keep* watching, at least until they believe you, which, if they have anything about them will take some time. You're going to have some hurdles to clear. I think they're going to make you sweat."

"I agree. Do we stay?"

"Sure. I think we can ride this out. Even if we did want to get away, it's risky. Especially now. If we get it wrong, then it's an admission of guilt, and we could end up like..."

"Yeah. I get it, yeah." Groucho's name didn't need saying. "So what next? Just wait?"

"Give it a few days. Don't do anything daft. Do some normal stuff. Coffee, gym, all that. We'll see what they do next. Maybe they try and turn the screws again. Or maybe they just go after Ringo and consider you in the clear."

"They might come after you again?"

"They might. It's okay. I'm not daft, Tone."

"I know, I know. Just..."

"...be careful. Look. They're like one of those coffee shops that sprouted up everywhere. Got big too quick, and have never had to get too smart, because it's been *easy* up to now. Woe betide them if someone sharp comes into this town. This lot sound like they are all just muscle and threats, and nothing between the ears. Why else let that big lump come and wag his finger at me on a busy street, for God's sake?"

"...which could help us. Perhaps. They're predictable. But dangerous."

"Yes, that's the thing to be careful of. I think we need to treat them like a toddler. All tantrums and smashing stuff, especially after they've shit themselves," she smiled, breaking the mood.

"You know how I feel about kids...!" He managed to laugh. An old line, recycled. They'd never gotten around to having kids, which other than the odd wistful "should we have?" wasn't contentious between them. They enjoyed the freedom, and light-footedness, that the two of them had. Besides given the line of work that Tony had found himself orbiting over the past decade or more, they could never justify trading off the lack of binding ties for someone that they'd have to worry about, if ever they found themselves in a position like this.

"How about you just take a few days for you? Keep your head down, nothing exciting, and then, end of the week, go to one of the places you know is theirs, and just see where that leaves you? I can't imagine they'd expect a guilty man to show up for work again, like nothing's happened? And even given how embarrassed they are, and how impulsive they might be, I can't imagine they blame you? You might just need to eat shit and grin for a while."

"Oh, I can do that. I can definitely do that."

He took another sip of her wine, smiled at his own impertinence, then pushed the glass back across the table to her. He had direction. He could cling to that.

18

Out of your routine, out of your surroundings, out of being able to remember three things of usual currency about everyone you saw in any given day, and it was easy to feel out of time as well. Cold Cut wasn't happy. He didn't really know where he was, he certainly didn't fully understand why he had driven himself here, to this arse-end of the country, surrounded by red-faced fat men in windcheaters, and passive-aggressive shrews in cars too big for them. The voices were ridiculous. Bumpkin clichés better suited to discussing lambing practice or smashing spinning jennies than intruding on his oxygen. He was relieved when he turned off hedge-bordered roads, to greyer, constructed surrounds, comforted by the cookie cutter appearance of council housing and brutalist flats.

King's Lynn. One of those towns that became small urban oases in a sea of green fields and long driveways. Dragged up when the ships and the field work demanded a relationship, but now withering on the vine, as circumstance and economics made the old ways increasingly pointless. Eastern Europeans had come over as cheap labour, picking the fruit the locals wouldn't touch, but even the immigrants were reconsidering, leaving just the hardy, the foolish and the stubborn, pressed together on estates, scowling at each other, suspicion aimed at any accent not identical to their own. Cold Cut didn't care about any of that. He hated them all equally.

He especially hated who he was living with. Six weeks he'd been living here, able to wield the word "family" like an oath, to people who still believed despite everything, that it was a word with actual weight and consequence. Cousins of an old scouse uncle, who fled the city at the soonest possible opportunity, and despite falling into an estate that felt like a tepid cover version of his streets back home, never shut up mythologizing his move as one of "clean air and good people" which, to Cold Cut's eyes, was either a long dead past, or bullshit from start-to-finish. But, family was family, wasn't it? He didn't have much of that left, as all those in his near orbit back in Liverpool had either been wrung dry of money, or of patience, or of life, and left him well alone. All of them except his mother, an empty shell of a woman, wheezing from a lifetime of cigarettes, and led by the hand gingerly around the most basic of care homes that she had been deposited in, and left to die, withering away like a forgotten plant on a forgotten shelf. He hadn't seen her in years, unable to face those vacant, glassy eyes, and wait for the clouds of confusion to part, even if only for a few minutes. And when she did recognise him, it was somehow worse, as the innocent confusion was replaced by that old expression of disappointment when she realised who it was sat across from her. So he didn't go anymore. She had nothing to offer him, and he had nothing he wanted to offer in return.

Here, now, these people had never been given the opportunity to grow tired of him, and after swallowing his pride to once again play the role of good-hearted naïf, which had served him so well in his teens, he was able to persuade them to take him in, if "only for a few days". Even better, dear old Uncle Knobhead had the added indignity of having to open the door to him in presumably reduced circumstances, with his tiny box flat a far cry from the mansion he had conjured up whenever a family event had previously brought them all together. Cold Cut nodded along to tales of hardship and double-cross, sympathetic on the surface, nudging and cajoling the conversation until his uncle had suggested that they go to the pub, and he catch up with his cousins, as maybe they could help him out?

Cold Cut was almost impressed. Whilst his uncle was there, the conversation ran on two levels simultaneously. Out-loud it was platitude, but underneath it was fencing and tactics, as his two cousins, twins Keiran and Connor, poked and prodded in their own way. Like knows like, and whilst Cold Cut never allowed himself to feel intimidated by these two, him being on their patch, them knowing their streets and their people, he did feel a feral admiration for them – they were more similar than he had expected. Maybe the apple doesn't fall far from the tree?

"Prick." Keiran went from jab to right-cross, as soon as Unc' had shambled off to the toilet, via the fruit machine, spoken over the top of his pint, just before pulling another sip from it.

"Yeah, prick. Fuck off home," Connor said following Keiran's lead and doubling down.

"We don't like you, we never liked you, we don't give a fuck who you are, and we want you to fuck off out of it."

Keiran leaned forward, underlining the point, then insouciantly slumped back in his seat. Over to you, Cold Cut.

"Boys, c'mon. It's just a few days. Help a brother out."

"Sort yourself out. Why'd you fucking come here in any case?" Connor said. He wore his dark cap pulled down, visor bent to a tight semi-circle on his brow. His thin, wiry face seemed to run in the family. Connor stared at Cold Cut. Keiran sipped his pint, observing the pair for now.

"Things got hot back home. You know how it is, right, lads? Got myself a little too...busy into something."

"Don't know what you mean," Connor said, knowing exactly what he meant. Maybe this fool would spell it out for him.

"Christ, boys. We're *family*."

"Fuck family," came back in unison, which led to stares from the twins, and silence, only interrupted by the ching-ching-ching of coins from the fruit machine as their father, Cold Cut's uncle, had a payout, which he would inevitably feed back into the slot in short order.

Cold Cut regrouped. Sipped on his rum and coke. Rotated the beer mat with one finger, wondering what cards he had to play.

He sighed.

"I can make things worth your while."

"Our while is worth a fucking lot, *Graham*," Keiran said.

Connor bounced in his seat, impressed at his brother's word play, such as it was.

"I fucking bet. Look..." Cold Cut reached inside his waistband, took a sip of his drink, and put his hand flat on the table, with something underneath it. No-one was looking at them, but he wasn't going to ever be anything less than careful, now more than ever. The two brothers, all pretence at street smarts washing out of them like a handful of sand in the rain, leaned forward, eyes fixed on Cold Cut's hand.

"...Easy." He didn't smile, but Cold Cut felt like it. This is all it took for these clowns to snap into line. He really was out in the sticks.

He lifted his hand, just enough, so they could see underneath. A plastic baggie, with a small amount of white powder in it. They saw it, understood it, quickly glanced at each other, then back to Cold Cut. He covered the packet again, then slowly removed his hand from the table, baggie taken along with it.

"So fucking what?" Connor said. "It's just some blow. Want me to show you ours? Dick."

"Patience, Boys. Okay. Now look at this." Cold Cut dug into another pocket now, and pulled out his phone, scrolling through, bringing up a picture from the photo stream. He showed the picture to the two men.

"That's a big fucking brick," Keiran said.

"Yes, it *fucking* is. It's somewhere safe. That's why I'm here. Got this from someone I know, and it's *so good* that all the faces back home are worried I'll put them out of business if I start slinging it around. But..." he leant closer, and lowered his voice, "reckon no-one would be any the wiser if we just slung it down here, right? Make a tidy amount." He said the word "we" with implied underlining. These idiots would take the bait.

"Give us that bag, and we'll try it first." The idiots took the bait.

Cold Cut smiled and passed the bag under the table to Connor, who was nearest to him, in the cushioned semi-circle of the tattered booth they were sharing. Time to show some "gratitude" as these marks were ripe for the plucking. He could spare a little bit of blow, and he knew enough of people like this, family or otherwise, that he could manipulate however he wanted, now they had revealed themselves so absolutely.

"Course, lads. Take the bag. It's yours. Just let me know what you think."

The twins scuttled off to the toilets, Cold Cut wincing at how embarrassing they were, not even attempting to hide their excitement at some free blow, "expertly" negotiated from this fool from the big city, who thought he could get one over the country boys. He reclined further into his seat, and scanned the pub, as he took another sip of his rum. His idiot uncle still transfixed by the lights and noises of the fruit machine, his idiot cousins barrelling past a couple of girls dressed in too-tight tops and too-short skirts, unable to resist a smile as he recalled what they would say back home about looking like a "burst sofa". Looking around, he started to appreciate that this pub was like hundreds of other pubs he had known, back in Liverpool. Perhaps this *could* work. A safe place for him to stay out of things, whilst his crew did the hard yards back home, finding Ringo, and finding him not only a reason to go back, but also, maybe, a way of climbing the ladder, all sins forgiven.

He had a brick of coke. Good coke. There might still be a way for him to not only make a *significant* bit of wedge on it, but also wield it like a magic wand, waving it at mouth-breathers, both here and in Liverpool, to get them to jump to his tune, maybe even without giving up too much of it. It was currency, and if he was clever, it was currency that he could use to buy his way out of this cesspit he had stumbled into. Drip-drip-drip a few grams here and there for the twins, to buy him bed and board, and promise the three clowns back in Liverpool the payout of a lifetime to be his eyes and ears. They were weak. Amateur. All of them. He deserved better, and he was going to get it, and he would step on their backs to get it, same as always.

"YES!" The pub turned as one, towards the fruit machine. His uncle had won the jackpot. All twenty-five quid of it. Small scale, but a win is a win. Cold Cut liked the omen.

19

E quilibrium was reestablished gradually. The whole sorry affair with Ringo, and Groucho, became *omerta*, for all manner of reasons. Not least because no-one quite knew how to square what had happened. One half of their double-act allowed a situation, seemingly motivated by the basest of reasons, to become so dangerous that his best friend ended up dead. If they avoided talking about it, they could avoid considering that it could happen to them. But even that paled when balanced against an even more pervasive reason to keep quiet about it – you don't poke and prod someone like Jim Stark and his boys. Especially not when they're embarrassed, unless you want to walk with a stick or breathe with an iron lung.

So, Tony found himself back in those circles before too long. After a week or so of conspicuous idling, he acciden-tally-on-purpose took a longer detour than usual on his usual walks around town, to ensure he walked past a few of the pubs and dens that he had been asked to work at with Ringo and Groucho. The lower-level faces that he'd come to recognise were sufficiently removed from the higher strata of the organisation, and so, had nothing to prevent them from a friendly nod, or a raised hand of acknowledgement as he passed by. The next day, those nods and waves became beckons and thumbs-ups, as slowly and surely, the thaw began – after all, if Tony was comfortably walking around town, and wasn't avoiding anyone, then surely he was away from the glare of suspicion? Surely he was okay?

His phone chirped with messages again – his conduit, Groucho, had gone, and Ringo wasn't replying again, but by degrees of separation, other names started to check in. Would he be interested in a night's work? Simple little door job? Tony had impressed many with his rise to trust in the organisation, so for him to be available again to those at ground-level was an opportunity for a safe pair of hands to be back in circulation, for however long he was deemed to have to stay on the naughty step, if that's what was happening. Tony presumed this was all done with someone's blessing, as making arbitrary decisions was a sure-fire way of accelerating towards the knock in the middle of the night. Everything was happening just as he and Eleanor had discussed, and hoped. But their eyes were open now – they were warier than ever, and made double and trebly-sure that any exit plan they had in place was primed and solid, should the need ever arise.

This had crystallised one thought in their minds, and they both seemed to make that conclusion independently of each other. Fifty years old this year, and still getting ribs broken, because of petty greed and pettier men. It had to be time to move away from all this, and stop talking about the future as an abstract, but as a real and definite time and place to work towards. "Soon" had to become a date ringed on a calendar, and once they both started to say it out loud, they were both comforted that neither one of them was putting up a fight or throwing a hand-waved platitude before turning over in bed, and switching off the light. They needed to get out of cities, and away from gangs, and fights, and turf, and bundles of notes, and all of that house of cards, and go and find that idyll that they so loved to daydream about. And once they had accepted this, and started to debate the practicalities, they realised that all they had been doing for years was hiding from a step into the unknown – it was doable, it was doable *now*, and all they needed to do was keep their heads down for a few months, convince those who needed convincing that they were on the up-and-up, and just smile and nod and play along until one day they could just vanish, leaving nothing behind but a few anecdotes and no forwarding address.

Tony found out about Groucho soon enough. His suspicions proved unfounded. No ultimate sanction for him; instead, he just never woke up from a blow behind the ear, when those desperate, deranged wretches had careered into the offices that night. There was the smallest kernel of comfort in that. He'd been tormenting himself with horror stories, his imagination spiralling out of kilter, based on the fairy tale of reputation that Stark had conjured for himself around those city streets. Images of pain, of fear, of torture, with the Red Pope's grin hanging above it all like the Cheshire Cat.

Tony felt comfortable back in the shallows, working inconsequential jobs here and there – nothing more stressful than having to scowl once in a while at some pissed-up suit or over-confident hoodie, who had either stepped where he shouldn't, or had overstayed his welcome after having his wallet cleaned at the poker table. He hadn't needed to ball his fist once in six weeks, and was getting regular work three or four times a week, banking the hundred or so quid each time, but more importantly, banking the goodwill he was getting, until, through a combination of solid work and his solid nature, and the general attitude of 'don't ask, don't tell,' it was like he'd never been under suspicion in the first place, at least not by the rank and file he was surrounded by.

He occasionally saw some of the faces from that night, but only ever on the periphery. A driver, or maybe even one of the hallowed "names" who made up the close circle that had attended that night. A Stark cab was hard to miss, given their ubiquity, but Tony made sure to keep an eye on them, out of the corner of his eye, as they passed, his cautious nature always making him ready to move if a car door sprang open a little too close for comfort. He thought he saw the tell-tale blond of the Red Pope on more than one occasion, but never close enough to be sure. It was a small city. He was being paranoid, most likely. But despite this, Eleanor and Tony reassured each other that being careful was not a handicap, especially given how tantalisingly close their exit was becoming. Head down. No mistakes. Then vanish.

Tony felt comfortable minding doors again. Back to the floor. Something he had done so often that it was muscle memory, able to steady out his thoughts, as he passed the time, counting down to the pat on the back and the folded twenties in his hand. This time it was minding the door at a "meet", which was ostensibly a formal strategy get-together for some of the lower-level sorts in this sprawling, inter-linked organisation, but would, after thirty minutes of posturing and boasting, devolve into piss-taking and gambling, lubricated by free-pour measures of the finest booze a supermarket could provide. It was almost comical, how performative it was – Tony could start a stop-watch and time each waypoint by how loud the voices were, or how screeching the laughter became. They all think they're the funniest, the sharpest, the bravest, but he knew, from many, many nights of experience stood outside, and occasionally inside, doors like this, in pubs like this, that it's all just the same merry-go-round, only with different faces and different accents. So what? He didn't care. Let them pay him, and he would get back to his internal musings.

Time wore on. The drinkers in the public bar, front of house, were shooed out into the night, and the staff busied themselves clearing glasses, a frantic ten minutes of tidying-up, in the hope that the sooner it was finished, the sooner they too could grab coats and escape into the night, tired from a long night of being on the receiving end of bad flirting or worse stories. The jukebox was unplugged, lights switched off, and the low-level hum of conversation had long since petered out, except for the buzz in the back room, where the meeting was just finding its feet. This was usually the part of the night where things got easy for Tony – no drunks staggering through to test him, or worse, engage him in small talk, and a locked door acting as first defence from anything more sinister. One of the staff had brought him through a cup of tea, which he had set down on the floor by his feet, no chair for him to sit on, as he was most definitely "on duty" and the bosses just couldn't let standards slacken off, now, could they? Let them have their little victories, he thought, but this was no real hardship for him.

Alone in the quiet, he pushed deeper into his thoughts.

A thump on the outside door centred him, reflexes kicking in, he scanned his internal checklist before investigating. Was it a distraction? Was it a drunk, after their forgotten coat left over the back of a chair? If this was sinister, what escape did he have? What weapons could he find?

How could he alert his paymasters? He worked it through, in seconds that felt like minutes, just double-checking all of those questions he asked himself over and over, on a night like this. One last time, before he moved things forward, once he was certain he was ready. The door thumped again and again, in threes, though Tony scrupulously refused to hurry himself along, just in case any haste allowed something to happen he would regret.

He walked around the bar, now dark, checking round curtains out into the street-lit street to see who might be out there. The bar was long, and wide-windowed, allowing views along the two streets that intersected on the corner on which the pub stood. The odd car ambled past, but he could see nobody unusual. He couldn't quite see who was at the door, though – just the back of a leg, obscured by the angle of the bay window. It was just one person, but who it was would remain a mystery until he opened that door. So be it. Maybe he *had* missed something, but he could do no more, and, whatever happened, he did have to open that door. Three more thumps. He unlocked the mortice lock, then reached up to the Yale, and turned it, opening the door at the same time. The thumps stopped at one, this time, as the door unlocked.

The grin. The hair. The scar.

"I thought you'd never open this door, son." The Red Pope leered down at him. He was dressed exactly the same as the last time he had seen him. Tony was sure that this was the sort of man who had thirty identical shirts and thirty identical pairs of shoes, in his wardrobes in whatever minimalist nightmare of a flat this idiot thought was cutting-edge. Unconsciously, Tony shifted his weight, and angled his feet; a subtle change of stance readying himself for whatever came his way, especially if it was another burst of violence.

He wasn't going to take another punch from this man without preparing himself for it.

"I'll come in, if you don't mind?"

It wasn't a question, but a statement, as the Red Pope walked straight into the pub, as a provocation, or a test. Tony closed the door behind him. As he did, the Red Pope turned his back to Tony transmitting bravado, hands in pockets, turning his head this way and that, as if a darkened pub was a source of great fascination for him, scrutinising the screwed-on sepia photographs showing the building through the ages. Get to the fucking point, already.

"Are they expecting you?" Tony said, trying not to rise to him. Play your role.

"Oh, never tell them you're coming. You might catch them doing something they shouldn't." He tapped his nose, and winked.

"Right, okay. Let yourself in, then?"

"Maybe. In a minute."

Tony waited. More posturing?

"It's you I wanted a word with, as it happens. I've been asked to invite you somewhere. Someone *very important* wants a bit of a catch-up with you, now we're all friends again."

"Who's that then?"

"No names, you know that. You're not stupid. Stupid is what your mate got up to. Stupid is not behaving. And you, Son, have been behaving. Keep it up, and you'll be fine."

Tony half-expected a cheek pinch, like a sixth-form Corleone, but it thankfully never came.

"Keep this safe. Read it later. It's a place and a time. An invite for you, and your lady, to meet someone. Attendance is mandatory." Pope reached inside his jacket pocket, and took out a folded piece of paper, which he gave to Tony.

Tony resisted the urge to open it and read it, and instead, slid it into the back pocket of his jeans. Eleanor, though? That was taking the piss.

"Not sure I'm bringing my missus. She's got nothing to do with this work. Or with you. Just so you know." Tony was digging in. Fuck them for thinking he was going to let her get involved – not more than she was already. Eleanor was smart, and brave, but they tried to strong-arm her on the street, of all places, and he had very much filed that infraction away for revisiting later. Possibly with a crowbar.

The Red Pope leaned down, looming over Tony, using his height as an exclamation point. "*Just so you know*, you're going to do as you're *fucking* told." He moved away, having made his point. Change of tone – the soft with the hard – "Now don't be a twat. This is nice. You'll see. Nice little get-together. More of a...social invite." The Red Pope flashed that grin Tony recognised far too well, just like before, but those shark eyes remained unblinking.

Tony said nothing. He knew this man was just an automaton in three-hundred pound brogues. Point-and-shoot, and off he would go, to do his boss' bidding, with nuance and reason alien to him. If he was told to stomp on someone's head, then he would crunch away until it was nothing but puddle and mush beneath his heel. But despite this, and despite his better judgment, he couldn't quite control the antipathy he had for this man from escaping from him. The eyes needed to be deferential, and obedient, but he could feel them steel, and burn, as he looked up at the Red Pope. His sensible side demanded a quiet end to this conversation, but his fierce ego, so often in check, couldn't resist a poke and prod.

The riposte from the Red Pope was the grin. Again. Flashed like a dagger being drawn from a sheath.

"Ha! Good man! I like you, son. No hard feelings from last time, eh? You took a good shot." He leaned in again. "Did I break anything? A crack maybe? Old bones, I expect." A wheeze of a laugh.

"No harm done. A job's a job, isn't it? Not my first time. Are we done now?" Tony angled himself between the Red Pope and the back of the bar, showing him towards the door.

"Yeah, we're done, son. Good man. Don't be late," he pointed at Tony.

Tony didn't move towards the door. Let this damn fool open it himself. A small inconvenience could be his small victory. It was noticed.

"I'll get the door, don't worry, son. You carry on. Only a few hours to go, I expect. Busy night for you, I'll bet."

Tony stiffened. Yeah, laugh it up, knobhead. I'm happy with my place. Just get to fuck, and let me have my peace.

The Red Pope opened the door, looked both ways, turned and grinned one more time for effect, raising his right hand to wave, before walking on, letting the door self-close behind him, with a thud. Tony glared at the door, and, under his breath, cursed at it.

He walked back to his station, realising his cup of tea had gone tepid, in stark contrast with his boiling blood. He knew he was in real danger of being irrational with that man. The punch was painful but predictable. The intimidation of Eleanor was similarly predictable, but still, a line was crossed. All he could see in his mind's eye was that grin – a haunted clown with bad aftershave, almost comically created to piss Tony off in every little way. His equilibrium had been nudged off-kilter, and his quiet, precise thoughts were now technicolour wish fulfilment, as he fantasised about small rooms, handcuffs, bats, knives, and knuckle-dusters. This flight of fancy kept him warm for a long ten minutes until reality snapped back into focus. The note! He hadn't even read it yet.

He reached into the back pocket of his jeans, and took out the piece of paper, unfolding it underneath one of the few spot-lamps still lit, that hung from arched arms attached to flock-wallpapered walls. Written in pen, in block capitals, it read -

"BUBBLETOWN KIDS CLUB

SATURDAY 10AM

BRING ELEANOR"

He read it again. And again. Soft play? A soft play centre? What the hell was this all about? His quiet thoughts had been nuked now. With the Red Pope fresh in his memory, and this curveball presented to him, he wasn't going to settle. Those hours ahead of him stretched into infinity, and his evening crawled. He needed to talk to Eleanor and work this one out.

20

Saturday came in a hurry, as if at such a pace just so they couldn't quite get their bearings. Of course, they went early, old habits dying hard, first doing a lap or two of the block, and then ten minutes before 10am, they walked into the car park, and quietly scanned the rows of Chelsea tractors and SUVs for a clue or a hint as to what this might be about. It was times like this they regretted not having a car, as they would have liked the opportunity to have parked up and sat and watched quietly for longer, without standing out to anyone who might've spotted them.

The play centre was a flat-roofed building – two storeys high. But looking through the high glass windowed front, you could see the first storey had been pulled out to allow for the tall slides and large network of tunnels and ladders that made up the bulk of the play area. Garish window vinyls had been stuck to the glass with gleeful, cross-eyed clown motifs and unicorns gambolling across the panes. From the car park, it was obvious that the centre was busy, judging by the frequent squeals and shrieks as the kids ran, jumped and slid on the obstacles inside. Tony glanced at

Eleanor, who looked back at him, both mirroring each other's expression of bemusement, so ridiculous it would've led to smiles, without the context of who had called them there – this was the right place, but was it *really* the right place? A children's centre? Seriously?

They opened the double doors and entered, all of a sudden feeling conspicuous by not having a child of their own in tow, but, in for a penny, joining the small queue at the counter, with put-upon and somewhat desperate looking parents lined up, hoping to get this transaction out of the way so they could head straight to the café counter, letting their children veer into the chaos of the ballpits and apparatus. The queue wasn't moving quickly, thanks to an increasingly irritated mum rooting around in her bag for a purse that had hidden itself under a juice box, a spare sweater and some angel wings, all deposited on the counter-top as the forensic exploration continued. She was also repeatedly interrupted by a little girl pulling on her arm, as if that would make the purse appear faster.

"...Wait. Wait," the mother barked.

The distraction was welcome. It bought them a few more seconds to scan around, again looking for clues, but none were forthcoming. It looked exactly like it should. No false walls, no sinister men lurking around the perimeter, no scared staff tapping out morse SOS on the counter. What *was* this?

They paid, smiling to the counter-staff who had far too much to juggle than to wonder why two middle-aged people might possibly be here, childless. And even if they did, it wasn't that unusual for 'auntie and uncle' to turn up to places like this. Someone had to be moral support for the parents on the other side of the turnstile. As aunt and uncle they got to top up on gossip, safe in the knowledge that they can hand the kids back after the hour or so. It was 10am exactly. Bang on time. They stood on the other side of the turnstile, and again scanned the room, trying to ascertain exactly why they were there. And then, from a table near to the café counter, a hand went up. Broad grin. A man and a woman. Tony didn't know the woman, but he knew the man. Jim Stark.

"...it's Stark," Tony whispered to Eleanor. He raised an eyebrow acknowledging Stark, from across the room.

"What? Seriously? Here?"

"Come on," Tony said and stood back, to allow Eleanor to take the lead as the gaps between tables weren't wide enough for two, even without considering the constant flow of racing children weaving in and out of the tables, after topping up on sugary drinks and crisps, before diving back into the soft floored play area. He gently squeezed her shoulder – we are together. We will cope with this, whatever this is.

"Excellent! Magic!" Jim called across to them as they got within earshot, clapping his hands together, then beckoning enthusiastically. The woman who was sat opposite him had also turned now, matching Stark's welcome with her own warm expression. As before, Tony couldn't help but marvel at the incongruity of Jim Stark, even admiring the chutzpah of hiding in plain sight – again, he looked exactly as you would expect someone who had made a career driving taxis might look. Practical trousers, high street shoes, a loose shirt and a quilted armless vest. The hair slicked back, and a grin matched by the sparkle from the garish necklace around his fat neck.

Stark stood up as the couple approached, "So glad you could make it. Great to see you again."

Tony inwardly cringed as he half-expected Stark to try

and lean forward to greet Eleanor with a kiss on the cheek, but, thankfully, he just extended his hand for a handshake. First for Eleanor, Tony noted both Stark's hands held hers. Then Stark gave Tony a particularly enthusiastic handshake, gently pulling him to a seat, and emphasising the greeting with a slap on the back. The woman sat at the table extended her hand to Eleanor, as Tony was being aggressively greeted by Stark.

"Oh, lovely! So nice to meet you! Jim?" The woman held onto Eleanor's hand, and turned to Stark.

"Manners, manners. I'm terrible, aren't I? Tony. Eleanor. This is my good lady, Jackie."

Jackie was the sort of woman who made an effort to go to the corner shop. Nails immaculate and lurid. Rings on most fingers. A tight, zipped salmon exercise jacket, and dyed-blonde hair pulled back into a ponytail. Her make-up was flawless. Clearly, she had the time for beauty treatments and the motivation for exercise and self-care to push back against getting older.

Eleanor played along. "Nice to meet you." All four sat down. The table was a mess of bags, sweet papers, brightly-coloured juice bottles, and crisp shrapnel. A couple of pink backpacks were on the floor underneath two of the chairs.

"Grandkids," Stark said by way of explanation, tipping his head at the mess of plastic and foam that made up the play area. He rolled his eyes, mugging to his audience.

"Right, of course." Tony was playing along, but what was this about? He knew Stark. He'd been working enough nights with people who, despite themselves, couldn't help but tell fairy stories about the sort of man Stark *really* was, and even if only five percent of those stories were true, this man – this grinning, hammy charlatan – was a stone-cold killer.

"So, sorry about all the cloak and dagger, but I don't get much time out of work, and this was the best we could do. Kids party this afternoon. Coof!" He scrunched his face, as if he had taken a bite of a sour fruit. Then, again, his grin. That laugh.

"I love 'em, though. God knows where they are!"

"He's a right softy with them. You spoil them, you old sod!" Jackie joined in now. An affectionate pat on Stark's hand as she playfully jousted with him. "Any kids yourself?"

"No, not for us. Think we've missed the boat on that one," Eleanor said. She was used to this sort of question, and as the woman, society seemed to expect her to have a good excuse why she hadn't been "blessed".

"Oh, no, love. Don't say that. You're never too old. Not with all that science they can do now."

"Well, we'll see. I think I'm quite grateful of the quiet, especially when I come to a place like this." Eleanor was gamely playing along. Tony and Eleanor were both fighting to ignore the incongruity of exactly who they were speaking to, and instead, were trying to play this drama at face value.

"I know what you mean, love! This old man still tries to drag himself up to the slides, you know. He really shouldn't, but he just can't say no, can you, love?"

"That's what Grandad does. He does as he's told," Stark laughed.

Jackie gave him an 'oh you' face.

"Look, I know you're probably looking forward to your weekend, so we won't keep you too long. Maybe you girls can go and grab a coffee and me and young Tony here can have a bit of work chat?"

"Come on, love. I know what you mean. Caffeine is an essential in these places," Jackie said, getting to her feet.

Eleanor had no choice but to do the same because

Jackie had linked arms with her. A subtle insistence that Eleanor stand up so 'the girls' could head across to the café counter and join the continuous queue of tired-looking parents trying to medicate their morning with strong, burnt coffee. Stark watched them walk off, warm smile on his face, until he felt they were out of earshot. He leaned towards Tony.

"I'm not happy, Tony. You can imagine why."

Tony said nothing. It's better to let someone think you're an idiot, than open your mouth. Let's see where this goes.

"Friends of mine – *good* friends of mine – lost a lot of money, and were made to look like fucking idiots, thanks, in no small part, to one of the men who recommended you to us. So, I'm thinking, does this fella – this fella we don't really know, who just turned up in town out of the blue, not all that long ago – have the brass fucking balls or the solid fucking brain to think he could get away with something like this, and then, presumably, fuck right off out of town again, never to be seen again?"

Stark hissed every curse, though for all the next tables could guess, he could just be talking about some car park indiscretion, or that penalty that wasn't given at the game last week.

"So, I'm sure you won't be surprised to know that we've been keeping an eye on you. Were you just unlucky, or were you just monumentally brain-dead? That one..." he nodded towards Eleanor, "is a game girl, though, isn't she? I'm sure you know another one of my friends had a chat with her as well. From experience, happy marriages are all about honesty, so there was no way you'd have a go at a job like that without letting your missus in on it."

Tony clenched his jaw. *Don't mention her. And don't you dare threaten her, or so help me, I'll pull you across the table, and beat the shit out of you, and screw where I am and who can see me.* Breathe. Control.

"And we kept looking, and asking questions. See, I know you know who we are. You're not stupid. You can't be. We've seen enough from your work – good work, as it goes. Quiet, sensible, *proper* work. But I don't take chances. Ever."

He reached inside his trouser pocket and pulled out his phone. A few prods and pokes, and then he turned the screen to Tony, so he could see the image he'd full-screened for him to see. As he talked, he swiped across, a narration to this particular story.

"So, we followed you. We followed your lady. Saw where you went and what you did. Who you spoke to, where you shopped, what you did when you went out."

Pictures of the back of his head in a convenience store appeared on screen followed by images of Eleanor through the window of her work, or the two of them in a queue at the cinema, lost in conversation.

Tony kept quiet, so Stark continued. "But nothing. You did nothing to give the game away. So, there I am, having a think, with some very angry friends of mine in my ear, and I wonder 'could be this fella is just unlucky, and his stupid mate has just done all this on his own, for God knows whatever stupid reason' and so, I've just thought, 'we'll keep an eye on him, but maybe he's okay with us, and can get back to being useful again.' But we had a *proper* look as well. Just to be doubly sure. And who knows? Maybe we could find that fucking *dead man* somehow because believe you me, he's dead when he pops his stupid little head out from wherever he's been hiding it."

Stark swiped the phone again. "You interest me, Tony. I like you. I was thinking you could do a bit more for us."

He angled the phone for Tony again. A picture now of

the inside of their flat. His fingers dug into his knees, below the table. Stark kept the phone held up, and turned his head to see where the women were in the queue.

"They won't be long. I do like to talk. Right, so, this is what caught my eye."

He swiped again, past pictures of the rooms in their flat – the kitchen, the living room, the bedroom, the toilet even, pausing on the hallway, and the display on the wall there.

"Military man. That's interesting to me. We get a lot of military men come to see us, looking for work." His finger pointed at the pendants and photos in the image on the screen. "But we don't get many from regiments like this, or squads like this. Busy men. Strong men. Men who do what they do without fuss. Do a particular *kind* of thing very well indeed, am I right? Good men to have around. Are you a good man to have around, Tony? Are you?"

He didn't finish his sentence. They were interrupted.

"Grandad? Can I have some chocolate?" A little girl had materialised next to Stark. Tony's vision was struggling for focus, as he wrestled with conflicting impulses, not least the feeling of violation knowing that people had been poking around in his flat, and in his stuff.

"Chocolate? Chocolate? Dear god, girl," Stark's expression changed instantly, the cloud of a scowl replaced by sunshine and smiles. "How much have you had already?"

"But I'm *tired* and some chocolate might wake me up."

Tony was invisible to the little girl. This transaction was all that mattered to her right now. Stark turned his head this way and that, as if looking for spies over his shoulder. He patted his pockets, and with the flourish of a pier-end magician, produced a chocolate bar from an inside pocket.

"There. Do *not* tell Nannie. Right?"

"Ok, Grandad. Thanks, Grandad." She skipped away, happy with her victory.

The clouds returned. Stark leaned forward again, lowering his voice.

"So, in a few days, or maybe a few weeks, I'm going to ask you to do something for me. And you're going to do it. Because if you don't maybe I'm going to start to get my doubts again. And maybe those angry fellas who are buzzing in my ear are going to get doubts again. You see what I'm saying? Could I be any more *fucking* clear?"

He made a very obvious turn of the head to look for the women, just to let Tony know that what he was intimating very much included Eleanor too, then pocketed the phone, sat back, and, again, warmed his expression as the two women returned with cups of coffee for all of them. The conversation turned to small talk, though wholly from the Starks, with Tony and Eleanor keeping quiet, and letting them fill the silence. Eleanor reached for Tony's hand under the table, and gave a little squeeze, a reassurance that they were strong and together, looking for their chance to regroup outside, as soon as they possibly could. They just had to endure grandkid tales and exasperated complaints about the eternal road working on the main road into the city for the length of a cup of coffee, though Tony was very aware that Stark was holding his gaze for just slightly longer than would normally be comfortable. I'm in charge, it said. I will scour you from the earth if you dare to cross me, it said.

Coffee finished, and they felt they could chance their arm to leave.

"Well, lovely to meet you," Eleanor said, confident as ever, getting to her feet first. Tony followed her lead.

"Thanks for the coffee," Tony said, trying to work out

how to explain the conversation he'd just had when they were both alone. "Nice to meet you, Jackie."

The Starks stood up, and came around from behind the table so handshakes could be exchanged. Stark patted Tony on the back again and Jackie reached in for a hug with Eleanor. She whispered something to Eleanor, before closing her eyes and squeezing, with a loud "mmm!" to underline this display of affection. That was the end of it. They could leave. Tony and Eleanor made their way back through the chairs and tables to the exit.

In the car park outside, Tony looked over his shoulder, but couldn't see the Starks anymore, due to the angle of the sun on the glass frontage. He reached for Eleanor's hand, and they walked away, not looking back again, keen to get to some bolthole to try and work through exactly what all this was about. Tony couldn't wait for safe haven though. He had to ask.

"What did she say to you? As we left?"

She puffed out her cheeks.

"She said if your man is stupid, he's dead and you're fucking dead as well."

21

They didn't say another word to each other until they'd made their way to one of endless cookie-cutter chain coffee shops on the way back from the industrial estate that the soft play centre was on, and back into town, feeling more secure in the crowds and banalities of a Saturday morning. Both gave each other the space to think, to be quiet, to weigh up their own experience of that surreal half hour.

"Special blend?" The barista, wearing a shirt that screamed BARISTA, asked with forced enthusiasm, for the hundredth time that morning.

"Mmm?" was the best Tony could manage, still away from himself.

"Sorry, Sir?" the barista said.

"Oh, oh. Right. No, no you're fine. Thanks."

Eleanor had sat down at a table for two, in the window, moving in just as the previous occupants had stood up to leave, with their cups and plates, stirrers and napkins, strewn across the table.

Tony carried two coffees, in comically huge cups, back to

the table, and sat down opposite Eleanor. Coffee black, and hot, and chosen absent-mindedly, just for something to do until they felt they could go back to their flat. Tony careered from anger to upset at the thought of how their home had been violated by Stark and his mob.

Eleanor spoke first, "Why soft play? What the fuck was that all about?"

"I don't know. I've been trying to think of the angle. Why show us the kids?"

"I can't understand it. What was he trying to gain? His grandkids, for God's sake."

"The only thing I can think of is either he wants us to know that he doesn't see us as much of a threat, or he just doesn't think of us as a threat *at all*."

"Christ."

Silence. They each took small sips of their coffee.

"They broke into our flat. He showed me pictures of the flat on his phone. Wanted me to see that he'd been checking up on us, digging around."

Eleanor took another sip of coffee, weighing up probabilities.

She spoke, unconsciously lowering her voice as a member of staff walked by, "Ok. We can deal with that. Nothing has been taken. I'm pretty sure we would've noticed. And I don't think they found anything that they shouldn't have done, as we would've noticed that too. So, the whole thing this morning was just intimidation. A 'we can get to you' warning."

"A test.", Tony said, nodding. He had come to the same conclusion himself, but was reassured that Eleanor had reached the same destination.

"Exactly."

Tony moved onto the next agenda point - "I think he

wants me to pass another test. Something about 'be ready' and 'we'll be in touch'. I don't like it."

"Me neither. I think we might need to get out from under this, and soon."

"That's not going to be easy, now. It's obvious we are still being watched, even if it's off and on. I'm not sure we can risk doing anything obvious until we are 100% sure that we can get away clean."

"That's why we have plans, Tone. We always knew we had to consider this. Light touch. No ties."

"Yeah, you're right. I know."

They both returned to their coffees, staring at the liquid as if it held the solution to all their problems. Tony couldn't help the scowl that descended on his face. He couldn't stay silent for long.

"But *fuck*. Who are they to do this to us? Jesus fucking Christ. We're not ready."

"We never will be, love. There's never a right time. There's just a time when you have to jump, and hope the parachute opens. We've always known this."

"Can we do it?"

"We can do it. We've got enough. We've got cash, we've got our accounts, and we've got nothing here to keep us. The only thing we need to be careful about is if we try and leave too soon. I'd not be surprised if there is someone watching the flat now. Hell, they could even be *in here too*."

"Carry on as normal?" As always, Tony wanted the reassurance that the pragmatist sat opposite him agreed with him.

"Carry on as normal."

They finished their coffee, and walked home in silence, words didn't come easy to either of them.

22

Cold Cut had been in King's Lynn for six weeks. It wasn't a pleasant transition for him. These weren't his streets, all new and so very different. The small town felt at odds with everything he had known before, and he felt adrift without the chaos and clutter of the busy street corners and constant hum of traffic 24 hours a day. Not only that, but the people only made things worse. They were as alien to him as the streets felt. These small-timers were only playing at being big-time, with their patois and attitude learnt from TV, bad karaoke versions of the real thing. Cold Cut himself was viewed with suspicion – he was seen as exotic, with his accent causing heads to turn, ruining any hope of camouflage or the quiet life. So he could only lean into it, which meant putting himself out there. The fact that what saw itself as the criminal classes in this town were so easily manipulated was a crumb of comfort, but still, he just wanted to get away from here, and back home as soon as possible. It was weird – routine and comfort seemed to be preferable to being a big fish in a small pond, or was it that he couldn't shake the feeling that this was a prison sentence of sorts, stuck out here, grey and cold and surrounded by idiots.

His days rolled into each other with no change in sight. Back in Liverpool, he at least had the feeling that he was in with a chance of moving up, and moving on. Here he just felt trapped.

Trapped on a worn-out sofa, feet surrounded by energy drink cans and discarded skins, in a small room dominated by a massive TV, constantly on, currently tuned to some dance music channel, though muted. Yet another night into the early hours, with the cousins plugged into their games console, being creatively homophobic with edgelord teens in Texas. Cold Cut sat removed, medicating his ennui with weed, a line or two, and rum. He lived in constant expectation of challenge, waiting for the moment when gears would click into place, and the cousins would push him for the location of the brick of coke he'd waved under their nose on more than one occasion with the photo on his phone. He was pretty sure they'd been through his bag, but, as yet, hadn't torn his car apart looking for it, but surely that had to come at some point? It was in his best interests to keep them supplied, both for their own use, and for selling around the estate, accepting a three-way split through gritted teeth. He wouldn't be here much longer. He couldn't be.

The cousins, Keiran and Connor, never apart, had put the kettle on, and were arguing over milk first or bag first, for the cup of tea they were about to ruin for each other. They wouldn't offer. So –

"One for me as well," Cold Cut called through.

"Fuck off. Make your own," Keiran called back cackling for both the cousins. Their humour was cruel. Nothing new though.

"One for me, knobhead," Cold Cut tossed the insult like

a grenade, a growl from alpha to beta, just in case the two cousins had any doubts who it was who held the gear, and so, the power to earn, at least for now.

"Yeah, yeah. Alright. Fuck," Keiran relented. A mug was dug out from the pile in the sink, and rinsed. It was going to taste like piss-water, but marginally less so now.

The tea was brought through, and dropped in front of Cold Cut with no ceremony, sloshing some of the liquid onto the table top, dangerously near Cold Cut's packet of cigarette papers.

"Christ, lad." He cleared the table of his paraphernalia, like a cardsharp clearing his cards after laying a hand. More cackling. The two youths collapsed onto the couch, failed springs seeing their bodies enveloped by the cushions as they folded in on themselves, mugs of tea held aloft like Olympic torches until they settled.

"We're going to need more gear," Connor said between slurps. "Got a queue building."

"Later. You don't need it now," said Cold Cut, digging in.

"Might do. Could do with a bump myself before I get myself ready for the day." It was noon.

"Where's the gear gone I gave you last night?"

Connor pointed at his nose. Keiran laughed. Bouncing in the seats like imbeciles.

Cold Cut sighed. "We need to *sell* it, for fuck's sake. This is the best stuff I've ever had, so don't stick it up *there* – get it fucking sold."

Cold Cut was losing patience, fast. He dug his phone out, absent-mindedly hoping that there was something on there, some text, some video, some update, that might, at best, get him home, or, at worst, just distract him from these gibbons screeching at him from across the room. Nothing. He went into his messages, and checked in vain to see if he'd missed some text message from the three he had charged with getting him out of this mess, and back home. Still nothing, his last message of "ANYTHING???" at the top of the page, read but unanswered. How dare they. He might be far away, but how fucking dare they think they can ignore him.

Connor and Keiran were flicking through channels on the TV, which meant he didn't have to respond to their chatter for a while. He took a sip of tea, and tapped another message on his phone.

Cold Cut – "GETTING FUCKED OFF. REPLY OR NO DEAL."

He threw his phone down on the table, catching the attention of the two brothers, who immediately started nudging each other, and sniggering. They just about knew better than to do any more than that. Just. Cold Cut took another swig of tea, four sugars sweet, and with a sharp aftertaste from the unclean cup.

Three dots. A reply coming. He grabbed the phone again.

Waiting. Typing. Waiting.

Acer – "THEN FUCK OFF"

Cold Cut – "DON'T FUCK AROUND. UPDATE OR NO DEAL"

Acer – "FINE. STAY THERE. FUCK ALL THE WAY OFF"

Cold Cut – "NOT JOKE. WILL FIND SOMEONE ELSE IF YOU SHIT OUT"

Belly – "NOT JOKE. FIND SOMEONE ELSE."

Cold Cut felt his fingers start to tremble. What the hell was going on? Who were these clowns to talk to him like this? When he got back he was going to...

Cosmo – "DON'T NEED IT. OR YOU"

Cosmo – "STAY THERE FOREVER. HOLIDAY BY THE SEA"

Acer – "LOL"

Belly – *cryface emoji*

Cosmo – *cryface emoji*

Cold Cut could barely hold his phone, it was shaking so much. He was angry. Furious. No. That wasn't it. He was *terrified*.

Cold Cut – "WHAT GOING ON? WE HAD DEAL?"

Acer – "HAD DEAL. DEAL OFF"

Cold Cut – "DNT UNDERSTAND"

Cold Cut – "WHAT HAPPENING?"

Belly – "ALL PAID UP. DON'T NEED YOUR GEAR. DON'T NEED YOU."

Three dots again. The anticipation of the next response unbearable, with Cold Cut staring at the screen, and watching the icons dance. Typing. Deleting. Typing. Deleting. Typing.

Cosmo – "FOUND HIM. WE FOUND RINGO."

23

"We found him."

Tony pulled himself in from the thousand-yard stare, as his brain struggled to turn those three words into a cogent message. Like digital to analog and back again. It fired out a vain, pathetic response to his mouth, which served only to give it more thinking time to properly understand the weight of those words.

"...who?" was all Tony could manage to say, even though he knew the answer.

"You know who. We just thought you ought to know."

He was stood a hundred yards from the front door that opened onto the stairwell and up to his flat, by a small square of green, loomed over hungrily by Victorian townhouses, desperate to swallow up nature and replace it with more bricks and concrete. It was evening, and dusk was drawing in, and, returning home after one of his long walks around the town, and the docks, he had been stopped by someone he had never seen before. Without saying a word, he identified them as yet another of those grunts, good for lifting and scowling, driving and punching, that seemed to serve Stark, and all those under him, so well. Same uniform, too – the black shirt, the shiny shoes, the gold chain around his neck – they all looked the same, with subtle differences that, if you paid attention, you could use to tell them apart. They all answered to one syllable names, if anyone ever took the time to learn them.

Tony enjoyed his walks. It gave him time to think, and, even if he couldn't solve a problem, it certainly helped him find the edges of them, hands stuffed in pockets, headphones in ears, and some loud drone or waves of music soundtracking his paces. The man had to say his name twice to get Tony to stop – the first time to break his trance, and the second time for Tony to fully appreciate that it was him being addressed. He'd never felt like this was *his* town, so never turned when someone called or stop if a car sounded a horn, as he just never assumed that he was the target. It was jarring when his name was called.

"Why are you telling me? What am I expected to do about it?" Tony responded, his bravado restored.

"You're not *expected* to do anything about it. Yet. I've just been told to give you this." The man handed Tony a folded note.

"Look," the man said as he took a small step towards Tony and lowered his voice, "from what they tell me, you're not on the block for this one. Well, they don't think you knew anything about it. And you've done the right thing. Got back to work. I think they liked that. Most of them just think you and the other one fucked up that night. You just need to keep eating shit for a while. Keep your head down."

"Right." Tony wasn't interested but either the other man didn't register that or he didn't care.

"I think the right people like you. Your name comes up a

lot when I'm driving. Could be you are good for some real business soon. Just keep doing what you're doing, alright?"

Tony half-expected a pat on the back, or a bump on the shoulder. His teeth ground together in anticipation of it, but it didn't come. The man put his hands into his jacket pockets, half-nodded at Tony, and then walked past him away from the illumination of the streetlight, and down a side street back towards the city centre. Tony watched him go, resting his back on the road sign for the street, preferring to keep this nonsense outside, rather than immediately bring it indoors, like tramping mud on clean carpets.

He looked at the folded note in his hand, flicking his fingers against it absent-mindedly, preparing himself for whatever message was on the inside. He yearned for the quiet life. Whatever was on the other side of that paper was most definitely not the quiet life, and like Schrodinger's cat, until he read it, it didn't exist. He puffed his cheeks and opened the note.

11PM

COME ALONE

BUSINESS MEETING

And an address. The same address from *that* night. Deliberately provocative? Or just a lack of imagination? The meeting was in a few hours' time. Time only to get his head straight; talk things out with Eleanor before he walked across town. The walk was vital. The walk would help him find those angles again, and prepare himself for whatever performance he was walking into.

"To the gallows," he chuckled to himself, and went inside his front door, home to Eleanor.

24

"Hi love. It's happening." Tony didn't wait to sit down before giving Eleanor a precis of what he had just learned.

"What's happening?" Eleanor responded, understanding from Tony's expression, eyebrows raised, that this was important. She turned off the TV, and turned to face him from her spot on the couch.

"Another note. And the bloke who gave it me said that they have Ringo."

"So, this is how they're going to test you, then. We knew it was coming."

"I guess we did." Tony sat down next to Eleanor, his excitement eased, now he had delivered his headline.

"Ringo might be there."

"He might," Tony replied, pinching the bridge of his nose.

"What are you going to do?"

"I don't know. I've got to go, that's certain."

"Yes. Definitely." Eleanor had put a hand on his knee.

"This could be it. We know how this might go. How it

might go," said Tony, again looking to his wife for a map through these trees.

"We talked about this, Tone. We're ready. We know what we're doing. Okay, so it's not ideal, but it never will be. We can't get trapped in this shit. I won't let us."

"I think they are going to push me into a corner on this and make me complete some kind of test of loyalty. Stark was pretty clear and we know people like Stark. Worse people than him, even. And when it comes down to it, they want to be certain that you're as *all in* as they are. He wants my hands dirty so we can't walk away."

"That's not going to happen, Tone. We can work this out. We're smarter than them. We have to be. They don't know where we've come from, and what we've had to do to get where we are. That's something. They just think we're fresh off the boat, and all you've ever done is bounce a few fellas out of doorways. Look at the sort of people they have around them. For fuck's sake, think about how they let themselves get turned over by a bunch of smacked-out scallies. We're better than them. Let's think this through."

"They might be watching, still, you know," Tony said, hunched over, sat on the edge of the sofa. Eleanor moved her hand from his knee and onto his back.

"Yeah, it had crossed my mind. They missed the bags behind the kitchen kickboards, though. I'm pretty sure of that. So, we have that on them. The trick is doing what we need to without them noticing. I know what I'm doing, Tone. I don't think we can be shy anymore. We might not get another chance."

"Yeah. Christ. How did we get here, again?"

"Road to Hell Paving Company, my love. It's always the way. You never know how deep you are in, until you try and wade back. It's not your fault," Eleanor said, having come to terms with what was facing them. Tony was almost there, but not without a few last kicks and scratches.

"Why couldn't I be happy being a fucking street-sweeper?"

"That's not you. It's fine, we knew the risks. You've never hidden that from me," Eleanor said, reaching forward to finally place the empty wine glass she had been cradling on the coffee table, more for something to do than anything else.

"I'm sorry. Sorry we're in this mess. Again."

"One last time. We play this right, and we're gone. Sooner than we planned, but we'll manage. We always manage," Eleanor again reassured, with her cool tone and confident optimism.

"Are you up for this?" said Tony, turning to face Eleanor.

"Guess I'll have to be. Don't worry about me."

"Ok. Get what you need together. Then let me get it straight in my head one last time. Okay?"

"Alright. Don't worry, Tony. We'll get through this."

"I know we will. Somehow," Tony, feeling solid again, wrapped his arms around his wife, and fell into the warmth of her embrace.

25

"Phone."

Tony turned up, five minutes early to the industrial estate by the docks, just like he had those weeks ago. It looked exactly like it had before, with the same evening quiet, and deserted car park, save for a couple of cars parked flush to the front wall of the building, in the disabled spaces. It was quieter, but even so, he could see one or two rooms illuminated from across the forecourt and from the service road.

The man on the door was the same lackey who'd hovered at the back of the room when he had been introduced to the Red Pope for the first time. A typical grasper, all bristling attitude and barely controlled bubbling rage, held in check only by deference to his own instinct for loyalty to his superiors, and by extension, a desire to keep his kneecaps attached to his legs. Constantly straining at the leash, desperate to be given permission to flail fists, hoping for some kudos to be thrown his way, like a bone to be gnawed. Every single one of these sort of people that Tony had met were blissfully unaware of how tiringly anodyne they were, a herd of testosteroned bull-necked thugs, hard of thinking but shark-like in their desires for money, and, as importantly, the nebulous concept of *respect*. Tony buried his loathing deep, but not so deep that he genuflected. He held the gaze, reached into the back pocket of his jeans, and pulled out his phone, handing it over. It was taken, switched off, and slipped inside the jacket pocket of the man, who offered a mirthless smile, then indicated that Tony should raise his arms to be patted down. Arms first, then his ribs, which still ached from that punch those weeks ago, then quickly up his legs. It was all over in seconds. The man stood up, satisfied, before giving a sarcastic bow of the head. He opened the door to the building and allowed Tony inside.

He stepped in. There was no-one around, and all the lights were off. He looked back over his shoulder at the man, who deigned to respond, pointing a finger up.

"I'll go upstairs then," said Tony, loud enough so the man could hear him. "In the conference room, is it? I'll head there. Thanks so much." He treated himself to some under-the-breath sarcasm. The expectation of what might follow had him feeling he needed to say *something* – whistling in the dark, maybe.

He exhaled, loudly, as he climbed the stairs, unsure what he was about to walk into, all his synapses were firing and the back of his neck prickling. He had a few seconds to himself as he climbed the stairs, letting him reach inside the waistband of his jeans. Breathing in, he pulled out another phone which he'd hidden in his underpants, gambling that any pat down would be so cursory that it would be missed. Tony was confident that machismo and insecurity would trump diligence. No fella round here was getting seen putting his hand on another man's junk. He switched the phone on and dialled a number before he muted the sound, slipped it inside his pocket and zipped it up. Adrenaline had him clear the last two stairs in one bound, and then, another puff of the cheeks, and he pushed the door open, firmly.

He expected what he saw, to some degree. He had run through as many possible permutations of what he might be walking into on the way here, briefly pondering what would be the most positive outcome from this situation, but unable to avoid dwelling again and again on the worst expectations he could conjure – violent and even terminal. These were the ones he kept coming back to.

The open plan office was a mess. The nesting tables and workstations had been pushed to the perimeters of the room, roughly. Chairs had been flung into piles. The room was cleared, and any concession to order and organisation ignored.

It was dark. Only one bank of strip lights were illuminated, bringing only the centre of the room into the light, darkness gathered around the edges of the room. No external light could sneak in as all the blinds were closed. The light was haloing a chair set on a tarp that had been unfolded across the floor. And on the chair, tied and bound with his mouth taped, was Ringo.

Ringo. He called him a friend. A fool, and a tiring one at that, but still a friend, the puppy-dog patter had eased past Tony's innate suspicions, and shyness, and done more than perhaps anything to convince himself that he could make this strange city home. And now here they both were. One summoned for God knows what, and the other, wide-eyed, bound and beaten, darting looks here and there to try, desperately, to think of a way to get away from here, alive.

There were others here, but Tony hadn't taken time to

try and identify them. All he could do was stare at Ringo who was in a bad way. Ringo, too, had seen Tony and was now staring directly at him, a look of complete desperation on his face, eyebrows high, sweat and blood mixing on his forehead. His arms had been tightly bound to the chair arms with gaffer tape. One hand was wrapped in bandages, noticeably dirty, more to stop the blood splashing than any obligation of care to Ringo. What had they done? A voice broke the moment –

"Mr Grace. Nice to see you. Prompt as ever." It was Stark. "As you will have noticed, we have found the snake in our garden, after he led us quite the merry dance." He stepped out of the dark, into the light, the strip light illuminating him like a lead on the theatre stage, a role that Stark was intending to revel in, enjoying the opera of the situation, performing to everyone there, now he could reveal his honest self.

"I can't abide greed. Ambition is fine, but greed? Especially stealing from your own family? I mean, that's what we are, isn't it? A family? We provide for each other, we look out for each other, and that means that when one does well, we *all* do well. See these men, Tony?" Stark waved to a couple of figures, still in the shadows, watching. "These men have been with me for years. Years! And everything we have has been built by us, brick by brick. And so, when one of our family, even some shitty little no-mark like this, who we barely know, let alone like, tries to hurt us, well, that's disappointing. Heartbreaking, even."

Stark had one arm behind his back, but he brought it forward now, revealing what he was holding. A knife. Tony had seen it before. Ringo spotted it in his peripheral vision, his eyes widening in terror. Tony kept looking directly at him, ignoring the knife for now, throwing Ringo a line, trying to reassure him, wordlessly, that he still had a friend in this room.

"And *this* one here," Stark said moving just behind Ringo. "Always fiddling with his little knife. I barely know the fella, but it used to wind me up something rotten. Picking away with his knife at his fingers. Pick, pick, pick. Learn some self-control, man. Christ. The first thing we did when we finally found him was take the knife away."

Tony said nothing. Don't fill a silence that was getting filled for you. Don't react until you have to. Watch. Listen. Think.

"I suppose we have to thank you for that, Mr Grace. Finding him, I mean. That and a public-spirited older lady, I should say." Someone chuckled in the shadows. "See, this one here, must've gotten impatient. Because, we threw a bit of money around, dangled a few carrots, and some little birds spotted you when you went to see the other one's mum."

Groucho.

"And it wasn't a massive stretch that this one might do the same. And, those good lads, all puppy-eyed over a few grand, hung about, day after day, until this sorry twat finally turned up. Big argument. 'Can I come in?' 'No, you can't' over and over, until he got the door slammed in his face, and we got the call quick enough to get a couple of our lads over there. And here we are! We found you, Lad. Silly, silly boy."

Stark kept talking. Tony was silent.

"Of course, what could he tell us? There's no-one he can give us. We found his mates *very quickly*. Stupid little fucks will always be stupid little fucks. Stupid to think they could rob us, and then, as if to make sure there was no doubt about their stupidity, they then immediately go shopping. And drinking. And 'you'll never guess what...?' to their equally stupid mates. That just left our friend here, all on his own. Pick, pick, pick, with his little knife. Well, no need for that anymore."

Tony knew what they'd done. The bandage on Ringo's hand was darkening by the second. The knife. His fingers. Ringo wasn't going to need to pick away at his fingernails anymore.

"Now I like to think of myself as pretty good at people, you know what I mean? Sizing them up. Doing my homework. And you don't seem stupid. So, I never really thought you could be in on all this. And I can see how the whole *incident* might have gotten away from you. It's not like you were on your own, was it? We've all been pretty embarrassed by it. But, having said that, I do like to be sure."

He beckoned Tony closer. Now a whisper –

"So, we know you've seen service. We know you must've been places. *Done* things. So this shouldn't be a stretch. A lot of our lads have done the same. Different rules out there. 'Shuffle off this mortal coil' and all that. We've opened our arms to you, son. Join the family. But a bit of tough love before you get the cuddle, okay? I'm going to give you this knife, and you're going to draw a line under this whole affair." He grabbed Ringo from behind, fingers in nostrils, pulling his head back, and exposing his throat. With the other hand, he offered the knife to Tony, hilt first. This was it.

"Now," Tony said one word.

"Yes. Right now, Boy. He's wriggling, so chop, chop."

"Now," Tony said again, more firmly. "Now."

"What are you fucking well on about, Son? Get to it." Stark looked at Tony, confused, knife still on offer, thoughts travelling across his expression like dark clouds blown across a city skyline.

"Now!" Tony shouted now, and lunged for Stark, and the knife. Stark, though, had found the way through his maze, and understood, sharply, that there was something else at play here, and taken a step back. Those in the shadows didn't need a second invitation. Two of them. Big men. One of them Tony had recognised as one of the drivers, the other, he had not seen before, but these were bone-breakers. Tony could see that.

The first one was on him fast, swinging a right cross at him. Muscle-memory kicked in, and Tony ducked under it, weaving and moving, as he knew the left fist was cocked and moving, and there was another man ready to swing in a fraction of a second. Be first, and be decisive; lessons learnt in a million back-alleys, or club doorways, or "late-night chats" with the wrong sorts – Tony kicked the first man as hard as he could on the side of the knee. There was a satisfying crunch as bones cracked and tendons snapped. The man yelped, and fell to the floor, just as the other man crashed into Tony, wrapping his arms around his waist, to tackle him to the floor. Tony fell backwards, purposely, using that momentum to surprise his attacker, hoping he could use it to roll through, and end up in a better position.

They ended up in a tangle of limbs, dangerously close to crashing into the pile of office furniture that was at the side of the room. No time for wrestling, or struggling, Tony knew he had to move very fast. At best, there was another man in this room, and he definitely had a knife, at worst, well, that wasn't worth thinking about. Wriggling to free his upper torso, he used that freedom to wind up, before crashing his forehead, as hard as he could, into the bridge of the nose of the man trying to pin him down. It was enough. The nose shattered, blood spewing out, blinding the man with pain, and snot, and tears, loosened his grip. Tony rolled free, kicking him hard in the ribs whilst he was staggered, sending him crashing back into the nest of tables and chairs behind him.

Tony turned back to the centre of the room. Stark hadn't moved. He was stood still behind Ringo. The first man was on his feet, though unsteady, unable to put any weight on his injured leg. A third man, who had been sat watching in one of the side offices, had now walked through to reveal himself. Of course, it would be him. The Red Pope.

He wasn't smiling this time. This was business. This was how he earned his place at the table. And his boss was here. This was also about pride. Reputation. *Respect.*

He strode past Stark, standing between him, Ringo and Tony.

"You're not what I thought you were, Grace," Stark said piping up. "I had hopes you wanted to be in this family. All the way in. It's a good career. Good prospects. Good life. But that's fine. That's fine. It's not for you. I can respect that." Stark nodded to himself. Philosophically, almost. Then he took the knife and cut Ringo's throat.

"Jesus Christ!" Tony rushed forward, too late to help, too late to prevent, but still unable to just stand idly by and watch it happen. It was a mistake.

The first punch lifted Tony off his feet, once again back to the ribs, an uppercut devastatingly fast. The second punch, a left hook, turned his head, split his cheek, and lost him a tooth. His head was foggy, and he was struggling to find his balance. Concussion? Cracked skull? It just fucking hurt. There was no time to dwell on it. Another punch landed on the same spot on his ribs as before. Then another. And another. He staggered backwards, hands flailing, trying to find a solid surface to grip onto, just so he could stand for just a few seconds longer, the longer he stayed upright, the more chance there was of some miracle happening. If he hit the floor, he was halfway to death. He knew that.

The Red Pope was mechanical and relentless. A death mask of emotionless concentration. A steady walk towards Tony, body perfectly balanced to strike from all angles. The bravado had fallen away, and, even as the metallic tang of blood filled his mouth, and pain seared his temples, Tony could understand why all that *personality* was tolerated, if this was who he really could be when he was called upon. This man was going to kill him. He was going to end up dead, like poor Ringo, bleeding out just yards away from him. Yards that could've been miles.

Three lefts rained down on him, crashing through his guard, clubbing the side of his head. His sight failed for a second or two, as his brain scrambled. Enough time to be lifted, seemingly with ease, and then thrown down and back. He bounced off one of the desks. No hurry, no urgency, just a steady, relentless disassembly of him by a man half his age, all muscle, skill and intent.

Time is the great illusion. Sometimes it flies past, loose and free like smoke on the wind, and other times it slows to a glacial procession, every second stretched out so tight it might snap. The whiplash between the two extremes was rare, but Tony felt it now. The fog of fury, in the middle of his beating, had left him clutching for coherence. But now, all of a sudden, everything slowed, as if his consciousness had left his body, to better process every little detail that was happening around him. Everything slowed because something had happened.

The building shook. An explosion. Windows shattered, then there was a pause that felt like the whole world was breathing in, before rebounding back as alarms screamed through the air. Finally, the Red Pope broke his gaze from Tony, the hypnosis of it lost, as he turned his head to try and work out what had happened. Stark, too, for the first time, had a confused, panicked look on his face, his eyebrows dancing above wide-eyes, and his mouth slack, reeling through the possible reasons, and not liking any of them. Tony had time to draw some conclusions of his own, but not enough that he could settle on any one in particular – all he knew was that this was his chance, and if he didn't take it, he really would be dead.

Tony found some cold comfort, in a body fizzing with pain. The Red Pope had left his legs alone. His ribs cut like glass with every breath, his head was fogged and on fire. Every movement saw a different part of his body add voice to the choir of angry muscles. He spat blood. But none of that mattered. His legs could move, so he dragged himself to his feet, desperate adrenaline readying him for one last effort.

They'd made one mistake in bringing him here. He had been here before, and knew it. Before the explosion had quietened, Tony took one gulp of air and was running, barrelling past the Red Pope, Stark and poor Ringo – now dead. The garbled gulps and chokes Ringo made as he died were silent now, his throat opened and his blood drained dry.

Don't stop. Keep running.

Tony crashed through the fire escape and down the metal stairs from first floor to ground, grimacing as his body bounced off the guardrail; speed was his only concern. He left the commotion behind him, the shock of it rippling through the men in the room as he vanished. He had to get away, somehow, or this was futile. A dead cat bounce.

And there she was: Eleanor. She'd pulled up in a car illuminated by the fire burning at the front of the building. Two of the cars parked there were in flames, one of them having exploded judging by the state of it.

"In!" Eleanor barked as she flung the passenger door open. Tony dived into the car. Eleanor hit the accelerator, the tyres screeched and the door slammed shut as they pulled away. Tony collapsed back in his seat.

"They killed him. They just killed him, there and then."

"I know, love. I know what they did. I heard over the phone. I heard everything."

"I thought you were too late. Thought I was never going to see you again..." Tony choked on his words, blood and emotion.

"I'm sorry. I couldn't get it to light. It's all I could think of doing to distract them."

Eleanor looked in the rear view, the building now a hundred yards behind them. The Stark cars were on fire, and, as they turned the corner onto the service road, a second explosion filled the air, as the second car went up. The ball of fire silhouetted two men – a tall man, and a shorter, fatter man. Stark and the Red Pope. They couldn't follow. Sirens were now audible in the distant, they had enough to worry about with a dead body in the building.

"Have you...?"

"I've got everything, Tone. Both bags. And a few more bits as well. I had time. They didn't see me leave. They don't know where we are going. They don't know anything about us. We can get away. Forget all this shit and start again. Just be us."

"That's what I want, love. That's all I ever wanted." Tony could barely finish the last word. He closed his eyes resting back in his seat. A few moment's rest, that's all he wanted. He felt her hand in his. A squeeze.

"Where did you get the car...?"

"I'll tell you later. You just concentrate on squeezing my hand, when I squeeze yours. Just for a little while. Don't fall asleep, okay?"

She squeezed. He squeezed back.

26

C old Cut's anger had peaked when he'd been away for a whole year. When it left him, all he had left was bitterness. He'd exiled himself from his home, unable to return for fear of who knew what and the consequences for letting the Stark lot down. So he'd found himself in bumfuck Norfolk, scratching out scams and dodges to keep the wheels turning, with his way home – his sure-fire way home – taken from him by the petty ambition of those who really should know better. He deserved better than this.

Bitterness had created lethargy in him. He'd taken years to hoard whatever goodwill or reputation he had back in Liverpool. With that wiped out, so far from home, he couldn't face the prospect of starting again in a part of the world that would always feel alien to him. Not least because whenever someone opened their mouth, accented words fell out with an accent so bizarre each syllable was like an assault. There was to be no nest egg or plan to work towards. All he had now was 'today' and all he worked for, if you could call it that, was the means to get through today, and to start again tomorrow.

Sure, he still kept in touch with events back home, but it felt like peering in through the window of an ex-lover. He'd get the odd text, or rarer, the odd phone call, from the handful of people who had any inclination to stay in touch with him. That enabled him to vicariously feel connected. Though each message gave him a pang of regret and feelings of impotence as they came and went without him being able to find some silver bullet he could use to buy his way home. He'd heard the whispers about Ringo, and how he'd vanished, into the boot of one of Stark's taxi cabs. He'd heard about the fella from out of town who had blown up cars and stood up to Stark. He'd also heard about the reward for his location, which just emphasised the myth of the man – the man who faced down Stark, then vanished, never to be seen again. He'd even had *that* photo, of this man and his missus, forwarded to him – fat lot of good to him here, but still saved to his phone, and stared at it intently from time-to-time, the cross on the treasure map that he could never locate.

He was still in the flat with his cousins. It reminded him of that old fantasy film his grandad would play on VHS when he was a kid – a blind beggar tormented by winged harpies every day, screeching and cackling. He embraced the melodrama of the simile. But with no fight left in him, he soon fell into the rhythm of their day – long nights in front of the screen, watching music channels, or pirate-streams of sport or endless, repetitive games on the console, all whilst under a fog of weed smoke, and the stink of days-old pizza boxes. The shame of it. The coke had sold through faster than he expected, but the proceeds were squandered just as fast. Faster once the despair gripped him and the urge to find anything – narcotic, preferably – to distract him from his situation was impossible to resist. That added to putting enough in the pot that his cousins wouldn't object to another night, another week, of him staying meant it was all gone.

"We need to get out of town. For today, like," Keiran said. He'd said it with some urgency, as the flat had slowly come to life around 1pm, recovering from yet another long night of indulgence. He'd appeared at the bottom of the pull-out sofa bed where Cold Cut slept, a pasty-white apparition, in baggy sweatpants and naked torso, all ribs and sharp edges.

"What the fuck...?" Cold Cut was bleary-eyed. He often was. He didn't sleep well any more, and especially not here. Every night he was the last one to sleep. He couldn't get any peace until the other two, and all of their entourage, had left the front room, giving him darkness and quiet.

Keiran waved his phone at Cold Cut. "It's rent day. Fucking rent day. Jimmy Grease down the road just text. Landlord doing rounds. We haven't paid him for three months."

"Three months?" Cold Cut sat up. "But I've been paying you every fucking month."

"Yeah, well. Shit happens, dude," he said with a leery smile.

"Christ..."

"Yeah, yeah, Mum. Who gives a fuck. Just get out for the day, and worry about it tomorrow."

"Out? Out where?"

"It's nice out. Your car still runs. Let's go up the coast."

"Up the coast."

"Yeah. It's good. I've got some weed. We can all go. I'll get the fanny, the weed, and you drive. Day in the sun. Get fucked up on the beach." The fanny. Not really selling it. Not selling anything more than chlamydia swabs, knowing this idiot, Cold Cut thought.

"Right. Whatever."

"Come on, then. Get a shit on. We need to get out. Like, before he gets here."

"Yeah, yeah."

Cold Cut took five minutes to get up. Slurped last night's flat cup of lemonade, weak with melted ice, which washed the taste of the night's sleep out of his mouth. He found a roll-up and he pulled some clothes on. They were out and in the car in thirty minutes.

27

Of course, the day had been a disaster. How could it not have been? To rely on those two clown cousins of his to organise anything was, of course, a mistake, but he hadn't really had a choice, other than to tag along, and grin and bear it. He'd needed a pint. Desperately. His small car, overloaded with four passengers – the cousins and two girls they had dragged along – as well as a snub-nosed dog, and a couple of bags of cheap cider and take-out. A ten-minute drive had turned into an hour, and this mythical, tranquil beach he had been sold had turned out to be a barren, windy mess of grass and sand. All this, to a soundtrack of bickering and flatulence.

Cold Cut had stomped off after ten minutes on the beach, after the others didn't put much in the way of a defence of the location. The Norfolk landscape could be like this – it promised much, but it could also change quickly as the weather shifted. From golden, open sands to unwelcoming and oppressive in minutes. He wasn't in the mood to hang around for another spin of that roulette wheel.

"I need a drink. At least one."

"Yeah. Good idea, Cut. Love it." said Connor, first to his feet, half-jogging to catch up, not risking Cold Cut leaving without them.

"Sound," Keiran said. The girls followed suit, the dog barking and jumping, fooled into thinking that movement would mean food, or at least, interaction.

They fell into the car, giggling and flirting, which only caused Cold Cut more irritation, gripping the steering wheel and grinding his teeth, a dark frown on his face. Keiran spotted the look from the passenger seat, and spun round to the back seat, with wide-eyes and an expression of joy on his face.

"Uh-oh! We've upset him!"

"Fucking hell, mate. Don't start crying!" Connor said, playing to their crowd.

That was enough for Cold Cut. The temper he had, never really that far from the surface, couldn't be kept quiet any longer. He spun around, his face a rich puce.

"You fucking little shits. You're a joke. Fucking gangsters? Big pimpin' is it? Joke. Out here, where you lot all just fuck the livestock because you can't tell them apart from your women, and you think that you run the streets? You think you'd last five fucking minutes in my town? Have you ever heard yourselves speak? And, what's worse – what's really fucking worse – is that I'm stuck with you lot, trying to keep my head down, and earn a bit of pocket money thinking I might be able to use it to get home one day. What chance of that, eh? Any money that I scratch together goes up your noses, or down your neck, so I have to wait another fucking night listening to your bullshit and choking on your fucking noxious fucking farts!"

Silence. The silence of a classroom after the teacher has lost it. The silence of that same classroom when that same teacher has sworn at, or worse, thrown something at the gobshite sat on the back row. A shocked pause; a pregnant one.

A loud parp bisected the quiet.

There's a pause, no one daring to react. Then an avalanche of high-pitched howls of laughter. Connor grinned. The whole car rocked as Cold Cut faced a battery of relentless shrieks and hoots. He couldn't help himself. A smile picked at the edges of Cold Cut's mouth, until he couldn't keep his anger boiling any longer, and then joined in the laughing, despite himself.

"You smelly bastard. Crack a window, for God's sake. I really need that fucking pint now..."

He turned the key, and drove out of the car park, to see which side-road would lead him to a country pub the fastest, the laughter having eased to the low-level inanity that had long since been the soundtrack to his days.

COLD CUT and his charges didn't struggle to find a pub. The county was full of them, dotted around the countryside, seemingly on every corner of every road, lane and track. A few miles and a few turns, and they had pulled up in a pub in the middle of a little village.

"Lager. Just a pint of lager, mate. I don't care what kind," Cold Cut said, leaning onto the bar.

"Sure I can't tempt you with our IPA? It's an award-winner, and we're all, well, I have to say, very proud of it indeed."

"Seriously, mate. I just want a pint of lager. And a bag of scratchings. Two bags. Please."

"And your friends? Can I get them anything?" said the

landlord, waving a hand towards the rest of Cold Cut's crew, who had loudly colonised a corner booth.

"They can get their own fucking drinks."

"Oof! Now, now, my good man. Mind the toilet mouth. I'll give you a yellow card for that one."

"Whatever."

Cold Cut looked away, refusing to give this too-friendly sheep-worrier the dignity of eye contact. He put a crumpled note on the bar top, annoyed that he'd have to risk further conversation as he waited for his change. Fortunately, none came, and the pint was poured and presented, and change politely put in his outstretched hand, all without any further interaction whatsoever.

This was not the sort of pub that he was used to. It was, he supposed, 'nice'. Back home pubs sometimes tried to ape places like this, with brick-patterned wallpaper, or generic sepia-tinted photos hung up around the place, but this pub wore its authenticity proudly. Hundreds of years of glacial change, and no desire for anything faster than that. That authenticity proved intoxicating for any of the passing tourists, or those second-homers who took to the cars at the weekend to find something they could call "our local" to visiting friends, with those who really did consider this a local, from generation to generation, wisely keeping their cynicism at the new faces who came in through the doors under wraps, knowing that the next week would bring a completely new set of faces, come what may, and it was best to just accept that. Cold Cut and his carload were fiercely incongruous – louder than they should be, drawing sideways glances, and shared eyebrow raises, with every too-loud curse. They hadn't quite tipped over the line that would require intervention, but the rest of the pubs occupants would be hugely relieved when they

this was the face that would buy him back to his town, and would buy him the rewards he knew he deserved. A ticket home.

He looked at the clowns on the next table, and couldn't help but smile. Maybe they'd respect him after all. Maybe they'd beg him to stay. It didn't matter. He'd struck gold.

He'd found Tony Grace.

28

Tony and Eleanor had allowed themselves to get comfortable. Their house felt like a home; a place to unpack all their boxes, put up pictures and add plants to a garden in the expectation of being around to see them grow, flower, and grow some more. Wheels were turning, but Tony and Eleanor had no idea or perception that they were still being hunted, not after all this time, and not out here.

Autumn was toying with the idea of making way for winter, but still had some warmth in the air, and Tony, as he often was, was walking around the garden, absent-mindedly picking at some invading weed, or tutting at a piece of litter that had blown over the pebbled wall to lodge in a bush. The sky was a Van Gogh smear of colours, as dusk settled. The trees on the horizon, towards the beach, faded slowly to silhouettes. He sat back on the wall, sipped his coffee, and looked forward to tomorrow and the menial chores that would make up his day.

Eleanor would be back in maybe an hour, ready for the chicken casserole that Tony was pleased he'd remembered to put in the oven. She was at the gym, fifteen miles away, but she felt comfortable there, and had made some acquaintances that she hoped would become friendships – each new name added to the contacts list in the phone felt like another little anchor that would keep them here, in this place they loved so much.

He heard it before he saw it. A faint siren, first sounding like some weird wildlife, from across the marshes, before repetition and timbre made it unmistakeable. Tony tried to locate the source, as the wide-open landscape bounced noise from left to right, east to west, making it difficult to understand exactly where it was coming from. The siren got louder. Tony got up from the wall, and paced slowly to the bottom of his garden, down to the back fence, to look out over a stretch of overgrown land, which stretched for about a hundred metres until it hit a decrepit wall, with the coast road on the other side. The road ran right, east, towards the village, or left back into the woods and the meanders for ten miles, until the next town. The siren was definitely coming towards the village, louder and louder now, becoming tangible almost, filling the quiet, dusk night with its insistent howl. But why? He looked towards the village. The light was fading, but he could still just about make out the outline of the buildings clustered a few miles away, eastwards.

Smoke. Human nature trying to piece together the picture often skewed towards the mundane, and he first wondered if it was just a bonfire, and the siren was nothing more than an odd coincidence. A second later, rationality spread, and he knew that something bad was happening. But his old, cautious, *safe* life seemed like it was hundreds of miles and hundreds of years behind him. He put his coffee mug down, hopped over the fence and jogged along to the road towards the village, at almost the same time as the fire engine roared past him, towards the same destination. The pub. The Shoggy Cut pub was on fire.

His running rhythm found his legs easily enough – the adrenaline of this, much more than just voyeurism, powered his tired muscles subconsciously, his eyes never leaving his destination, with every step causing him to push on. Each step closer he hoped there would be a happier outcome than the one he feared. He patted his pocket searching for his phone to tell Eleanor where he was going, but immediately cursed himself. He'd left it charging on the kitchen counter back home, angry that he had done nothing about that old phone, even though it was desperate for a new battery. Maybe it was just a fire. After all, the pub might not have been open yet. Jack tended to play fast and loose with the opening times, especially out of tourist season, and especially on a nothing-doing kind of midweek evening like this one.

The layout of the village delayed confirmation, and stretched hope, for a few hundred yards further, as the outlying cottages, and the turn of the road, prevented clear sight to the pub, though smoke had now established itself as an ominous pillar stretching from behind the roofs and chimneystacks, a Victorian villain swooping over its prey, cloak outstretched.

He knew what he might see, but even so, as he turned that final corner, the sight of it rocked him on his heels. The pub faced him, adjoining some terraced cottages on the left-hand side, with a fenced off beer garden to the right, and a twenty-vehicle car park in front of the building. The fire had taken hold of the pub completely. Smoke poured out of every window, the thatch on the roof had ignited, and flashes of angry reds and oranges burnt through the black to show that the fire had taken hold of the rooms inside. The scene was the kind of quiet bedlam that typified any disaster in England. The neighbouring houses had emptied, with people stood on the pavement, and across the road, wearing whatever they had on, but with a practical coat as well – both understanding the urgency of evacuation, but not at the expense of warmth, given that this was likely to be a long night. A huddle had formed, some distance away from the fire, with opinion and pointing well underway. Cups of tea were grasped, brought outside from warm kitchens. A few kids were blearily disciplined, after being dragged from their bedtime routine when the scale of the situation became clear. The fire engine nudged its way through the impromptu cordon, half on the pavement, half on the car park, with the frenetic efforts of the fire crew at odds with soporific incongruity of the crowd, knowing they could defer responsibility to the specialists.

Tony moved forward, edging past people, sharing looks, but not stopping to talk. Tony was one of those people who tried to rail against the tyranny of the crowd. He tried to be the sort of person who stepped forward to help the fallen pensioner, or stop the car so the child could cross. Eleanor did this without trying, and it had rubbed off on him. He needed to help. His friends lived in that pub. He wanted them safe, and wanted to know that he'd done everything he could to ensure they were.

Trance-like, he inched closer to the front of the pub, pulling away from the cluster of people like a rocket pulling away from the gravity of a planet. His feet moved unconsciously, his eyes scanning the windows for signs of life, hoping to see friends alive, or best, safe, maybe wrapped in a blanket and led away to be cared for.

Maybe Jack had gotten out early? Maybe he was

watching his life go up from the crowd? Tony turned away from the pub and back to the crowd, slowly, just to be sure, just to scan faces, desperately hoping he could stand back. To let the building reach out for life from the fire crew who were now pulling hoses from the back of the fire engine and passing out fire axes and breathing equipment, and just take solace from the fact that no-one was hurt.

The faces opposite him were all staring at the fire, tiny licks of red flame reflected in their eyes. A murmur rippled through the crowd, punctuated by the odd shriek or gasp as the fire burst a window or exploded an appliance. They were rapt. Unable to tear their gaze away. All of them except one.

The fire found the spirits behind the bar and exploded them like bombs, sending a roar of flame and noise into the night. The blast illuminated the faces, wide-eyed and open-mouthed, as if they were watching a firework display. And at the back of the crowd, hovering at the very periphery of all this, he locked eyes on someone who was staring directly at him, ignoring the conflagration behind him. Even after all this time, all the distance. Connections slammed together in his memory, and the reality of the situation fell into place.

The man was in black, wearing that de-facto uniform he had come to resent – black shirt, black trousers, dress shoes, jacket. The cropped hair, the scowl, all added to the unavoidable familiarity, especially incongruous away from the big city, framed by the stone cottages and overhanging trees of Norfolk. This man worked for Stark. He knew it. They'd found him.

A salvo of thoughts crashed together in his head. Tony was rooted to the spot as questions demanded immediate attention, too many to process, but, in reality, all in a heart-beat. Why was this man here? What did he want? Were there more? What should he do? Was Eleanor safe? *Was Eleanor safe?*

The man knew he'd been spotted. The hard-wired human response to a shared stare was to look away, to feign insouciance, but Tony couldn't play along. The shock of the fire, the explosions, and now this, all pretence at social norms had long passed. Tony hadn't broken his gaze away from the man, who now, stared back at Tony; both aware that the other had spotted them, their eyes locked from fifty yards. Then, suddenly, the man lifted his hand to his mouth, put two fingers inside, and whistled shrilly, twice, a noise to alert, but also to break Tony free from this stasis. He needed to get out of here, back to Eleanor, as fast as he possibly could. If they could find him, then she was in real danger as well.

Two more men revealed themselves from the shadows, one from the left, one from the right, emerging like predators. Tony was flanked on each side, the burning building behind him, and the crowd in front. The man he'd first spotted, manoeuvred his way through the throng, straight towards Tony.

Tony had the crowd, and the fire crew, as some sort of protection against any violence, and presumably, the police wouldn't be far behind, but what he couldn't rely on was the predictability of these men. He knew that they must've been looking for him all this time, and the prospect of any escape might well make them desperate, not least because they knew time was short. They couldn't risk Tony getting away again. Desperate men made bad decisions. Violent ones.

No-one was paying any attention to either Tony or the three men. The fire was the only show in town. Once those in the crowd were safe knowing the fire was unlikely to put their own homes in danger, given that the pub was set back from the nearby houses, it became vaudeville entertainment, with the crack of wood or the whoosh of heat eliciting woos or gasps, like some kind of impromptu bonfire party. In addition to the spectacle, gossip bubbled, the onlookers speculated over what might have caused it, or, for those more cynical, why it might have been lit in the first place.

Eleanor. Tony needed to make his play. To get away, to warn her, to escape. The men were still inching forward, at a steady, relentless pace, coiled springs ready to do God-knows-what if he was to try and take them head on. He couldn't rule out that these three were the last of them either, and the longer he waited, the more desperate his situation would become. And then he answered his own question – an unmistakeable figure, at the very back of the crowd. Tall, powerful, and, with another pulse of fire, caught by a gust of wind illuminating the night, unmistakeable. Blond hair, blue, unblinking eyes, and that criss-cross scar on the forehead. The Red Pope was here. He looked at Tony and grinned.

That was Tony's cue. They were making their play, and he needed to make his. No second thoughts, no caution, he just had to run. He turned on his heel, to face the burning pub, and ran straight for it.

His sudden movement was noticed by the crowd wondering what this peculiar man was possibly hoping to accomplish, and by the fire crew too, who were torn away from their routine and preparations for entering the building to stare. The shadowy men orbiting the scene threw off their careful scrutiny and started to run themselves.

The burning building loomed ahead of Tony. The fire seemed to have every brick and beam in its grip. He had a plan, but in an almost out-of-body state, knew just how ridiculous it was. He was going to try and escape injury, or death, from those who wished him harm, by plunging headlong into a fire. Pulling his sweatshirt up over his mouth, he took one last long lungful of clean air, before closing his eyes, and barrelling into the heavy, inward-swinging doors with as much force as he could muster.

He could see nothing, the smoke had claimed whatever light was available. But he knew this building. He'd been in it enough times, and like many others before him, been roped into helping out with a barrel change, or some other bit of manual graft by Jack, so he was familiar enough with the rooms behind the public bar as well. With his eyes shut tight against the smoke, all he had were his recollections of how the pub *should* look, overlaying it onto that darkness. He plotted an approximate route, from front door to pub counter. He'd have to feel along the left for the bar hatch, go through a back door and into the kitchen where a smaller door opened out to the bin store outside. Then into the beer garden. Behind that was a disused trainline, which he could follow away from the village and back home.

He went as fast as he could, but the heat and the smoke were crushing him, forcing him to a low crouch, unbalancing him, the hand not clamped over his mouth touching the floor to help propel him forward, and maintain some sort of balance, as he made his way through this hell. He knew they could well be behind him or even finding some alternative route to the back door. It didn't matter, he had to push on or he'd die tonight.

His fingers found the counter, but as he was searching for the counter hatch, he'd tripped over a chair, crashing onto it, winding himself. The air he was hoarding in his lungs, escaped into the smoke. It was only a painful desperation that got him back to his feet. His head was swimming.

The smoke was insistent, tempting him to take a few gulps of the polluted air, but grinding teeth together, he pulled himself up, and into the back room, just as a huge part of the plasterboard from the ceiling crashed to the floor behind him, as the pub gave up its integrity.

The back room was slightly less chaotic with hard brick and more sterile furnishings, that didn't offer as much fire fuel as the comfortable furnishings of the public bar. The smoke was everywhere, nonetheless. His lungs burned with the filth he'd gulped down, and the strain of not breathing more than he had to. His eyes were streaming, his ribs ached from his fall, and sweat had soaked his clothes, and all this in the space of what could only be thirty seconds. He just needed to get through this room, and then he had a chance to get away, back to his wife, and warn her of the crosshairs that they found themselves in.

The proximity of freedom made him careless. He tried to run for the door, not checking his footing, and just as he was within an arm's length of the door, he tripped over something heavy and solid, crashing down just bracing a catastrophic fall with his outstretched arms.

Tony felt around him, to try and understand what he had fallen over, and to reorientate himself in the room, to find the side wall that he could follow to the corner door. His hands searched for the flat ground, but then found the shape of what he had tumbled over – he knew what it was with the first touch. But he continued to pat the outline for the avoidance of all doubt. A foot, then legs, then up to arms, braced across the belly. It was hot, and wet. The wet sticky, down the front of the chest. A man's chest. Tony reached up to the cheek, and then there really was no doubt. He felt Jack's sideburns, his mop of hair, and that wide nose. He was dead. One last reckless touch confirmed that. He knew he couldn't afford to waste any time here, but he had to know. Gentle, probing fingers felt under Jack's chin, and found the corners of a gaping wound, that had spewed out the hot blood that covered Jack's chest and belly, him being left to bleed out like an abattoir pig in his own kitchen, as his home burnt down around him.

Tony battled a wave of sorrow that curled up into anger. A feeling that became the fuel he needed to drag himself to his feet again and give him the final impetus to get out of this place. All this chaos and carnage, delivered just for him. His friend at his feet, dead, and this village that had welcomed them in, at risk, all because of some small-minded thugs who couldn't let them just *be*. The desperate immediacy of having to navigate the burning building could pass now, as he fell out of the back door into the outside air, and it was replaced with a burning rage of his own.

He was going to find his wife. He was going to get her safe. And then he was going to kill every one of these fuckers.

The beer garden was narrow, and short, and he could get to the back fence in maybe thirty strides. His aching muscles responded to the adrenaline and anger that burnt through him, and he managed to run. Five strides, ten, and then he was taken off his feet. One of the men had hedged his bets, and found a way around the perimeter of the building, those crucial seconds spent with Jack enough for the man to close the gap, and tackle Tony from behind as he made his push to escape.

They rolled and tumbled, the surprise of the attack allowing the man to throw a few punches as they fell. Tony felt nothing. If anything, he felt rewarded. His anger now had somewhere to go. The man, this brute in black, had managed to leverage himself into the stronger position, cocking his fist for more now that they'd stopped moving. Tony didn't wait. He punched again and again and again, aiming at the space the man's raised arm had exposed, under his armpit. Tony didn't care that his eyes stung, or that his lungs burnt, or that his hand might shatter if he hit the man as hard as he wanted to. As far as he was concerned, this man was wholly responsible for the death of his friend, simply by being *here*, in front of him, right now. And there was no force on earth that was going to stop him.

The man winced, and yelped, and then covered up. Tony had heard something crack during his assault, seconds passed, but no pain came. It was the man's rib, and not his own fingers. Spurred on, Tony didn't relent. It was his life or this man's. If Tony stopped he was dead. Tony swung his other hand up, straight fingers dug directly into the man's Adam's apple, squeezing, and at the same time, forcing him off and down to the ground, giving Tony a precious, hard-earned window to find his feet again. To stand was to win, and nothing was going to stop Tony, as the man struggled to fill his lungs through his ruined throat.

There was a disturbance behind him. Tony looked over his shoulder. The other men Tony had seen in the crowd, the Red Pope at the head of them, had found a side way around the perimeter of the pub garden, pushing through hedges to gain access to the beer garden, as the external gate had been locked for the evening, and the internal route was no longer passable as the fire continued its destructive attack on the pub.

"Grace." The Red Pope didn't shout, but his voice carried. The grin had gone. The Red Pope knew he too was racing against time. This stunt of theirs, this trap, had its own time limit. Each passing moment increased the chance of delay and inconvenience or at worst, police would be called, and that would be the end of their whole gambit; Tony would be lost to them.

It had to be now. Tony looked at the Red Pope, twenty yards or so away, and went to run. The choking man half-heartedly tried to grab his ankle, but Tony wasn't in any kind of mood to let this broken fool keep him here any longer. A left hook, aimed downwards with all his power, knocked the man out cold. Tony ran.

Noise erupted in the beer garden. Some of the fire crew had made their way through to the garden to form a perimeter around the burning building and to chase down these idiots endangering themselves. One of the fire fighters put himself between the men and Tony and was trying to shepherd them away from the garden and back to the street. This was all the distraction Tony needed. He hurled himself over the back wall, and down the overgrown siding of the disused railway cutting. The Red Pope burst past the fire-man, his lackeys trailing behind him, but the moment had gone, as Tony had vanished into the dark of the old railway route.

"Back to the car. Except you. You follow him. And someone drag that useless fucker back to the car."

Tony hadn't gone. He knew that's what they would expect, but the low light was now his ally, and he could hide amongst the chaos of decades of uncared for bushes and shrubs, the soot and blood smeared on his face a small consolation, offering him camouflage in the now-dark night. One of the black-garbed lunks slid down the siding, in his flat-soled slip-on shoes, swearing and crashing into mud and nettles, before getting to his feet, trying to pick a direction – left or right. Tony let him stumble out of sight, before climbing back up the siding, then along the perimeter of the beer garden, then on, past two more gardens, hopping over a fallen fence panel, and into a garden.

What would they have done? Where might they have gone? Back into shadows, and back onto the roads, he imagined. He hoped. If he kept to the back gardens, and went into the fields parallel to the road, he might just be able to loop round before they could set up a perimeter, if he stayed low and quiet. How many would they have brought? He could only hope it was one car load, and that they would stretch themselves too thin trying to close off all routes out of the village. He was gambling on their arrogance. A sensible, pragmatic man would have scouted ahead, and spent the time in finding the lay of the land, but the sort of people who blew up pubs and murdered a man in cold blood, might not be the sort of people who took the time for cold logic. That was all he had to cling to, but it was enough to keep him going.

He cleared a couple of low walls, crossing back gardens quietly. The fire kept the village people distracted, and would for a while yet especially now he could hear the hiss of hoses above the crackle of the fire. He had time to get clear of the village, and into the fields before Jack would be found and the police were called in force. Once that happened, escape would be more difficult, cornering him and leaving Eleanor exposed, with Stark's dogs running.

He reached the fields, running on the other side, away from the stone wall that ran parallel to the road, and by the copse of trees that created a border on the far side, between the field, and the marshes that ran down to the sea. The trees offered safety, and by keeping close to them, he traded some speed for the darkness they gave him.

Ahead of him was one more wall, which, when cleared, would have him at the junction from the main road to the small track that led to their cottage. He assumed the Red Pope didn't know where he lived. Otherwise, why go to all the trouble of destroying the pub, to draw him out, if they could have just done it quickly and quietly when they were sleeping in their own beds. As long as he could get to his house without being seen by any of the men, making sure to avoid the main roads that he presumed they would be patrolling, then he could at least warn Eleanor, and try to stay safe until he could make his own escape.

But there *were* only a few roads out of town, and the house was close to one of them. And as the fear crystallised a large SUV blinded him, by switching its lights on. It was idling on the grass verge on the main road, its headlights illuminating the road back into town. He instinctively crouched down, and crawled back into the treeline, hoping he hadn't been spotted.

He couldn't risk breaking cover for the house, as this would surely escalate into some kind of endgame. He was outnumbered and outflanked, but had to warn Eleanor away before she unknowingly entered the drama. He needed to think fast. He needed a phone.

Desperation gave him a renewed energy – he could feel the passing of time with every hammering heartbeat; each one inching him closer to disaster. Caution would have to wait, he broke cover and ran as fast as he could back the way he had come, back towards the village, desperately scanning left and right for anyone he could borrow a phone from.

It didn't take long. Across the field, on the other side of the perimeter, he saw an incongruous figure, resting against the wall. Garish cap, pulled down low on his head, and similarly neon tracksuit, all illuminated by the occasional reds thrown up by the still-burning fire and the tiny orange glow of a roll-up cigarette, and joyously, the white glare of a phone screen. The man was far enough away from the car that Tony felt safe to approach, hoping not to spook him, by slowing his pace, and trying to be casual, as he walked up to the metal gate, that opened out onto the road, close to where the man was standing.

Why was he standing there? What was he doing here? He looked odd, unusual even, dressed like a street-corner rogue, out here in the rarefied Norfolk countryside. No matter. He had no choice.

"Mate, look. I can't explain, but I really need your phone. Just for a minute."

The man spun round, shocked, completely unaware of Tony's approach. The cigarette fell to the ground, as his mouth dropped open with surprise. The man, an unexpected fear on his face, offered the phone, with shaking hand. Tony had no time for niceties, and took the phone before the man could change his mind.

No sooner had Tony taken the phone, than the man had backed away, before breaking into a run, back along the road, towards where the car had parked itself. He began waving his hands, and shouting, trying to get the attention of the occupants, from the half-mile distance away.

"Here! He's here! He's here!"

It was the accent. A thick, high scouse. Liverpool back street timbre on a country road. He didn't know who this man was, but he knew who he was with. The car had seen him too, and started driving at pace back along the road, to intercept Tony – he had maybe a minute before it would reach him. He dashed back into the field, phone in hand, now trying to get away whilst desperately trying to summon up the digits of Eleanor's number.

But no-one remembers phone numbers anymore. His mind was blank all except for one number. His old home number. The number his mum still had, which she'd had since he was a boy. In that moment he was so grateful of her stubborn nature when the prospect of her moving to a care home had been angrily rebuffed when it was raised.

He dialled, trying not to think of the car, the occupants, and anyone else who might mean him harm, all homing in on his location. A thin voice answered the phone.

"Hello?"

"Mum, it's Tony. Tony! Look, stop, stop – this is important."

"Tony? What? It's late..."

"Mum, listen. I need you to help. It's important. I need you to call Eleanor. Right now." He looked over his shoulder, spurred on when he spotted the SUV turning into the field, with a wheelspin and a rev of the engine, headlights swinging round to illuminate his route out of the field, and towards the treeline. "Stop. Stop talking! Tell her 'pillbox', okay? *Pillbox*. Do it now, mum. I'll explain later. Just do..." Three beeps. Call failure. Signal lost. Something he had welcomed once – the technological isolation of countryside life – now something that might end up costing him everything.

He'd sent his message in a bottle, and had to take solace in pulling the men away from their proximity to his house. Maybe Eleanor would breeze through this whole business without knowing how close to danger she had come. Maybe. He slipped the phone into a pocket, and crashed into the trees, hurdling bushes, knowing that he would soon be in the marshland, where he could slip down to the beach, if he was careful, and then make an escape along the coastline, maybe all the way to the next village.

A crash of branches behind him warned him that his pursuers were close, perhaps fifty yards behind or so. His immediate need for pace meant stealth had long since stopped being an option, so he had to rely on making good ground from his pursuers first before attempting to lose them in the dark again.

He put the trees behind him, and entered the undulation and uncertainty of the marshland. Shallow pools of water, and soft ground slowed him, but he'd walked this ground hundreds of times before. He knew it was firmest around the tall reed beds which he could still make out in the faint moonlight. He also knew that it was only a few hundred yards to the gravel public footpath that wound down from the road to the beach, and if he could clear the next few pools, and the next few banks, he could join part way along giving him firm ground he could use to extend the distance from those behind him.

He staggered over a patch of uneven ground and slipped. A slip that brought him to his knees. He struggled not to slide backwards into the deep water he'd just jumped, his soles struggling to get any purchase on the wet mud. Suddenly, he found precious grip and hauled himself up and onwards. He didn't dare turn to see how close to disaster he was. The desperation gave him fresh energy, and he found the path at a sprint, turning towards the sound of tides and wash.

His thoughts were narrow. One step followed by another. Get to the end of the path. Get to the beach. Keep running. Get safe and call Eleanor. He heard voices behind him, maybe a few hundred yards or so, near enough that they would soon catch him if he dared slow. The path became a tunnel in the dark – one side banked by the marshland undulations, the other by a row of trees, with the path falling away downwards to beach level. The camber forced Tony faster than his legs were ready for, his momentum almost taking him off his feet..

The beach opened up, impossibly wide, illuminated by a moon that had crept out from behind the clouds, dark silhouettes of trees now behind him, and a faint red glow a mile or so away, back towards the village. Turning right would have him back towards that glow, so turning left, and into the sand dunes, was the safer route, putting the village behind him, running from colour and life, and into the monochrome world of the moon and the dark; a thought so sharp that it flashed in his mind, despite the adrenaline and the desperation of his situation.

All Tony had left was the hope that his message had reached Eleanor and she understood. Half a mile more of burning lungs, and burning muscles, and he would know. Anything less than that and he knew he would likely end up face down in the sand, good for nothing but gull food, that's unless he was taken away from here, for a slower, more painful end.

He had two advantages – he had the lead, enabling him to wind through the sand dunes, in and out of sight-lines for anyone following behind, and he had a clear idea of his destination. He walked these dunes most days, letting his thoughts fly free, almost as if they were spread wide across that sprawling horizon, the slow pace of everything drawn in like the first breath after swimming underwater. Even now, the focus solely on pushing himself forward, his feet remembered the ebb and flow of every dune, weaving this way and that, keeping him ahead of the chasing pack he was straining to hear above the wash of the waves.

And there they were. A yell then another shout, and then, he knew, they were coming in his direction. It was impossible to hope the dunes would be his salvation on their own, but even so, hearing the commotion behind him, like dogs after a fox, pushed him, fear and determination dragging more out of his tired legs and his smoke-blasted lungs. He was on fire. Pure pain. Hot tears were streaking his face now, his teeth gritted, his fists balled, pulling at the air, trying to keep his pace and balance.

He scanned the beach ahead of him. The half-mile seemed like an impossible distance, his destination a mirage he couldn't hope to find. And then, he noticed something, which became a more tangible destination, pushing him on. There, ahead of him, was a bonfire. The irony didn't occur to him until later, that he found himself escaping one fire that had tried to claim him only to head towards another one which instead offered an escape.

As he drew closer, he spotted figures around the fire. Three, maybe four people, all stood up, staring at the strange man running as if the hounds of hell were on his heels. Four kids – teenagers, two male, two female – wide-eyed and open-mouthed, holding bottles of beer and fruit cider, a few hundred yards ahead of him. He daren't look behind him, but he knew what was coming, and he knew he needed to warn them and get them away to safety.

"Get off the beach! Get off!" He waved his arms, frantically, a tiny voice inside him telling him that all he was doing was encouraging curiosity, making these oblivious souls more likely to remain than escape. It was the same instinct that made someone turn their head after being told not to look.

"What? We're not doing nothing, mate." The most confident called back, still not quite finding the answer to the equation being presented to them. "It's a public beach!"

One of the girls tugged at the boy's arm, clearly a couple of steps ahead of him. The man running towards them was not running *to* them, but *from* something. Tony couldn't hear what was said to the first boy, but he could imagine. *Come on*, she'd say, *perhaps we should just go*.

He was close to them now. Perhaps a hundred yards away. He saw their faces, their eyes widening, and from that, he knew that his pursuers had come into view from behind the undulating landscape. The bizarre scene writ large across their faces, their expressions exaggerated by the bonfire, like torchlight held under a chin at Hallowe'en.

The shot rang out, announcing itself to its small audience like a ham actor on first night, loud and jarring. The scene froze, as the players all found themselves detached, processing the noise, the shock and finally, the impact.

The Red Pope emerged from between the dunes, onto the flat sands of the beach, gun in hand, and seeing Tony, silhouetted against the fire, so close to more cover, and worse, the chance of escape, he did not pause, and fired, certain that he could bring him down, and be done with this tiresome chase, and the whole sorry expedition, which was becoming louder and messier by the second. Let this be the full stop to the ugly, meandering sentence, and get away from here, back to his kingdom, in Liverpool.

Cold Cut had followed the rest of the chasing pack after he had alerted them to Grace's location, a mix of obligation and terror demanding that he stay with these men who scared him so much, as they chased their quarry. He was close enough behind them all when he saw the Red Pope reach for the gun inside his jacket, his legs slowing as it dawned on him what was happening. He wasn't sure what to expect when he followed the Red Pope down to the beach – it was a lizard-brain impulse, to just follow. But after he'd waved Pope's car down and pointed Tony out as he fled towards the beach, Cold Cut hoped that whatever happened, if he was there at the end, then he could get the absolution – the reward even – and get home. Pulled along in the slipstream, eyes only ahead, hoping that, when all was said and done, he would be in good graces, his luck finally turning.

Tony turned his head at the same time as the shot was fired. That risked look gave clarity to the vague, shapeless fear at his heels – he saw exactly what was behind him. The Red Pope, gun in hand and striding forward, one shot fired, and ready for a second, a third, a fourth. No option but to turn and push; to run harder, even though his whole body rebelled against him.

The teenage boy, Chris, couldn't believe what he was seeing. Their quiet evening huddled around the fire sharing sips of piss-weak beer had been shattered. The delectable drags of a tightly wrapped spliff, handled like a porcelain heirloom – despite it being filled with only a passing resemblance to weed – had been ruined by whatever chaos was approaching them. One man running as if death itself was at his heels, waving at the group like he would bowl into them like skittles. Seconds later, another figure, blond-haired, gun in his hand, looking like a character from a late-night gangster film had walked off the screen and onto the sand. A real gun. Chris didn't believe the bang could have come from that gun actually being fired. He didn't believe any of it, right up until the force of another shot tore into his shoulder, lifted him off his feet, and dropped him, bleeding, back onto the fire that burned behind him, in an explosion of sand, blood and ashes.

Cassie screamed as her boyfriend fell to the floor. Tony had seen her before. She was the girl that Eleanor had helped back at the festival, a few months back. Tony finally reached the kids and now completely aware that the Red

Pope had no hesitation jeopardising the lives of innocent strangers if it meant a chance at taking down his prey, thinking no further beyond that. The thought of more blood on his hands, even if unwittingly, caused Tony to veer away from the group, the three teens stood stock still and terrified, except the injured boy who writhed on the floor from the gunshot. Tony had a goal in mind, and he knew he wasn't far from it, though salvation seemed like catching smoke.

The treeline loomed, with another break in the trees ahead of him, three bollards sentry-like at one end of a tarmacked turning circle, next to an overflowing dog-bin, at one end of a road that led away from the beach and back up to the outward road out of town. Just to one side of the bollards, almost obscured by a clutch of overgrown bushes, was an old, wartime pillbox, slots like eyes, scanning the horizon for invaders that had never come.

Behind him, the Red Pope, Cold Cut following behind him, had slowed to a walk. They set a remorseless, considered pace, in order for the Red Pope to better aim his gun after the unfortunate attempt before. The teenagers had regrouped, pulling the stricken boy from the floor and along the beach by the shortest possible route. All of them oblivious to the fact that they'd obscured the Red Pope's aim at Grace. The last shot was a frustration. But despite the adrenaline and ill-concluded confidence, it was beginning to dawn on the Red Pope that a dead kid on his hands would make things intolerable for him and his employer.

"Get out of my fucking way!" The Red Pope cursed with the ferocity of a gunshot. It was severe enough to make the four teenagers scurry faster, kicking up sand as they struggled to gain purchase in the fine grains underfoot. The Red Pope bobbed and weaved his head, trying to get a clear eyeline on Grace, his back to him, dangerously close to reaching those bollards, and potentially, the shadows and escape. Finally, he had a shot. Take your time. Take a breath. Kill this motherfucker.

Grace didn't know how close he was to dying. He didn't know that the Red Pope had clear sightlines, had steadied his aim or slowed his breathing. Nor did he see the slow smile play across his lips as he twitched his trigger finger. It was certain death for Tony. Almost. Almost.

Then pandemonium.

Two red lights lit up the darkness underneath the trees. They were coming from the lane that led from the beach to the road. A hatchback car reversed towards the bollards, an animalistic whine screaming out of the engine. The passenger door was already open. Tony saw it first – salvation – gritting his teeth and ignoring his burning muscles he flung himself towards the door.

The Red Pope had him, cold. Gun trained on Grace's back, primed to take him down. One shot and instant death. The Red Pope was calm, no longer needing to worry about his prey escaping him, him dead in his sights. The gun was cold in his hands, his grip relaxed, and his trigger finger tightening, waiting for the perfect moment to fire.

Suddenly, the gun was knocked out of his hand. One of the group of fucking children, the girl whose scream had shredded his ears, and his nerves, had smashed into his arm from his peripheral vision and the dark, growling like cornered dog, knocking the gun clear and away, before running back to catch up with the rest of her group, who were dragging that feeble slab of meat that had gotten in his way mere seconds ago. These children were irritants, but how he regretted not dealing with them with the brutal contempt they deserved.

He was bigger than the girl, far bigger, but the ground here was treacherous, and this slight girl, at pace, had been able to knock him from his feet, down to one knee, and to his hands. He looked up to see the back of all of those he had slowly faced down on the beach, as they clustered around the red glow of the brake lights of the car, maybe twenty yards from him, which could very well be twenty miles.

Tony reached the passenger door. Eleanor was poised, inside, foot on the accelerator and the engine revving, and just the handbrake engaging that was preventing the car from slingshotting away from danger, and up the lane and away.

"Get in! Tony!" She was not going to wait a moment longer than she had to. She had seen what was going on – Tony racing for dear life across the beach, a man – that man – stalking from behind, and, worst of all, that horror sound of gunfire that had cut through the noise of the engine and her desperate thoughts.

Tony clutched the open door with his left hand, the roof with his right, and through tortured gasps, said one word.

"Wait"

Eleanor looked at him with wide-eyes, and unsaid questions, willing him to speak, and quickly. She knew they had seconds to live or die.

"The kids." Heavy breaths and a pained expression. Bare teeth and blood on his lips. "He'll hurt them."

Eleanor swung her head around, and took in as much as she could in the pale red glow of the brakelights, and the moonlight reflected on the sea. The Red Pope was pushing himself back to his feet, one hand at a time, his second hand snatching the gun from the floor. He was the distillation of everything they'd hoped to leave far behind – the cold remorselessness of the city come to stake a claim on the quiet safety of this rural nowhere. He was death Himself. In front of him, obscuring the Red Pope and his hideous intentions, were the four teenagers, one injured, one stumbling, and the others helping one or other of those along as fast as they could; scared witless judging by the looks on their faces, but still, admirably, certain that they would all escape together. They had seen the car as well, and saw it as something to chase towards, as a lighthouse in a storm, and were now at the bollards, just a few feet from the bumper of the car.

"In. In. In!" Tony had turned, pulled open the rear passenger door, on his side, that action making all other decisions moot for the teenagers, wounded Chris half-lowered half-thrown into the back seat, two more falling in behind him horizontally, a tangle of legs dangling from the door, and just Cassie, brave Cassie, still to enter. She was tantalisingly close. Like someone drowning reaching for a lifeguard, she stretched out her arms. Behind her, the Red Pope's figure was fifteen yards back, readying to fire again.

She jumped for Tony, and he braced for her, falling backwards into the front passenger seat. With her in his arms, pain lanced through his ribs, radiating around his body, forcing a yelp from him. A shot fired, and glass shattered, tiny nuggets spraying onto the three in the back seat. The bullet left an improbably small exit hole in the front windscreen. Another bullet ricocheted off the driver's headrest strut. It went unnoticed by all except him – a measurement of fractions between life and death for Eleanor, lost in the maelstrom of noise and panic.

The car was full of screams, pain and fear, the car symbolising safety, though a safety that seemed tenuous and temporary at best, with a killer yards away. Cassie was the first one to find words again, imploring this woman to drive, with a voice hoarse from stress. Then, suddenly, the handbrake was released, and the car sped forwards, like a sprinter out of the traps, leaving the Red Pope, Cold Cut and all of those other invaders behind it. The feeling of movement was a comfort for all inside, the car reached the top of the lane trailing exhaust fumes and glass behind it. Eleanor steered hard right onto the main road away from the village and danger, to safety.

29

Time was elastic. It slowed and sped up, all at once. Everyone inside the car was willing it to go faster, to be away from the beach as fast as possible. They needed to find some dark, quiet place to stop, think and to start breathing again. But each one of the people inside the car were also beset by so many thoughts and fears that they felt like a flimsy boat buffeted on a stormy sea, no sooner having considered one factor before twenty more crashed down on them.

The car slalomed down dark country lanes as fast as Eleanor dared drive it. She'd cut the lights as soon as she'd found the high gears to make speed. She needed to get away, quickly, but they also needed to avoid detection, especially given how terminal that would be – they were in no position to put up any kind of fight.

Cassie was still clinging to Tony both for safety, as they had no time to secure the seatbelt, and through some kind of unconscious fear response. Everyone was silent, concentrating hard on the road, in both directions, until Chris groaned. The rustle of smashed glass filled the car as he writhed in pain, shaking them from whatever grip their thoughts had them in, back to the here-and-now of inside the whining, battered hatchback. Eleanor spoke first, reaching up to adjust the rearview mirror so she could make eye contact with those on the back seat.

"Try not to move. I know it hurts, but moving will make it worse."

Chris groaned through gritted teeth. He was lying across the boy and girl who were trying to keep him still by wrapping their arms around his torso and legs. The boy holding him was quietly sobbing.

"Can someone tell me your names? Do you know who we are? My name is Eleanor. This is Tony. You're safe now, I promise."

As soon as Eleanor said this, Cassie eased her grip from around his neck, embarrassed, but trying not to show it, as if saying his name had stopped him being some abstract figure, and somehow more real. The boy in the back seat was still sobbing, and Chris was hissing through his clenched teeth.

"I know you, don't I?" said Eleanor. "It's Cassie, isn't it?"

"Yes. And that's Chris lying down, and..." Her voice broke as she realised the *why* of Chris' situation, taking a gulp before continuing. "...and Coney and Bex. We weren't doing anything. I don't know what's happening..."

"This isn't about you." Eleanor was concentrating on the road, but made sure her voice was soft, and calm. They were in shock. They might all be in shock. "Look. Cassie, you know us, don't you? I know your mum, too. She runs the gallery in the village, doesn't she? Her name's Melody, isn't it?"

"Yes," she gulped. "Yes."

"And you know Tony, don't you? He helped with a bit of damp-proofing in the gallery, didn't you, Tone?"

"Few months ago, something like that." Tony knew it was best to let Eleanor manage this. She knew that too, so they both found their roles, and Tony spoke when he was invited to.

They'd driven for fifteen minutes, leaving the main road after a few miles, to try and flit across the fields using the spiders web of single lane roads that criss-crossed the county. Eleanor was doing her best to find eye contact with all of the kids in the car, but the rearview made it difficult. She felt safe enough to pull over next to a siding that led to a metal-gated field. She dropped the car into neutral and turned to look at each of them directly.

"This is all about us. And we need you to help. Chris, I'm sorry, but just hold on for a little bit. Just two seconds, because I need to talk to you all first."

Chris hissed and wheezed on the back seat, but he managed to hold Eleanor's gaze as she spoke to him, acknowledging he understood, just by dint of not turning away.

"Those men that were chasing us, shooting at us. They are bad men. I don't need to tell you that. And they are desperate men. So what you choose to do now is really important, and I want you to be safe. They've been looking for us for a long time, because we didn't do what they wanted us to do. And now they've found us. They're going to keep looking for us until we can convince them that we've left. Which means they're probably going to be around the village in the next few days."

The boy, Coney, sobbed a little louder at this.

"It's okay, love. Don't worry. If you listen to us you'll be fine." Eleanor reached back and squeezed Coney on the knee, making sure to look at him whilst she was doing it.

"What we're going to do is go back to where they come from, which is the other side of the country. We're going to give them what they want, and go to them. That means they won't need to be here anymore, and they definitely won't need to come looking for you." Tony knew what she was doing. This was a Trojan horse – on the surface, reassuring, but there was something to focus the mind implicit in that statement – 'follow our plan or they'll be back'. She was good at this. Much better than he could ever be. A scalpel versus a hammer.

"We're going to have a look at that wound of yours, Chris. We don't want you going to a hospital, as that is going to raise a lot of questions, and it might also give them something to look for. I can't imagine too many people get shot round here. If I can get the bullet out, then we can make up a story, and you will just be any old hospital admission."

"This could be bullshit!" Bex piped up from the back seat, silencing both the sobs from Coney and the hissing from Chris. "You could just be telling us all this to shut us up. To scare us."

Eleanor closed her eyes, for a second to keep calm, the little voice inside her desperate to be a loud voice on the outside, to shout at these children about how they could all be killed if they didn't do as they were told.

"You're right. It really could be. But look at what happened. They were chasing Tony. They shot at him. And then they shot at us, because they didn't want him to get away. They don't care about anything else, which is why young Chris here has a hole in his shoulder. And why they'll keep looking because they know how close they are to getting us once and for all."

The girl's forehead furrowed, as the undeniable logic of what she was hearing started to sink in.

"I don't know what they'll do next for definite, but I know what I'd do. I'd find the kids on the beach who saw me. Who saw me shoot at someone. I know one kid was shot and got away, and I know that another stopped me from killing the man I've been desperate to kill for months. I'd know that this is a small village, and these kids would have more they could tell me. I'd want to have a chat with them."

Coney sobbed again. Cassie tried to shift her seat so as little of her was sat on Tony as possible.

"That's only part of it. We love it here. We got away from some bad men. And we need you to help us. I know what you kids are like, status updates and posts and the like, but please, you have to promise not to talk about this. If not for us, then for you. And yours. Just keep your heads down for a week. Don't go out. Go to a relative's house or something. Say nothing. Let it blow over. I promise you we'll make sure those men never come back here, but we just need a few days to do that, okay?"

Eleanor looked at each one of the teenagers as they glanced at one another. A long moment followed until Cassie spoke, comfortable to take the lead.

"We can do that. We won't say a word. We promise." She turned to the rest of her group as she said that last word, prompting.

"Yes, we promise," said Bex. Coney nodded, a drip of snot on his nose. Chris nodded, too.

"But, Chris needs help?" Cassie looked at Eleanor, and Tony, hoping they could give a good answer to that problem. Hard to even conceptualise – a gunshot wound.

"I know. Tony and I are going to have to have a look at that shoulder of yours, Chris. We need to see if we can get that bullet out. If we're really lucky, it's gone in and gone out."

"Can you just get off for a second, Cassie?" Tony shifted his legs, as an additional prompt.

"Oh, right, sure." Cassie popped the door and stepped out into the still night, stretching to full height and taking a deep breath of cold air into her lungs, sobering her up.

"Tony? Have you got your lighter and your...?" Eleanor didn't say "knife". He knew what she meant, and there was nothing to gain by saying that word out loud. "Get it clean, love."

Tony climbed out himself, gingerly, still feeling the beating his body had taken not half an hour ago. He dug around in his pockets, pulling out the penknife he always carried, and the gas lighter that he was given as a 45th birthday present, which he carried with him, in the usually fruitless hope that someone would hand him a cigar to smoke every now and again, never able to justify the cost to himself of buying one himself. His fingers also found the phone he'd taken from that odd man. He'd forgotten about it. He wouldn't again.

He flicked the lighter on, a blue flame whooshing out, which he ran up and down the opened blade of the knife, until it glowed red under the heat. Coney was still in his sorry trance, but Bex was staring, wide-eyed, at Tony, or more particularly, the knife. Fortunately, Chris didn't raise his head to see. Tony turned his back on the car, just on the off-chance he might.

Eleanor opened her door, and climbed out as well. She walked around to the back, opened the boot and rooted around clanking bottles and rustling bags as she searched through the shopping she'd picked up on her way out to the gym that evening. The boot shut, freeing a few stubborn glass fragments that were clinging to the edge of the back window frame.

"Shit. Sorry, everyone." She had a small bottle of vodka in her hand, and a couple of rolled up towels from her gym bag.

"Tony, come round to this side. Chris, love. We're going to have a look at that wound of yours now. And, I'm sorry, but it's going to hurt. I need you to pop this towel in your mouth, and I'm going to wrap this other one around your shoulder. Be really brave. This will be over as quickly as we can make it."

Tony and Eleanor manoeuvred Bex and Coney out from under Chris as gently as possible, sitting him up so they could slide out. Tony then climbed in beside him, sliding one arm under one shoulder, and guiding Chris forwards, so he was slightly bent over, exposing his shoulder for Eleanor to inspect. Tony's grip was firm but not constrictive, trying not to hurt the boy any more than was necessary, but not letting him hurt himself by struggling.

"OK, Chris. Bite down. I need to just poke it a little bit."

Everyone sniggered. It broke the tension. Chris even managed a smile, even if just for a second. Then his eyes watered, and his ears reddened, as his shoulder felt like it was being torn apart.

30

"Do you think we can trust the kids?" Tony was absent-mindedly rubbing his arm, sore from any number of possible causes.

They had taken the most circuitous route they could think of to join one of the few major roads that led out of the county and west. Eleanor was trying to find the perfect balance between the speed of a major road, and the inconspicuousness of the smaller roads, especially given the ruined back window, and the spider-webbed cracks of the front windscreen, emanating from the hole where the bullet had exited. It was late, and the road ahead was a monotone, illuminated by the headlights, the view only changing from two-lane to one-lane depending on the road they were following.

Tony preferred the single lane roads. It made him think of his childhood; fond memories of long days with his father, on some weekend holiday away, driving back to their bed and breakfast at night, along those single lane roads, a tunnel of overhanging trees, and the flick of the headlights from low-to-high beam which made the trees burst into view, as if apparitions come to act as sentries for the travellers. He felt safer here. Hidden.

"I think so. I think they understood what was at stake, and I don't think they would fancy another run-in with our friends back there. Even if they went to the police, which they might, I'm not sure what they would tell them that would cause us any more trouble than we're already in." Eleanor flicked the indicator on, and joined a slip-road back to a main road, which would do for another ten miles or so. "To be honest, I don't fancy another run-in with that lot either. Not until we can think things through."

"I know. We're going to have to, though. I just won't let us live the rest of our lives skulking about," Tony paused and looked out of the window at nothing. "And they need to be dealt with. They killed him."

That last sentence seemed to echo, as if it was as loud as a scream, even though Tony barely raised his voice beyond a whisper. Eleanor moved her lips, almost imperceptibly, as if she had a rush of words but couldn't settle on the right ones. Finally, she spoke –

"Who? Who was killed, Tony?"

Now it was Tony's turn to pause. If he said those words, then it became real. Each second he stayed silent he could hold onto some hope that what had happened could somehow be negotiated out of reality. "Jack. They killed Jack. Cut his throat and burnt the pub down with him in it."

"...Jesus," was all Eleanor could manage.

"All for me. To call me out. They didn't need to kill him. Why did they kill him?" His voice rose, pleading. Tony was a stoic, but not impossibly so.

They were silent for long minutes, the only sounds were the rumble of tyres on the road, the whoosh of air through the back window, and the low chug of the engine.

"I don't know. They don't care about anything other than proving a point. They want to punish us. And everyone who knows us. That's their message. Fuck you, and everyone you know for being alive."

Eleanor gripped the wheel until her knuckles whitened, railing against her own tumult of emotions – anger, fear, and above it all, a paralysing sadness, a guilt even, that the quiet decision to move to the village had left such injury and hurt behind them. Her eyes stung, and she instead concentrated on the road ahead to give her something to focus on rather than drift into her own thoughts. She found her equilibrium, like coming round after a deep sleep, and her eyes cleared. Tony was pinching the bridge of his nose, his broad shoulders shuddering as huge, quiet sobs shook his body.

She knew this man better than anyone. She had long since understood that the inscrutable exterior was a defence, and inside, he *felt*. Those who somehow made it into his small inner circle were cherished and protected and valued. His scowl was his shyness manifesting, but those who were nimble enough to sidestep those defences or perhaps like Jack, simply crash through them, were members of a lifelong club. Tony had let him down. Just by *being* he had killed him. He would be his own purgatory.

Eleanor snaked a hand around his back, rubbing his shoulders, and massaging the back of his neck. Touching him, reassuring him, that they were together. That they still had each other, and still had ways out of the corner they'd been backed into.

"Oh Tony, my love. It's not on you. This wasn't you. It was *them.* And we are going to sort this."

Flicking her eyes between Tony and the road, she could see with each glance he was regaining his composure like the slow progression of frames in an animation. The tell-tale sign? His hand dropped from his face, to mirror his other hand, clutching a knee. His fingers flexed, and dug in, pushing at the muscles, as hard as he could, the pain a sobering crutch for him.

"That's exactly what we are going to do. We are going to sort this. We are going to go back to Liverpool, and we are going to finish those motherfuckers."

Eleanor moved her hand back to the gearstick, and put her foot to the floor.

32

"How do we get to go home after all this?" Tony put voice to his fears, hoping Eleanor had some solution she'd kept to herself until now.

"We can. We will. We know what we have to do. We have to make them go away. Leave us alone for good."

"And then what? What about the police? About Jack?" Tony had so many questions, and whilst he knew that he might not like the answers, it was preferable to being trapped with his thoughts, and the hum of the tyres on the road as they drove.

"Look, do they actually know? What can they prove? You'll have been identified as the man who ran into the pub, but everyone knows you and Jack got on, and everyone knows that you're the type of silly sod who would do something like that for one of his friends. We can explain that away." Eleanor spoke with confidence, even if Tony suspected that she might be projecting, whistling in the dark for his benefit.

"And Jack?"

"We can beg ignorance. What can they prove? Pretty

sure they can't tie you to the murder, and the crowd definitely noticed those clowns lurking around, and making a nuisance of themselves once you'd turned up," Eleanor said, changing lane with care, careful not to draw attention to themselves, and the battle-scarred car they were driving in.

"The kids? They might talk?" Tony said, testing another strut of his argument.

"I don't see it happening. They were scared, love. Really fucking scared. And I think we are going to have to trust them. They know us, and let's not forget, we know them as well. They've seen us around. I think they believe us and more than anything, they were shit-scared of the Stark lot. Who knows, maybe they're a little bit scared of us too."

"It's risky. I just want an easy life. A quiet life."

"Don't we all? Let's just be brave. We've been careful. Our money is safe, and everything from before we moved to Liverpool is packed away. As long as we stick together, I don't see Norfolk coppers pushing into us too much when some crazy Scouse murderers are about. But all that's got to wait. The most important thing is that Stark and his lot know where we are now. So we need to do something about that. Then we'll know where we are."

That was enough for now. A problem for another day. One thing at a time, and the big conundrum needed to be addressed. They could have avoided it – take a left turn, head south, and start again. But did they want to start again? If Stark had found them once, he could find them again. A reward could be put up, people could gossip, and those shadowy threads could lead all the way back to Liverpool. Only next time they might not see Stark coming. There was something else as huge as dawn on an open horizon pushing them forward: revenge.

"I've still got their phone," Tony said.

All hot emotion had passed, and cool analysis was occupying both their thoughts, as they continued to drive. Both of them took solace in the familiar, comfortable pattern of planning – they liked the process of organisation, each stress-testing the other, testing for weaknesses and opportunities, though they both thought that the days of planning revenges and survival were behind them. It was a muscle memory they fell back into, able to slip into the critical thinking of murder with a disconcerting ease. Who were they? Which aspect of them was their truth? The quiet, contented warmth of the Norfolk cottage, or the practical brutality of their younger days, when the circumstance of their lives saw them through military experiences, to big city tear-ups, and the controlled violence of the grey edges of criminal life. Both of them wanted to believe they were the former, easy and charming, and their old lives were an aberration, a means to an end, to be put away and forgotten. But as the car drove on, they knew they couldn't let go of the people that they'd tried to forget.

"How did you get it?" Eleanor asked.

"I saw this lad, up on the road, as I came out of the village. I didn't realise he was with them, until I took his phone off him, to call you. He ran back to the Red Pope as soon as he could."

"Did you know him? Recognise him?"

"No. I don't think so. No mistaking the voice, though. Or the look of him. He couldn't have been more obviously Scouse. I wasn't really thinking straight, to be honest." Tony replied, shifting in his seat as bunched muscles started to make him feel uncomfortable.

"I don't blame you, love. You did rather have other things on your mind." Eleanor replied, with a wry smile.

Tony managed a smile of his own, of sorts.

"Can we use it?" Eleanor asked.

Tony dug into his pockets, and pulled out the phone. It was still on, lighting up with a touch of the finger, a cannabis leaf screensaver flashing to life as Tony pressed the screen. A swipe of the finger, and a keycode prompt replaced the tawdry graphic.

"There's a code. I dunno."

"We can try and get it unlocked?" Eleanor said trying to be positive even though they were facing a dead-end. This tiny bit of advantage looked doomed. Without access, the phone was just a pointless plastic brick of wasted opportunity. Tony looked out of the window, staring into the dark away from the road, trying to reorder his thoughts to look at some other angle, but mainly to hold onto some reserve and refuse to buckle to yet another disappointment. He looked back at the phone, his fingers twitching and tapping the side of the handset, like hounds eager to be off their leads. They tapped away, almost unconsciously.

Tony entered a code, and tutted. Incorrect. His eyes rolled to one side, looking away from the phone to think of another set of four digits. He knew he only had a few attempts at this, before the phone would lock him out for a time. After that, a few more, and then it would lock him out permanently, and it might as well find a new home on the central reservation. He tried again. Wrong again.

"Anything?" said Eleanor, more in hope than expectation.

"Nothing. Maybe we could find someone to jailbreak it?" suggested Tony, but he was unsure even when he said it.

"I think we could do without any added suspicion at the moment," said Eleanor, saying what Tony was thinking.

They sat in silence for long minutes, the headlights illuminating the road a hundred yards ahead of them, as if the light itself was conjuring the road into solidity from the nothingness of the dark that surrounded the car; as if their world was tenuous and would vanish the moment they switched the lights off.

Tony tried the phone again.

The phone screen swooshed as it came alive – a table of icons now filling the screen, apps ready to be opened, to order food, to place bets, to waste time.

"I've done it. It's unlocked."

Eleanor half-spluttered, half-laughed at this.

"How the fuck have you managed that, Steve Jobs?"

Tony laughed now, too. Showing their age.

"It was four zeroes. I mean, why bother?"

Eleanor screeched, banging the steering wheel, gleefully. This little ridiculousness was irresistible, Tony finding it impossible not to laugh. A low snigger becoming louder, and higher, until both of them were laughing and whooping, every lull just a pause before one of them to started laughing again, which, in turn, set the other one off.

When the laughter passed, they returned to thoughtful silence. Tony was scrolling through old messages, and investigating the numerous messaging apps on the phone, all the time trying to build up a picture of that curious creature he had taken this phone from, and looking for anything they could use to their advantage. Eleanor was furrowing her brow, speculating on the traps and risks, one looking at positives, the other looking at negatives. She found her negative first.

"Find My Phone," she said, turning to Tony.

"What do you mean?" Tony was several steps behind her, and looked back at her quizzically.

"Find My Phone. The..the..oh, you know...when you lose your phone? You can track it remotely? If it got stolen?"

"...Shit." Tony held the phone as if it was hot. He flicked a switch on the passenger side door, and the window opened, an almost-ridiculous movement, given the state of the other windows in the car.

"Wait!" Eleanor knew what he was going to do, but she had found her own angle. "Don't! This could be useful. Just switch if off for now. Keep it safe. They might be able to track us, but that's not necessarily a bad thing. Maybe there's going to be a time where we want to be tracked."

Tony looked at her, understanding in his expression. This could be an advantage, after all.

33

C old Cut had spent long nights staring at the ceiling in that hateful, squalid flat in King's Lynn, fantasising about a similarly squalid flat, a few hundred miles north west. His flat – where every pile of unwashed clothes was his Capability Brown landscape, or Tetris stack of pizza boxes were his castle walls. To be away from those two quarter-wit brothers, with their inane bickering, and yokel inflections was very much the "push" but the "pull" of being back amongst his things, and on those streets where he not only knew everyone's name, but their family, their job, their fling, their betting debt. But now, any thoughts of relief that he was finally back within city limits in Liverpool were asphyxiated by the terrible and pervasive fear that this return might result in him having soil fall over his dead eyes, illuminated by the headlights of a CityArrow cab, as some low-grade lackey was tasked with burying him under hometown soil, forever. The fingers of the monkey's paw had closed, all at once.

The trip back was long, like a voyage across a huge and dangerous ocean. There were long periods of quiet with a cloud of dread never far away. Cold Cut knew that he was in a car with dangerous men. Men he'd failed. Equanimity was a concept that, even if they understood it, had no place in their world; a world of predator succession, the path to any success was a ladder built of corpses. Cold Cut concentrated on being as unobtrusive as possible – he understood he couldn't talk his way out of this car, and certainly not without risking the snap of a finger, or the loss of teeth, so instead, he slunk back into his seat. He both willed the time away so he could escape this plush, movable cell, and wished it would never end. What came next was likely to be more dangerous, maybe terminally so.

There were interludes on the long drive where the low-level dread was replaced by wide-eyed terror. The Red Pope was frightening. He had a dangerous inscrutability; a feeling of unpredictability where all practical considerations could be thrown out, as a rage could broil like a tropical storm, without any cues or warning. There was an episode, parked at a late-night motorway services, where a phone call had sent him into such a rage, he screamed curses as he kicked a dark green plastic bin until it shattered sending burger cartons and dog-eared newspapers into the air like a murmuration of refuse gulls. A few concerned looks from other twilight commuters were met with the fiercest of glares and low-growled threats, leaving them in no doubt that any further enquiry into the explosion of violence would be met with escalation, and in their direction. As this tantrum was going on, Cold Cut noticed a shared look between the driver and the man sat next to Cold Cut. The look said that even for the Red Pope, the outburst was unusual in the scale and fury of it.

Cold Cut drew his own conclusions, but from the quiet deference of the phone call to the handbrake turn of the rage, it was obvious the Red Pope had been reporting back to his boss. To Stark. Could there be anyone else who commanded such deference from someone as dangerous as the Red Pope, and only after the termination of the call did the explosion occur - the slammed door of the grounded teen. The Red Pope scared Cold Cut. But Stark scared him more – anyone who could keep this rabid hound on a tight leash was deserving of being the bogeyman that he was often conjured as, if anyone ever invoked his name in whispered street-corner fairy tales. He was scared that he might find himself in front of Jim Stark, soon. It wasn't the simple act of meeting Stark that terrified him, per se – he knew hundreds of people who had some passing acquaintance with him. But that was what made him the most dangerous man in the city – he hid in plain sight, challenging the rumours and the suspicions, maybe even absorbing them and sending them back out onto the streets, fed and angry, as if to say "I know what you say about me, and you are right to fear me, because here I am, and I am not scared that you know this about me." To be in Jim Stark's presence wasn't terrifying in and of itself. What was terrifying was context, and that was what Cold Cut was really afraid of. The Red Pope was unpredictable and violent, but that was animal impulse, and because of that, Cold Cut felt he knew how to behave around him. He'd been around people like that his entire life - step-fathers wrapping belts around their knuckles, or the bigger kid extorting lunch money in a bike shed crucible. Stark *really* scared him because of who he was, how he was, and what he must've done to get there, and to stay there.

A fragile calm permeated the car, with the darkness isolating those inside, unable to see any landmarks or buildings, that might orient them in the night. That feeling of being cut adrift, trapped in this metal box, with at least one sociopath, made the drive back to Liverpool seem interminable, and fraught with risks; risks Cold Cut couldn't quite bring into sharp focus. After maybe an hour, of Red Pope demanding complete silence as he weighed all options, he turned and spoke to Cold Cut directly.

"We're going to see Mr Stark when we get to Liverpool, and we're going to discuss how you're going to use this phone that those bastards have *somehow managed to obtain*" – those last four words were sharp, designed to eviscerate – "to get them to do what we want them to, and draw a very thick, very final line through this annoying little affair."

Cold Cut searched for a word or two, like bars of soap that evaded a firm grasp. He managed to nod, though this was a poor offering judging by the stare that the Red Pope was aiming in his direction, pulling out words from him like fingernails with pliers. Like a drowning man, Cold Cut managed to gasp for air, and spluttered out something, anything, to get that man to turn his gaze away from him."Yes, Pope. Of course. Whatever it takes," was the best that Cold Cut could offer.

"Whatever it takes. Yes, that's the right answer. Whatever it takes."

34

Tony and Eleanor didn't make the mistake of going back to their old flat. They had no need to, and even a casual drive-by, long odds though it was, might have put them in a position of fight or flight. This was a city that had hundreds of pairs of eyes either in Stark's direct employ, or only too willing to whisper a tip to the right person to see someone taken away in the boot of a car for an envelope of notes. Even so, implicitly, they knew they had to make some concession to masquerade and disguise themselves. Tony had found a cheap baseball cap at one of the motorway services, dark blue and with "NY" emblazoned on the front, incongruous as it was, seeing as he had bought it just outside Birmingham. Eleanor had made her own changes, pulling her hair into a tight ponytail, and swapping her contact lenses for glasses that she kept in her bag. It wasn't much of a change but it was something and that would have to do, for however long they were going to be there.

The car was more problematic. A small cosmetic change

was off the table, given that the car had no back window and a gunshot through the front. Circumstance intervened. As they drove, just past Stoke, the trees cleared from one side of the road, and Tony spotted a sight he had driven past hundreds of times, but had forgotten about until now. A scrap dealer car graveyard that clustered around the treeline like an erupted sore amongst the greenery, with a mobile number hand-painted on the side of a white car perched atop three others. Tony knew a few places like this, dotted around the country, and had no reason to believe that this one was any different. It was easily found, once they had pulled off from the motorway at the next junction, driving back against themselves, following an old road that ran in parallel to the bigger roadway. After an hour sat in a portable cabin, drinking piss-weak tea from a plastic cup, their old car had been "disappeared" and an equally non-descript, though thankfully, intact, car had been presented to them to drive away. A handful of crumpled paperwork paying lip-service to any kind of legality, but most importantly, no questions asked. It would do for what they needed, and could equally be left to burn in a disused car park or even back into the rust and shadows of a scrapyard like the one that spawned it, until the next person appeared needing something quick and easy and impossible to trace.

Neither of them cared about cars. It was a good job. If they knew the scale of the comforts that were available to the discerning driver, perhaps driving this rattling automotive corpse, reanimated by a particularly careless mechanic-cum-sorcerer, would have seemed even more demeaning than it already was. The heater spewed out the wheezes of an asthmatic; the windows didn't wind all the way down, and even then, there was a real chance that, if opened, they would never close again. But it drove, and that's all that was needed for now.

Tony and Eleanor skirted Liverpool first, taking a few days to think things through. They stayed in a cheap hotel on the fringes of Birkenhead, knowing that to some, the Wirral, 'over the water' was akin to being on another planet for many of those in Liverpool itself. It wasn't completely safe, but far enough away it would do for now. Besides, what choice did they have? Their minds were made up. They had to reach some kind of permanent conclusion. Still confident in themselves, and most importantly, in each other, they knew they could get through this and see off Stark and his vulgar, brutal intentions once and for all, and find themselves back in the low-wattage comfort of their new life.

The hotel room served as their base of operations. They bought street maps and inventoried their possessions. They purchased a few essentials - changes of clothes and toiletries from a padded envelope full of banknotes they'd kept stuffed in the padding of one of the back seats of Eleanor's car. It wasn't enough to start again, but enough to keep their wheels turning for a few weeks at least. Getting hold of anything else would constitute too much of a risk, until they understood the full scale of things. Using their bank card might alert the police, if they were looking for them – which was entirely in the hands of the kids they had left wide-eyed and tearful hundreds of miles east. Going back to the house in Norfolk, or even the flat just across the river in Liverpool, to equip themselves with more money, supplies or even to grab passports and vanish abroad, would have them run the gauntlet of, at best, the police, and, at worst, those who had put them on the back foot by crashing back into their lives in the first place. They would need to be creative.

But they had a plan. Of course they had a plan. Hot emotion always cooled quickly, and two pragmatists took turns to build a structure to operate in. Each of them sense-tested the other's work, prodding and probing until they were certain that it was sound. Neither spent any time trying to understand quite how they had been put in this position. How some butterfly effect had delivered that particular tropical storm to their idyll in Norfolk. What was the point? They had no-one to interrogate, save each other, and so settled on dealing with the problems of the here and now, leaving the whys for another day. A mistake had been made, somehow, so both made allowances to each other, unconsciously, to stifle any irritation when the same challenges were put forward, again and again, so a mistake wouldn't be made again.

Finally, after sipping vending machine coffee with the suspicion of a medieval cupbearer, Eleanor closed the notepad, slid the pen into the wire spine binding, and sat back in her chair. They were talking in circles, and she'd decided that they'd put enough meat on the skeleton of the plan that they'd created between them. This was their final opportunity to abort this course of action, and cash their chips, hoping that they could relax into a life that always had them looking over their shoulders. What was said next would define that.

"Are we agreed? Are you sure that this is what we want? To take them on?" Tony was always one to ask the question, needing reassurance that they were in total lockstep. He sat down on the side of the bed, facing Eleanor sat in the chair opposite.

"We don't want it, love, but it's how it has to be. I can't bear the thought of us double-checking behind us, or living in the shadows for the rest of our lives, and I certainly can't bear the thought that someone might come after us again and cut another of our friends down." Tony choked that sentence out. Jack, Groucho and Ringo flashed in his mind, like a zoetrope designed to torment him, alternating images of them alive, then dead. He looked out of the window, until his eyes stopped stinging.

"OK. That's settled then. I know this could very well be the end of us, Tone, but you're right. Those bastards killed our friends, and they are going to go on killing people, good people, until someone puts an end to them. We have to cut off the head." Tony turned back to Eleanor when she said this, seeing the determination in her face, which gave him the surety he needed.

"They're not smart. They've never had to be. This plan can work. They're so arrogant they won't consider someone might take them on," Tony said, speaking it out loud, convincing himself as much as he was trying to convince Eleanor.

"There'll be others, you know. A new crew. It'll never end." Eleanor sipped at her coffee cup, though all that was left were the cold splashes at the bottom of the cup. No matter – she needed something to do with her hands.

"There always is. But I want Stark finished. Then we can go. No-one will care about us after that. Why would they?"

"Okay. But we've not a lot left. Not that we can get a-hold of," Eleanor said, with a wave of the arms, the sum total of all they had managed to cobble together from their escape from Norfolk. It didn't look like much. The wad of notes was dwindling – there was maybe a grand left.

"It's enough. It has to be. We daren't try and get anything else – not until we're sure that we've seen the back of Stark, and then we can worry about what the police do or don't know about us. We know that Stark is our problem *here*, and the police are our problem *there*, so at least we only need worry about them one at a time."

"That makes sense. But I think we are going to need some help. I'm going to see the family."

Tony paused. Quieted. He hadn't really considered that Eleanor might want to get them involved. It opened them up to all sorts of other problems, but the situation was difficult, and he had to concede that they needed all the help they could get. He still couldn't help the sigh escape his lips, or stop his hand reaching up to pinch the bridge of his nose.

"I know, Tony. I know you don't want to get them involved, but they can help us, and they owe us. I won't ask for much, and I won't tell them too much about what's going on. I know what I'm doing. You know I do."

"Alright. How long will you be?" Tony couldn't argue with the logic, even if he was frustrated that it had come to this. There were very good reasons why he hadn't even raised this as a possibility, but they were up against the wall, and needed all the help they could get.

"Give me a couple of days. We've got pay-as-you-go phones, so I'm not going to be out of touch. I can get the train south tonight and come back tomorrow."

"What should I do?"

"See what Stark is up to. Scout the location. If we're going to call Stark out, then we need to check every possible angle. The longer we leave it, the bigger the risk, so be careful, but see how the city is looking."

"When are you going?"

"Give me fifteen minutes, then you can walk me to the station."

"I better not. I'll walk *behind* you to the station. Just to be careful."

"Good point. Careful it is then!"

They didn't laugh, but they did manage to smile at each other. Tony reached across from the bed to Eleanor, on the chair next to it, and squeezed her knee. She put her hand on his and squeezed back. This was them, chips all in. The stone kicked down the hill, and unstoppable now. So be it.

35

E leanor had taken most of the money, after spending a few notes on a change of clothes, some travel essentials, and a few other oddments with the goal of making her as unrecognisable as possible. The train station was busy, as it always was, though Tony had to pause, and slink away when he saw the row of CityArrow cabs queued on the taxi rank on the incline to the station. The hardest lesson had been learnt – small odds did occasionally come in, and Tony wasn't about to test his luck by being overly brazen and walking past them. He was safe in the crowds, but then so would anyone be who came after him. It was more important Tony saw them coming rather than feel a knife in the ribs from behind, with nothing left but to curse his luck as he bled out on the steps of the station. He saw Eleanor turn towards the ticket desk, and out of sight from the other side of the crossing. Though it hurt not to see her face, he was pleased she hadn't turned back to wave, or acknowledge him at all, despite the flicker of pain it gave him. The next couple of days were going to be kicking an anthill to see what scurries out. He kept an eye on the reflection in the glass for as long as possible as he walked away, down the bank towards the city. He was perversely comforted that his intuition was confirmed, noticing that his movement away had inspired some hand-waving, pointing and no little agitation from the driver. The last thing he noticed was headlights blinking on, and the car attempting to reverse back out of the tightly compressed queue of cabs onto the road which sloped down to the traffic lights of the junction. He needed to get away from here and lose himself in the city crowds or everything was over for him and Eleanor.

Anything other than a steady walk would exacerbate the situation. He was prepared to bolt, but timing was key. He needed to find enough people to safely lose himself in, safety in numbers, a magic eye picture in reverse. Every instinct was pushing him to run, though. He set his jaw, a conscious distraction from the impulse he was trying to resist, concentrating to keep his movement to a steady stride.

The city centre was an island – a pedestrianised land-mass surrounded by a moat of traffic circled around it. He would be safer away from the roads, able to find thorough-fares and cut-throughs to hide amongst, provided he was quick. The danger was that cars would be summoned, arrive, park, and empty, those inside with their bad inten-tions also able to find anonymity amongst the scrum of bodies, and get close enough to him to make any further hopes and plans beyond a few more snatched breaths irrelevant.

There was a crossing just along from the road junction between the station slip road and one of the roads that circled the shopping centre. But that would involve him heading back towards the queue of cars looking to join the traffic from the station slip-road. Back towards the City-Arrow taxi. He couldn't risk giving the driver absolute confirmation of his identity. Any doubt over his identity, however tenuous, was a currency of pause that he may need to capitalise on. In the other direction was a less formal crossing – more traffic lights, controlling the flow both back and forth, with an island between the lanes. He could cross there at a half-jog, without obviously playing his hand, just gently flouting the law, such as it was, jaywalking around the front of the waiting cars across to the steps that led down to the main shopping centre.

The cab was second from the front in the traffic queue to join the road Tony was now crossing. Unable to resist any longer, Tony turned his head back, as he was crossing, trying to look as if he was taking care to assess the movement of the traffic, but instead sneaking a look back at the driver. The driver didn't appear to have let Tony out of his sight, and was still talking on the phone. No doubt now – this was real, and he had been seen. He indulged wasteful thoughts, self-flagellating again with histrionic self-accusations of how he had risked everything, even though just being in the city *at all* was a risk. How could he be so stupid? How could he be so stupid *again*?

Focus. Escape. Play the odds. They were still in his favour. Stark would have expected something surely, and knowing that Stark had clearly made preparations for them, sending out this approximation of an all-points bulletin to his fleet. If Stark had made allowances, then Tony could make his own, provided he could retreat to the staging point of the hotel across the river, where he might not be safe, but would certainly be safer.

He descended the steps on light toes, with the square

opening out in front of him, two shopping mall entrances yawning open to his left and his right. Mobile fast food stalls had been arranged to greet those coming down the steps, the smell of fried onions persuading the impulsive commuter that they deserved something quick, greasy and substantial, and they could afford to forgo the drudgery of a clean salad in exchange for a crumpled note or a few scattered coins. Interspersed with the stalls sweeping sizzling onions here and there on identical hotplates, and sideways glances at their immediate rivals, were the carnival colours of the replica shirt stalls, winding down their day's trade. The commuter buzz was at odds with the casual family groups they enticed with easy football banter aimed at the smallest in those groups, encouraging sleeve-pull entreaties just by mentioning the form of the star striker. A wall of commerce, "hello, sweetheart" and every trick in the book to pull the queues to them, something that Tony could use to his advantage.

He weaved in and out of the clusters of people hovering around the stalls, momentarily joining a queue at one burger stall, to enable him to look back along his route, and up the steps, to see who, if anyone, was following him. He wished he hadn't.

Two CityArrow cabs had pulled up at kerbside, close to the top of the steps, with both driver's doors open, and the drivers themselves pulling themselves from their seats, phones clamped to their ears as they scanned the scene below. They hadn't seen him yet, but even amongst the hundred or so people milling about, he ran the very real risk of being found, and soon. There were no doubts at all now, and his disguise, if you could call it that, was well and truly blown. Ducking out of the queue, making sure he was between one of the stalls and those at the top of the steps, he removed his cap, and folded it in on itself tightly enough that it could fit inside his jacket pocket – he might need it again, and it couldn't hurt to give himself the option of change further down the line, however long this episode lasted, anything that might help him however small the advantage.

Any sudden movement would be a giveaway, even amongst the sharp eddies and swells of the home-time commute. He was careful to join the crowds matching their pace, manoeuvring himself so taller people were both obstacles and camouflage, hoping that removing his cap was the vital concession that would allow him to slip away, before others arrived.

There were a few options – he could follow the crowds that were heading towards the Central train station, slightly upbank of the main drag. The alternative was following the main street down heading towards the docks against the main flow of the foot-traffic, negotiating the slower moving late-evening shoppers, and those heading for a drink, quiet or otherwise. On the one hand, the busier route allowed him more opportunity to try and blend into the crowd, but crowds need transport, and he would almost certainly have to pass other CityArrow cars before he could sneak away down one of the lesser side-streets, or even dare risk the train system, closed environment though it was. On the other hand, there were more opportunities to weave through shops, safer amongst the cameras and security of the shopping centres, and, crucially, it might be what they *weren't* expecting. No time to weigh things up any longer- if he wasted any more time considering probabilities and options, he would be lost. Instead, he needed to roll the dice and seeing what numbers stared back at him.

He turned towards the shopping centre, and down the

main street, past the huge glass fascias of anachronistic fashion boutiques, clinging to life one "SALE" sign at a time. The windows were even more of a boon than the grimy pub windows he'd used a few minutes earlier, especially as the night was darkening the sky quickly, allowing the bright lights of the street to make mirrors from almost any angle. It occurred to him that even as the crowds thinned as he pulled away from them, space was as much of an advantage as a disadvantage. Yes, he might be more visible, but then, so would anyone following him. A spider-web of streets and doorways available to him if he did see anyone closing in.

Still attempting to maintain the air of someone oblivious to those circling him, he made do with the protection that those reflected scenes offered him. There was no-one following him closely and overtly, affording him time, and crucial yards, before he made his move to escape the net closing around him.

The street was wide, with clusters of people like islands dotted here and there, with the footfall of customers ebbing and flowing like a waterway incising through a countryside scene; all meanders, pools and rapids, dependant on the obstacles ahead. These small crowds were lollygagging around different points on the broad avenue – one crowd was giggling and nudging each other as a haggard, messy, bearded creature was tunelessly yelping into a plastic microphone, singing along to a backing track with impressive gusto. But, judging from the continuous jingle of new coins dropping into his upturned hat, he was going to have the last laugh. Slightly further down, on the other side, two teenagers were dancing awkwardly, to an insistent beat, rapping verses about Christianity, as accomplices pressed leaflets into the hands of anyone who made the mistake of stopping for more than a moment. Both of these entertainments demanded a wide circle of onlookers. People didn't want to get too close as, in both cases, those passers-by did not want to be seen to associate themselves with them, for fear of crossing the line towards overt approval, or worse, some forced interaction. This meant that in order to continue along the street, Tony had to veer from left to right then left again, turning to slalom through those watching in places where the logjam had gathered. He took advantage of this, as he turned, by looking back along the street to see if he could identify anyone following him.

Further along, at the T-junction he'd joined the drag from, he spotted two men talking with one of the drivers. As always, he was grateful of that de facto uniform that the Stark men insisted on wearing, all black shirts, black jackets and tailored trousers. This trusted inner cadre, in black like shock troops, had clearly never understood the strength of subtlety, and now, when subtlety would be a fatal advantage for them, Tony had the upper hand. He could see them, yet had the benefit of the crowds around him to mask his non-descript appearance.

Tony stared at them, as he inched around one of the circles of onlookers, briefly looking to his destination, before returning his gaze back to them. They were scanning ahead, looking for him, with one of them pointing and waving his hand whilst loudly talking into a phone held in his other. More reinforcements being summoned, no doubt. The noose was tightening. He had to make a move and fast.

Still keeping them clear in his eyeline, he moved sideways, his goal was a huge metal and glass awning that covered a wide entrance way into a covered shopping area. If he could make it into there, and through the labyrinth of cut-throughs, escalators and shopping displays, he knew he could evaporate into the early evening dusk, and make his way back over the water in his own time.

Careless.

"Jesus Christ, get down with his love!"

Tony had crossed into middle of the circle, gathered around the Christian rappers. The crowd were happy to manoeuvre him, clearing away from him at just the right moment, to corral him with the preachers. The voracious cynics in the crowd could see that there was some fresh meat they could toss to these so-called "street entertainers" and maybe, just maybe, it would be worth filming and sharing with their friends. As soon as he had become separated from the security of the crowd that swelled and heaved like some mythic monster, the two rappers had no choice but to acknowledge him. Broadly grinning, they bounced over to him, call and response lyrics to-and-fro between them, with one of them wrapping an arm around Tony's neck, to try and encourage him to sway along with the beat, running long odds that he would be the passer-by who would greet their attempt at conversion with patience and warmth. The response was as far from their vain hopes as possible.

Shocked by the physical contact, Tony span around to see who had grabbed for him, then violently recoiled when he saw these two long-limbed clownish figures gurning merrily at him. Had he been expecting it, and had he not had adrenaline bunching his muscles, he might not have pushed the nearest one away from him, and he certainly wouldn't have done so with as much force as he did.

There was no weight on the boy – he flew back, losing his balance, and crashing backwards limbs flailing, his baggy clothes exaggerating the collapse. The crowd reacted with a gasp, which soon became the cheer of a mob, most of whom were reaching for their phones to grab as much of this scene as possible to share for the thumbs-ups and LOLs. That was it. The starter's pistol. Tony had blown any hope of cover, and giving himself just a fraction of a second to verify that he'd been spotted, knew it was time for him to lose all pretence of a careful exit and run.

The crowd could still be a help to him. They could see he was a source of potential for new drama, far more sustaining than the musical group they had been patronising. As Tony pushed back through the perimeter ring of people around the impromptu stage, they closed behind him, craning to see what he would do next, oblivious to the other players desperate to make their own dramatic entrance, pushing through the close-shouldered group that had closed behind Tony like water closing around a diver entering the pool.

Tony ran through the wide-open doors of the nearby shopping precinct. He'd decided to head for one of the large department stores that anchored the sprawling open-plan shopping centre that clung to the main shopping thoroughfare of the city like a school-shy toddler to a parent's leg on their first day. Chrome and glass blurred past him as he felt he ran at hundred-mile-an-hour speeds, but these were adrenaline tricks, narrowing his vision to just his destination.

He didn't realise how far ahead of the two black-clad men he was. Mere inches or whole miles, it was irrelevant to him. Just the impetus to get away and get to where he could reset, and find his camouflage again. Unconsciously, he weaved through the streets, and around pushed prams and dawdling lovers, lefts and rights, until he spotted the broad doorways of the department store ahead of him. He came at it from an angle – even bursting with panic, chemicals bubbling in his brain, he was aware enough to know that bursting through the doors straight on would only add more eyes to the pursuit, waking up idling security guards from their CCTV caves, as if a goat was trip-trapping across their buffed and polished floors. Instead, he arched his run so he came to those doors side-on, decelerating as innocuously as he could manage without causing an attention-gathering crash of his soles on the pavement.

His forehead was beaded with sweat, sweat that also broke cold on his body, a slow drip running along the small of his back. He knew that this in itself was enough to draw some attention, if someone saw fit to scrutinise him in any way, given the chilling air of late-autumn outside. He concentrated on his breathing, trying to calm it down to a steadier rhythm, as he idled away from the main cleared routes through the store, and into the forest of offers and mannequins that sprang up around the entranceway of the shop floor.

He must've been seen entering the store. There weren't enough people around to obscure his entry, and, at the very least, those on his heels would check in here when they saw no sign of him on the throughfares that led away from the building.

He'd been in here several times. Dragged around by Eleanor who took perverse pleasure in laughing at the preposterous prices on appliances that could surely only perform the same functions as well as equivalents that were cheaper to the power of ten, the swollen price tag simpatico with the clean lines and faux 50s chrome bodywork that every item had. This huge cathedral to the pointless, ostentatious purchase, with Tony and Eleanor as naughty school-children giggling and nudging each other through the sermon. This helped. He knew the layout, and had a good idea of the best exits, and with good luck and abundant care, he might be able to navigate his way through the consumer maze, around mannequin crowds, and up a few levels to the walkway that led to the higher levels of the shopping centre outside. From there, he had more options, and a far better chance of melting away before more cars unloaded their black-clad passengers, all with fierce intent on their minds, and the prize of kudos from Jim Stark, the king of these streets.

Tony weaved around the walkways, moving across the sales floor in a chess knight pattern, aiming to get to the back stairs quietly and steadily. Once he'd made it three-quarters of the way to his destination, he chanced a look back, peeking through the gap between a summer scene, plastic dummies pointing at an imaginary sun, in shorts and pastel shirts.

Two men had entered the store, and were stood in the open space in the lobby area, scanning for any sign of him. One nudged the other and indicating left, the other man went right beginning a sweep of the floor. The sales floor was sprawling, and littered with displays and stands, enabling Tony to feel, at least, as comfortable as he could be, given the situation, that he had the measure of his pursuers, with maybe ten more metres to go to the stairwell. That feeling was a cold comfort, though. There was no time for any kind of reflection of the precarious nature of his situation. The adrenaline flooding his body, his eyes wide and focused, as he picked his route around the store, each step a reassessment of his route, and a judgment on the obstacles ahead of him.

He reached the bottom of the stairwell. It was quieter here. The majority of the shoppers used the escalators that dominated the centre of the shopfloor, which Tony hoped would draw the attention of the men he had seen enter the shop. Given there were just two of them, and they would have to play the percentages as well. He chanced another look behind him, and could just make out one of the men, looking across to where the other man, out of Tony's eyeshot, must be. The man had communicated with a wave of the hand toward the escalators, which meant that Tony's decision to use the stairs had been a wise one – now he could continue up those stairs, bypassing the first floor completely, buying some more time, and exiting via the second floor. He waited until the man had moved out of sight behind a display, and headed up the stairs.

Tony heard voices. Hard voices. Coming down from the stairwell, echoing against the tiled floor from above. One was a voice he'd heard too often and hoped to never hear again: The Red Pope. Of course, it had to be him. Tony almost laughed. Laughed at the idea that his escape was assured, and laughed at the notion that he'd ever encounter this man on anything like his own terms. He was a thunderhead, rolling across whatever landscape Tony found himself in – an inevitability that could only be weathered, rather than avoided. The crumb of comfort was, like a thunderhead, the Red Pope never felt the need to be subtle. Instead, his way was the way of noise and chaos and destruction; the louder the better. It had served him well, it seemed, and he had no reason to temper that *sturm und drang* with any lighter phrasing.

"...I'm at the stairs. Just mind the escalators. He has to get past one or other of us. If he's upstairs already, then he won't get past the exits."

God bless his indiscriminate mouth. It was a bad situation, and getting worse, but even in the depths of it, knowledge can never be underestimated – it could be the key to a lock that Tony hadn't found yet.

The Red Pope was coming down the stairs, judging by the squeak on the stairs above him. Tony couldn't pass him on the stairs – he couldn't risk any sort of physical confrontation for several reasons – he was outmatched and outsized, and even with surprise, which was unlikely, he would have seconds to best his opponent before he was swamped with others, drawn to the noise. Could he cause some sort of distraction? Possibly. Were there any other exits? He feared his chance at taking them was closing faster than he could match. Exits closed above him and behind him. Even the comfort of this public space was a falsehood – these were men who burnt pubs down and fired shots at strangers. Not only would they be unafraid to leave Tony bloodied, or worse, here in this department store, but this was their town, and knowing how towns like this worked, Tony was fairly certain that the security guards here would not only know of Stark and that terrible reputation he'd built, but may very well be in his employ, to a lesser or larger degree. He couldn't count on any favours from them. He was a rat in a maze, and the exits had been shut.

He returned to the ground floor trying to reorient himself against the other pieces on the board. He couldn't see them. Any of them. But he had the Red Pope and his orders, so could be certain that the escalators and stairs up were covered, and exiting by the doors he had entered by would most certainly lead to a painful conclusion. What options did he have left? Could he hide somewhere, and let that storm blow over before making his way out? As an option, this was merely a delay to the inevitable – like waiting whilst a door slowly shut in front of him, as the Red Pope being here meant that the whole Stark crew would have been alerted, and no doubt, lethal men would soon be closing off every possible route out of the store, and the city centre. It was escape or nothing. Chips all-in and the longest of odds.

Just by the entrance to the stairs, were two doorways – one led to some toilets, and the other to changing rooms. He had to chance one or other of those.

He walked through the doorway to the toilets – an open arch, with two pedestal barriers designed to bleep if someone tried to sneak goods into the stalls to stash them about their person, before attempting a brazen exit. A wet floor sign was in the middle of the corridor, as well as a cart, laden with cleaning items and replacement bin bags. This was the first turn of luck in his favour since the chase was on. He'd worked in places like this before, as security, covering for friends who had ducked away to make a better buck doing less reputable work. The modern stores were laid out with an eye for presentation – whilst cleaning toilets was unavoidable during the day, despite how distasteful it might be for the corporate branding and the customer experience, it would've been worse if the toilets were left until after doors closed each evening. Tony knew full well how these rooms could get, especially on a busy day. The task of cleaning the toilets, with a grubby cart wheeled by a minimum wage employee, was one that should be out of sight and out of mind as much as possible – one that should not dirty up the clean lines and regimented displays of the shop floor. Because of this, there would be a doorway to the back of house in the same corridor of the toilets, to prevent the cart needing to cross the floor during opening hours. If Tony could make his way into the warren of corridors running behind the walls the public could see, then he had a chance to make it out, perhaps by a service bay or fire exit.

He found it: 'Employees only'.

It came to him, quickly. The door had an analogue push-button door code – five silver studs, marked one to five, sequentially, in a downward pattern by the door handle. These had to be pushed in the correct order to allow the lock to release, and the door to open. Human nature was his best hope – in the same way that the most popular pass-words to an email account were the words "password" or "default", he had to hope that whoever had installed this door, used by the most junior of staff, that they would be prone to that same mindset of "tomorrow" and can-kicking. The door lock had a default sequence – two and four together, then three on its own.

Doing his best to radiate confidence and belonging, he keyed the sequence. The press-buttons clicked, and he turned the handle. Nothing. Trapped.

Looking over his shoulder, and back towards the shop floor. One of Tony's pursuers had a phone pressed tight to his ear, clearly talking to someone who was directing traffic and organising the shutdown of exit routes. At the precise moment Tony saw the man, the man's eyes locked onto Tony. A wave of recognition lit in the man's eyes, straight-ening his searching meander into a firm, direct walk across the shop floor towards Tony. The man was fifty paces away, but surely his accomplices were nearer. The Red Pope defi-nitely was.

Given how embarrassed the Red Pope had been, those hundreds of miles away, to have let his prey slip through his fingers, and the recriminations that followed, he'd vapourised any temptation to maintain social niceties the moment he heard Grace had been spotted, in this rabbit warren of polished tile and sale banners. He pushed past people, pushchairs and products, to ensure he could claim his trophy. He was all haste. All anger, grinding teeth, ready to envelop Tony fucking Grace in threats and pain and out to a waiting car, where he would have time in abundance and sharp knives for company.

Tony was desperate. Panic fizzed his brain with new energy, an adrenaline jolt like grasping live wires forced him back to the door and the keypad.

Idiot. This was a newer kind of keypad. The *other* kind. A different default. He still had time. Fingers clicked the push-buttons again, slowly pushing them in in order, making sure that each push fully registered to the mechanism. There was a buzz of voices behind him, as two women exited the toilets, eager to get back to the sport and the spoils on the sales floor, if only as backdrop for their conversations. He turned the lock and pulled.

Nothing. He had put the default code in correctly. He knew he had. He pulled the door again, harder, rattling the door against the frame, but it wouldn't open, even though it had to. It *had* to.

"Fuck," he hissed loud enough to draw a tut from the women behind him, already inconvenienced by having to walk around Tony to make their way back along the corridor. . They passed him, side-eyeing him and then, conspiratorially nudged each other, waiting until they were a safe distance from this odd man, pulling hopelessly at a locked door, before restarting their gossip.

The Red Pope turned into the archway at the exact moment the two women exited and bowled them over with a crash. He lost his footing in a tangle of legs and bags. His feet slid over the polished tiling and a triangular yellow "wet floor" sign clattered off behind him as his legs kicked out.

At that same moment, the service door had opened, surprising Tony, his attention having shifted to the melee. A small, cheery face appeared from around the door – Tony's salvation was five foot six, grinning, and bearded.

"They've changed the code, haven't they? And never told anyone. As usual,"the man said.

Tony didn't wait. He shot through the door past the man stood in the doorway and broke into a sprint putting the bright lights of the store behind him as he fled into the breezeblock austerity of the service corridors. He stopped, a final indulgence, perhaps. He was doubling down on his winning hand, and hard. All his life he had been blessed - or maybe cursed - with a face that could transmit sincerity and certainty. That "work-face" countenance that made him hard to get to know, until the brave or the persistent dug a little deeper to the good man underneath. He had long since learned how to use it to his advantage, delivering stoic instruction with a look of rock-solid confidence, that asked the recipient to take a great stride forward to even think about challenging it. And at the same time, this also sang to that truest of human behaviours – if someone looked like they had an unassailable right to be somewhere, then would anyone dare to challenge that? Would they risk making an enemy of this person, when plausible deniability was still the best defence? Tony relied on human nature, looking back at the cleaner holding the door open with one hand, and securing his wheeled trolley of detergent and spare toilet rolls with the other, who must've been baffled that Tony - a solid, serious man - had burst past him, and then, turned back towards him, an unblinking stare demanding full attention.

"Shut the door. And keep it closed." A brief pause, as the man weighed up this instruction, and the man giving it. The man let the handle slip from his grasp and the door clicked back into the place, the lock reset with a quiet whirr.

The man looked up at Tony, his mouth pursing to form a quizzical "but" but Tony knew to sideline any objection before it could be fully formed. If that door opened again, he was dead. He had his hands around a golden thread in the maze on Crete, and he could not afford to let it slip, especially with his Minotaur, snorting and fierce, trapped on the other side of the door.

"Shoplifters. We've got them cornered, but they're trying to get into the back. I'm going to get Colin from this side" Tony threw a plausible name down, like a grenade – "but do not open that door."

The cleaner nodded. Tony knew how the hierarchy of places like this worked. The man may well resent his lot, but not enough to leave, glad enough of the comfort of his position. He wouldn't want to risk rocking the boat, and certainly not by being difficult in a situation like this. To reinforce what Tony had told him, a perfectly timed thump crashed against the door, as whoever the ne'er-do-wells were on the other side of this door, they were now trying to get through it, exactly as he had been told they would. The cleaner looked along the corridor, in the dim light of cost-cutting and minimum safety standards, at Tony's back, who was about to turn out of view around the corner, towards the junctions that would lead him to the service yards or the fire exits, and couldn't resist throwing an assurance at him – perhaps there was a chance of a back-slap and an anecdote in the canteen for the next few days in this for him.

"Don't worry. This door stays shut!"

36

T ony finally relaxed when he had put a mile under his shoes away from the city centre. He looked unremarkable enough, and was wise enough not to look like he was in a hurry, or wary of bright lights or clusters of people. He made sure not to look over his shoulder, and, instead, dug his hands into his pockets, and kept a steady pace. A drizzle had wandered in along the Mersey, demanding that everyone he passed shared the same gait as him – hunched over, collar pulled tight around necks, walking with the purpose of finding a set destination. He allowed himself a smile knowing that he was as safe on these streets as he could've dreamed of being, given how near to disaster he had been twenty short minutes ago.

The drama in the department store corridor was the perfect distraction he needed to make his getaway. Basic though they were, the back-of-house corridors were signposted and practical, and led to a communal service yard that hosted a procession of delivery vans, from the small to the gargantuan, with a pervasive smell of oil, cardboard and pastries.

News travelled fast about the group of men who had attacked those two poor women in the toilets, scrabbling around the floor with them, before one of them had gone mad, trying to smash a door off its hinges in his haste to escape. Staff had cornered them like mad bulls at Pamplona, trying to keep them corralled, but not getting too close to risk their own safety, clinging to the hope that more support would be on the scene shortly, and would know what to do.

Before long, this big man with the scar, was shaken from his rage by one of his accomplices, a sobering act that had him realise his own predicament. Five, maybe six of these men, not mere youths as the wildfire whispers had suggested, had all converged on that toilet corridor, pushing through the cordon of gawkers and staff, around the big totem of a man. When it was clear they weren't going to find the thing they'd been hunting, they all left as one pushing back through the growing crowd and exited the front door, daring anyone to stop them, before dispersing into the night like ghosts.

Tony didn't know any of this beyond the fact that he'd made it away. However, he knew enough about the Red Pope to know that his lack of subtlety would play to Tony's advantage. He knew this would give him extra precious minutes to navigate away from that kill zone. Eleanor was safe, he was pretty sure of that, and he was still free, and so, despite the shopping centre chaos, nothing had changed. The plan could still work. If anything, it made his foes more predictable – time and again they had shown themselves creatures of the brainstem: all instinct and reaction. Yet another narrow escape would simply turn the temperature up, and make them even more likely to react in an impulsive way. Predictability could be exploited. And now was the time.

Tony reached into his jacket pocket, and pulled out the phone, snatched from the hand of that incongruous refugee from Liverpool on that night in Norfolk. He powered it up. The phone screen lit his face as the screen started, with various apps and functions blinking into life with pings and tones as the phone restored connections, sounding almost irritated to have been starved of data interactions by the luddite brute holding it. There was a pause, then a deluge of alerts.

The phone had connected to the network, and all of the apps were updating; messages of all varieties filled the screen – a tessellation of notifications, obscuring each other before they were given fair chance to be read. Tony got the gist of them as he skimmed the growing pile. The choir of voices communicating those messages thinned until just one loud voice remained, text message threats layering on top of one another, each more gruesome and definitive than the last. He could read them later – Eleanor had reminded him, and shown him clearly enough how to disable the data stream to camouflage it from those searching for it, but that would have to wait. He knew he was exposed, as his location would surely be triangulated and shared almost as soon as the phone was on, but this would only take a moment, before he could detach himself from the network, and disappear again. Just one message.

The last text read – "WE KNOW YOU ARE HERE NOW. WE SAW YOU. WE NEARLY HAD YOU. WE'LL FIND YOU AGAIN, AND WE'LL KILL YOU IN FRONT OF HER"

Laughable, really. He could've guessed every word of that. No matter. This was not about what they had to say, but what he had to say to them. He highlighted the message, and clicked the "reply" icon, and typed.

"WE NEED TO TALK. SOON."

37

Cold Cut had been too scared to be bored. He should have been bored. He tried not to dwell on his situation, but occasionally, the lack of anything approaching stimulation, and the unchanging fact that the door to the outside that he stared at was to stay closed for fear of some unknown but inevitably painful consequence if he tried to walk through it. It made his eyes sting until he gulped back whatever feeling of helplessness and hopelessness were trying to manifest. He couldn't show weakness. Weakness was the worst sin, because weakness could be exploited. Once that balloon had been sent up and the men he had fallen in with had seen weakness, his chances of ever walking free, or smoke a roll-up under a high street awning, or bite down on a greasy kebab, or any other of the mundane treasures he yearned for, would fast approach zero. He had to be a soldier. A soldier for Stark, and his desire – his need – to impress was paramount. Careful what you wish for. He'd always wanted to be recognised, maybe even lauded by these sorts of men. It was an ambition he was hungry for, but now, in this little room, frosted and wired windows only hinting at the passing of time, he desperately wished the monkey's paw would unclench and take back the wish.

Cold Cut was in one of Stark's CityArrow taxi offices, in one of the satellite districts that clustered around the city centre, entwined like a rat king with the neighbouring streets. The offices were sandwiched between a betting shop and a takeaway, the two constants in every single shopping precinct and high street in every single post-industrial northern town, like cockroaches after the apocalypse, parasites left to extort the last few coppers from the hardscrabble residents of these streets, providing promises of little dopamine rushes to distract from the water torture rent increases and tax demands. The door to the street outside was always open, dirty light pushing through wiremesh glass which sat in chipped paint window frames, and the garish, simplistic font screaming CITYARROW with the same ubiquitous phone number it had used for years.

The reception area of the taxi office was small, with a long bench underneath the window and a shelf loaded with pawed-over tabloids. There was a small teller-window where a rogues gallery of faces took turns in delivering monosyllabic service to whoever has the patience to wait for a response. The bottom corner of the window cheerfully displayed a "how was your experience?" sticker, the five-digit text number scored off the sticker by bored receptionists.

Behind whoever was manning the service window was a collage of muted colour chaos. The back wall displayed a chipboard noticeboard, with a years-old faded calendar buried under a snowfall of different coloured notes, addresses and numbers scribbled on them in all manner of spidery shorthand, with any bare space filled with cock and balls, or football club initials. This place had looked like this for years, and probably always would. Stark was perfectly happy that the continuity was the best camouflage for any inquisitive types who may have heard stories and took the foolish decision to poke their nose into his business.

Beneath the slovenly, haphazard first impression, the essential facets of the Stark business operated with brutal and watertight efficiency. False walls, packed envelopes, coded ledgers, all managed by a trusted crew, who had worked hard to earn Stark's trust, and now it was given, abundantly aware that it was a lifetime commitment – the length of that lifetime wholly dependent on them keeping their mouths shut, and their eyes open. Because of this, each office rarely saw change in personnel, the only changes being Dorian Grey in reverse, as the faces drooped, puffed and lined over long years, overseen by the faded, smiling, young faces on the photographs of the "Here To Help" display, to the left of the customer window.

And opposite that window, at the back of the office, was a solid door, then a heavy filing cabinet, and next to that, another wire mesh window, this one frosted and impenetrable. Behind that door, sat on a tattered faux-leather office chair, was Cold Cut, next to a beige sofa, that he'd been using as a bed – when he was permitted to close his eyes and get some rest over the best part of a week he'd been there. He wasn't under suspicion, and he wasn't aware that he was being otherwise scrutinised; instead, Cold Cut had decided he was seen as some kind of asset – not only did he have a different network of eyes and ears than the CityArrow drivers, but he had the passwords that enabled him to monitor for a tell-tale ping that would alert them to Tony Grace's whereabouts once he switched on Cold Cut's phone. Sure, someone else could have handled the monitoring, but why waste a perfectly useful body on that, when Cold Cut was available, obedient, and acutely aware of the Sword of Damocles that hung above him.

Cold Cut would get a polystyrene carton of chips and indeterminate meat slapped down on the floor in front of him a couple of times a day, from the takeaway next door. Their own offended noses insisted that the staff there also allowed Cold Cut to wash up in the damp and mould-ridden toilet that led off from a different door in the back office.

Of course, Cold Cut was told, he wasn't kept there, he could leave when he wanted. There was no need to worry. But make no mistake – Cold Cut knew he was in a cell, and he knew that the key to that door, if there even *was* a key, was if he could present Mr Stark, or whoever reported to him, information that led to Tony Grace being bundled into the back of a car, and driven somewhere dark, lonely and final. If he didn't, then that fate was his.

Cold Cut even started pining for his mother – his thoughts drifted behind those small four walls, a combina-tion of "if I get out of here" and "if only I'd done", making deals with God, Allah, Jahweh or whoever else might be listening; deals of how he would be a better man if only he could get away from this hole he had fallen into. He thought of his mother, trapped in her own prison – a body that wouldn't listen, and a mind that had long since fallen into fog – and made sincere promises that he would go and see her, and make things right, and show her the love that a good son should have for his mother.

He had a phone, presented to him, boxfresh, by one of the blackshirts who strode into the back room a few hours after he had been deposited there. The first hour was spent fiddling with SIM cards and passwords, as he hurried to get the phone working, and all of his many apps and accounts live again, so he could not only monitor for Grace, but also send out digital tentacles to his address book of reprobates, the Stark name a powerful motivator that would ensure that everyone he contacted would suddenly find good cause to walk around the city with head up and eyes open. He fantasised about triumph, and of being able to bang on the door to demand that whoever opened it stop what they were doing and immediately call Stark, as "he'd want to hear this now".

Refresh all info, and be thorough. Be methodical. Work through his contact list, and check off every part of the city, a Big Brother network in cheap trainers, covering as much ground as possible. Once he set those hares racing, he would go back to the Find My Phone app, and feel his heart sink at the lack of update. The phone had not been switched on in days.

The taxi office staff changed over every eight hours or so. Occasionally, there was a low rumble of hubbub as *other* business was managed, and despite the intention of playing it cool, those handling Stark's real business couldn't resist speaking in whispers until whatever was delivered was locked away, or handed over to a different courier on collection. The light outside changed as the day progressed and if he concentrated, Cold Cut could make out the change of radio station as the shifts changed, with the new cab controller flipping to their channel of choice. Still no change from his phone – his window to the world. False alarms were quickly discounted, and street corner rumours debunked. With each passing hour, a desperation descended on Cold Cut, hope fading that he'd ever leave this room. He was finding it hard to shake the thought that the only way he was leaving was as a failure, and he knew the consequences for that were ultimate.

PING

A notification message: "Your phone has been found"

He stared at his phone. He was tired, hungry, scared and panicked. Was he conjuring this up? Had his mind given up on him as it had given up on his mother?

"Your phone has been found"

"Your phone has been found"

It was real.

He banged on the door, it taking only a couple of fierce knocks before an angry face appeared in the crack of the door.

"What the fuck are you doing making a din?"

"You need to get Mr Stark. Like, now. He'll want to hear this. Now."

"You're going to see him. Directly," the Red Pope said.

Cold Cut had seen the knife-edge he was expected to dance upon. He always suspected that getting out from the situation he had found himself in would require the right words at the right time, like disarming a bomb. But everything was out of control, and he found himself wishing he could go back to the background static hiss of the fear he felt trapped in that little room.

Fifteen minutes after he had banged on that door, the Red Pope himself appeared, *careful-what-you-wish-for* manifested, any friendly façade jettisoned, and replaced with the volcanic frustration that Cold Cut had been near to too often in the past few days. Cold Cut wasn't stupid enough to ask what had caused Pope's mood, but gathered from the few terse words he'd overheard that Grace had wriggled free of them yet again.

Cold Cut was beckoned, a firm hand had rested on his neck as he was steered out of the cab office, onto the street, and then into the back of a waiting car. He hadn't expected to meet Jim Stark in person. If he ever did, unlikely though that was, he hoped – dreamed – Stark would garland him with praise for a job well done. This was something else.

Cold Cut could barely concentrate as the car wound its way away from the hubbub of high street into suburbia, with even Cold Cut losing full grasp of his surroundings, given he rarely, if ever, had any excuse to come to these parts of town. Landmarks passed irregularly, enough he had a rough idea of his whereabouts, but not enough to be able to place exactly where he was going, or where he'd been. Finally, the car turned into a pleasant enough cul-de-sac, ten-year-old houses, still new enough to feel modern. They had colourful brick walls, and novel driveways patterning a uniform on the street. Every house had more than one car, and every house, despite the best intentions of the occupants, resembled the next, impossible to shake off their off-the-shelf design from when they were built – the estate expanding quickly, like a diner loosening their top button after a heavy meal.

They pulled up outside a house with the downstairs windows all illuminated. It was tea-time, and inside was active – one last chore before everyone could kick up their feet on the sofa and flick channels for a few hours. The Red Pope got out of the front passenger seat, the driver remained in the car. The back-passenger door was opened, and Cold Cut tentatively got out. Who lived here? Wouldn't the feared and mighty Stark live somewhere grander? More imposing? A Transylvanian castle or undersea submarine base? What was going on?

The Red Pope returned his hand to the back of Cold Cut's neck, and gripped firmly. Firm enough to transmit the potential for pain, but not firm enough that it couldn't be waved away as friendliness. Cold Cut was steered to the front door. The Red Pope knocked on the door with his free hand. The frosted glass darkened as a figure came to the hallway, and the door opened, and a jolly, portly face filled the gap.

"Gentlemen! Good of you to come! You got here quickly! Excellent. Excellent," Stark said. The only man on the planet the Red Pope would knock politely for. The Red Pope underlined his manners by bowing his head and wiping his feet as he stepped inside. Stark ushered him through, clapping him on the back as he passed.

"And you. I've heard about you. Graham, isn't it?" The smile was warm, but the eyes were lasers. Cold Cut tried to hold the stare for as long as he could, but it wasn't long before he had to drop his gaze, and stare at his feet, defeated. He felt judged. Assessed. And Stark knew his name. *No-one* knew his name. Or so he'd thought.

"Yes, Sir. It's...nice to meet you, Sir."

"Sir! Sir! I'm not your school teacher, my man. Jim will do, in these four walls."

Agog, Cold Cut saw the Red Pope slide off his slip-on shoes, nudging the gleaming leather to the end of a line of trainers, adult and smaller. He looked back at Cold Cut, making it plain that he was expected to do the same. Even with the terrifying and discombobulating scenario he now found himself in, and after the events of the past few days, he couldn't help but redden with embarrassment, taking off his worn and scuffed old trainers, to reveal white socks that had long since turned grey and threadbare.

"Good men, good men." Stark had opened the internal door, from the porch into the house itself, indicating that the men were to follow him through. The kitchen door was open, the pots and pans of the night's meal piled up next to the sink ready to be washed alongside a stack of plates bobbing in water, like a row of shark fins. The other door to the front room was also open, and Cold Cut could see a large L-shape white couch, dominating the corner, opposite a large TV fixed to the wall, blaring the applause and synthesised fanfares of a quiz show. A middle-aged woman, dressed in a tracksuit, was sat, feet curled underneath her, on the angle of the L, flanked on either side by a child – a girl of maybe seven to one side, concentrating on a bowl of ice-cream cradled in front of her, and a boy of maybe nine on the other, staring at a handheld game that illuminated his face. Stark ushered them along, and past, the woman noticing the guests, and waving a hand happily.

"Just the men, my love! We'll be in the conservatory!"

"Cups of tea, Jim?"

"No need. You just put your feet up and mind the monsters!" The girl giggled playfully, though the boy showed no indication that he'd even heard what was said, enraptured by the screen in front of him.

Cold Cut managed a wan smile at the woman, as he passed the doorway, and trooped after the Red Pope who knew where to go, both carefully deferential. Cold Cut had heard that those who had actually met the real, honest Jim Stark were few and far between, irrespective of the ubiquity of his name. Certainly, those who had were scrupulous about keeping that fact to themselves. Stark liked to have a name that commanded respect and fear in equal measure – it was good for business. But Cold Cut had never heard of anyone actually being invited to Stark's house. In his mind, hardwired for survival, he knew what it meant. It meant that Stark was God. Look upon my face and despair! It meant that Cold Cut was a moth pinned to a slide, to be scrutinised by an unforgiving and unyielding lens. You have come to my attention, and you must not fail me, for the price of that failure is everything you are. So, this was it. No half-measures. Success or death.

They silently walked into the conservatory, Stark looking over his shoulder to make sure that everyone else was as he had left them, before pulling the double-glazed door closed behind him. He indicated for them to sit in the wicker chair arrangement that looked out over Stark's average-sized garden, the back fences just about visible, illuminated by the lights from inside the house.

Cold Cut said nothing, wisely. The Red Pope sat down next to him, reached inside his jacket pocket, and pulled out his phone, swiping and pressing until he found the screen he was looking for, before turning it around and sliding it across the glass and wicker table so Stark could read it. The Red Pope then snapped his fingers, glaring at Cold Cut, and beckoning him to do the same with his phone.

"Show him what you showed me." He remained terse.

Cold Cut fumbled for his phone and tapped through to a screen that displayed a flashing icon, on a map layout of the city, indicating a marker by the river, near the docks. He mirrored the Red Pope and slid it across to Stark as well, the two phones next to each other on the glass.

"Mr Stark," The Red Pope said. This was business now, and business demanded the correct respect, with all pretence and play-acting left to one side.

"That's the message Grace sent me. He sent it from the phone this idiot gave him. We gave the idiot a new phone, and from that, we were able to track Grace."

Stark leaned forward, peering down his nose at the two phones, like a dimestore detective looking for a clue.

"I see. And what can we conclude from that?"

Silence. Possibly a rhetorical question, and neither the

Red Pope and especially Cold Cut were going to chance their arm on the off-chance it was.

Stark looked at each of them in turn, then answered his own question.

"So, is he stupid enough not to disable the location program on his phone? Possibly, but likely not. Is he stupid enough to think we wouldn't be monitoring the phone? Again, maybe, maybe not. He's certainly stupid enough to come back to the city, judging by today's little escapade. So maybe he *is* stupid enough?"

Stark pushed both phones back across the table, and reclined back in his chair, turning to look out into the night, one finger tapping on the arm of the chair as he sat. Again, silence. If his audience of two had any doubts about staying quiet before, they certainly hadn't now. Stark steepled his fingers and spoke again.

"What I do know is that we may very well have an advantage that we can use. Several, in fact. Firstly, he was spotted near the train station, alone. So, where was the wife? Why would he risk going to the station unless he was with her? So we can presume that she was on a train. That's fine. We've got more than enough eyes on the station, and we can pick her up if she tries to crawl back into Liverpool that way. Second, he's trying to arrange a meeting. If we assume he'll want to be close enough to the city to get in and out quickly, but not stupid enough to get a room in the city centre, then we can start to look at some of the places on the main routes in and out of the city – looking at this location map, he's near the tunnels, so it's likely that he's actually over the water in Birkenhead. Long shot, but you never know. We found him today, after all, and it's not like we don't have the numbers. Thirdly, he wants a meeting. If he *is* stupid, he'll give away his position again. If he's more careful, then we just need to be able to move fast when he does make his play."

The Red Pope nodded along dutifully, a leashed dog in his master's company.

Stark issued his orders - "I want constant surveillance on every train station in the city for the wife. Make sure everyone we know has a copy of their pictures and double the reward, particularly those who are over the water. And lastly, I want all of the full-timers to stay together in one of the pubs in town – no excuses –I want them to move quickly when Grace gives his position away again."

Stark looked at each of them, wide-eyed, then clapped his hands together.

"Now!"

The Red Pope and Cold Cut found their feet with a start, and hurried out, opening the glass door and marching back to their shoes. Stark hovered behind them, like a wraith in bad jewellery, watching them struggle and hop with their shoes, before opening the front door, a further indication of his lack of patience. Cold Cut scurried out first, in a monkey-lope, with the Red Pope following behind him. As he passed Stark, Stark grabbed for the Red Pope's elbow, pulling him close. Cold Cut was a few yards ahead, but could still hear what was said.

"And for god's sake, get him washed."

39

G race did nothing that night. He'd bus-hopped back through the tunnels to Birkenhead, getting off as soon as he could, at the most non-descript stop on the fringes of the town, so he could take a long and circuitous route back to his room. It was real now. He had survived the latest brush with Stark, and he just about felt he still had some control of the situation; as much as he could say he had any control at all.

When he had made it back inside his room, he took out his pay-as-you-go phone. His direct line to Eleanor. Even here, he didn't think it wise speaking about any of this out loud in case walls really did have ears, so started tapping out a text.

Tony – "NARROW ESCAPE AFTER STATION. THEY WERE WATCHING FOR US. DON'T COME BACK ON THE TRAIN."

The seconds passed like glacial shift, him staring at the screen willing it to flash into life, just so he knew she was safe. Finally, after a handful of heartbeats loud enough to spin his head, a reassuring beep.

Eleanor – "ARE YOU OK?"

Tony – "FINE. TOLD ME WHAT WE ALREADY KNEW. THEY ARE LOOKING FOR US. HARD."

Tony – "SO I GAVE THEM SOMETHING TO THINK ABOUT. SENT THEM TEXT FROM OTHER PHONE."

Eleanor – "ANYTHING BACK?"

Tony – "NOTHING AT ALL. IT'S BEEN READ THOUGH."

Eleanor – "SO THEY'RE THINKING?"

Tony – "RECKON. PROBABLY RINGING THE BELL. GETTING THE WORD AROUND."

Eleanor – "THAT'S FINE. KEEP THEM ANGRY. THAT'LL WORK. "

Eleanor – "WILL YOU BE OK UNTIL TOMORROW NIGHT?"

Tony – "YEAH. NO NEED TO LEAVE THE ROOM UNTIL TOMORROW. I'VE GOT SANDWICHES AND TEA."

Eleanor – "I CAN MAKE MY WAY INTO THE CITY ANOTHER WAY. NO NEED FOR TRAIN. STICK TO THE PLAN?"

Tony – "STICK TO THE PLAN. IF WE'RE RIGHT, THEY'LL COME RUNNING."

Eleanor – "ONE MORE DAY THEN. BE SAFE. LOVE YOU."

Tony – "BE SAFE. LOVE YOU TOO."

He put the phone down on the bedside table, and reclined back on the bed, shoes and jacket still on, for now. He stared up at the ceiling, letting his mind drift as he pondered the cracks and old damp patches, as they presented a Rorshach vista for his eyes to wander around. He had a plan, and, as far as he could be, he was content. At least he had direction, and come what may, he took solace from that at least, rather than thrashing around trying to make order appear out of chaos. Until tomorrow, when it was challenged and tested, the plan was a comfort and he found a peace in it, until his eyelids leadened, and he fell asleep.

40

C old Cut had, at least, made it out of that little back room. He was now in one of the many pubs that had served bad pints to the angry, the lonely, and the wistful for decades. It had been "closed for a function", an all-caps sheet of A4 taped to the window, and the draw-bolts pulled firmly across all of the doors. He found a quiet corner, tucked away in one of the booths as far from anyone else as he could manage, but close enough that he could respond to the all-too-frequent enquiries for updates as he scrutinised his phone, both willing it to life, and wishing it quiet, at the same time.

The great and the not-so-good of the Stark empire were milling around, helping themselves to snacks from behind the bar, and punctuating their frustrations with outbursts of cursing or impotent displays of violence towards the bar furniture. These were Stark's attack dogs – the blackshirts, a hardcore of hard men, six in total, including the Red Pope. These men were used to the hard and final *doing* of things, and having them all cooped up in here, all wannabe Alphas and YouTube messiahs, was like shaking up a can of lager, before jamming a pen through the tin. Their one true Alpha was the Red Pope, who wasn't saying anything to anyone, and wisely, everyone else was leaving him be. Cold Cut had seen several tantrum-like outbursts from one blackshirt or other cut down cold by one glare from the Red Pope. There was no doubt in anyone's mind that the psychotic rage bubbling behind those eyes was now pushing the needle into the red and nobody there wanted to be collateral damage when he blew. That pleasure would be reserved for Tony Grace and his stupid wife.

The day dragged. Stark had ordered that nothing be done until the city had been swept north-to-south and east-to-west, with every person with even the smallest debt to Stark be given the clearest expectation of what they needed to do, knocking on doors, calling associates, and walking streets, in the hope that someone, somewhere, had seen Grace in the last 24 hours. But it was a big city, and all they had was conjecture and theory. Their belief in Stark being one step ahead, was being tested in whispered conversations, safely out of earshot of the Red Pope.

Afternoon became evening, and Cold Cut took advantage of yet another argument to sidle around the bar and grab a few bags of pork scratchings, the first food he had had since half a sandwich he'd scavenged this morning. Like a returning late-night reveller lit up by a surprise flick of the light-switch, caught tiptoeing through the house after dark, he froze when he realised that the Red Pope had spotted him, turned to stone by a word.

"You."

The snacks fell from his hands. He turned to face the Red Pope. Better to see his face, he thought, then instantly regretted it.

"Has there been anything?" The question was delivered

as if it was Cold Cut's fault that Grace had gone silent. He was scared to answer, but he had to say something, even if it was clearly not what the Red Pope wanted to hear.

"Nothing all day."

The Red Pope just stared at Cold Cut, unmoving. Unmoving, that is, apart from the whitening of knuckles that gripped the side of the bar counter, gripping so hard it seemed like he was ready to tear the wood from its fixings and hurl it overhead.

The atmosphere was pregnant. Cold Cut needed to say something, but daren't say anything, so instead froze, cycling through progressively more hopeless options in his brain. Suddenly, a beep, back from the table that Cold Cut had colonised. It was all the cue he needed, scurrying across to investigate. He quickly tapped the screen, looking back to the Red Pope when he had opened the notification, shifting screens and accessing pages as rapidly as possible, as the Red Pope moved towards him with the certainty of a tidal wave.

"He's sent a message! Grace! And...and a location! I've got a location!"

The heavy hand fell on the back of Cold Cut's neck again, as it had before. That squeezed threat returned, and had the desired effect – Cold Cut found his focus.

"What does it say?" The Red Pope leaned over Cold Cut, pulling him close, looming over him, a devil in black, come for judgement.

"He says 'Me and Stark to meet tonight. 10pm.' Where, though?"

The hand squeezed. Don't ask questions, Cold Cut.

"He's sent another text. Says 'I'll say where later'."

"And do we have a location?"

He flicked his finger across the screen, selecting Find My

Phone, which brought up a map of the city, with a flashing marker now displayed. The Red Pope reached down, took the phone from Cold Cut, and zoomed in, to be absolutely sure. It was the office building on the dock road, where the Red Pope had first looked into Grace's eyes after that shit-show of a heist, and the same building that they bled out the stupid bastard who let himself get caught for it. So Grace had a taste for the theatrical, then? Very well, thought the Red Pope. *Grand guignol* it is. He looked at his watch, then looked at the room. No-one was talking anymore, and they were all staring at him.

"He wants us to meet him at 10pm. Stupid twat got there early, so we need to get there before he gets settled in. He might be stupid, but I'm not letting him get comfortable. Get your shit together, *now*. We leave in five."

He dialled a number on his phone.

"Mr Stark. We know where he is. We are going now. Can you meet us there? Now, Sir."

Location shared, the Red Pope put the phone back in his pocket, and unlocked the pub door, walking out into the evening gloom. He could be there in fifteen minutes, maybe ten, a good ninety minutes before ten, and a good ninety minutes that Grace wouldn't have to get comfortable. Would Grace know they were tracking his phone? Maybe, maybe not. If they were lucky, he would be able to walk up behind him and choke the life from him without Grace even know-ing. Save the sharper, slower work for his wife. If it was a trap, he was still only one man, against six. Six hard bastards, all of whom had blood on their hands for Mr Stark.

The pub emptied, the door swung shut, and Cold Cut was left on his own in an empty room. He stood still, uncer-tain if he still had a ball and chain around his leg, or a knife at his throat, until his legs started shaking. He tried a tentative step forward, and didn't fall into a fiery pit. Another, then another, all the way to the pub door. Carefully, he inched it open, poking his head round, scared that they had left mustard gas to kill him dead if he stepped outside. Nothing. Nothing except for the Red Pope, half-in half-out of a waiting car, boring holes in Cold Cut with a look that could grind diamond.

"Get the fuck in. And bring the phone."

41

T he Red Pope hadn't been back to the office
building off the dock road since Grace's bitch-wife
had blown the cars up, and they'd escaped. He
had no reason to come back. He lacked the imagination for
remorse or self-reflection, and he certainly wasn't going to
go back without instruction from Stark himself. The place
was scarred by the events of that night. Scaffolding laced
around the building like a steel web, and the quiet of the
road, out of trading hours, was only broken by the flap of
plastic sheeting tied to the metal poles as the wind gusted
off the river. The side of the building in particular had
received close attention – the explosion had threatened the
integrity of the wall, and it now needed securing and
rebuilding. Otherwise the whole place needed levelling out
and starting again, but progress was slow, as if all sides had
lost interest, embarrassed by the monument to failure.

Two car loads of Stark's closest, most trusted men,
pulled up at the forecourt entrance, parking bumper to
bumper to block the open gate, the chainlink fence ensured
there was no other obvious way out from the forecourt. The

Red Pope got out of the car, a cue for the other doors to pop open, and the other blackshirts to get to their feet. Their faces all transmitting the potential for sharp violence. They were coiled springs with bad attitudes. The Red Pope waved hands and the blackshirts split in different directions, forming a perimeter in the forecourt around the building, thirty metres from the walls.

A snarl revealed itself on the Red Pope's face. He'd noticed a light visible on the first floor of the building, illuminating some of the clear windows still intact, and shining a dim blue through the plastic sheeting that covered a large hole in the side of the building, where a new window frame was being built. Grace was here. As he had hoped.

A car turned into the road, its headlights spotlighting the Red Pope where he stood, like Agamemnon or Alexander at the head of his army, ready to go into battle against a mortal foe. It pulled up a few feet from the other cars, and a window wound down.

"He's here?"

"Yes, Mr Stark. We think so. His location came up when he sent the text, and there's a light on in there."

The Red Pope walked back to the car he'd arrived in, and stared at the back passenger seat until the door opened. He snapped his fingers, and opened his palm. On the back seat, Cold Cut, found new reserves of terror. Nervously he handed the phone over unlocked so the Red Pope could access as he saw fit. The screen displayed the location map, the marker remained steadfast in the same position as earlier – inside the building. The Red Pope walked to Stark's car and offered the phone as evidence.

"The phone is definitely in there, that's certain. We have to presume he is, or very close," the Red Pope said, as Stark took the phone from him.

"Let's hope so. I've left a Viennetta on the table back home, and this little shit has ruined enough of my nights already."

"Please stay in the car until we've made it safe, Mr Stark. He will almost certainly have something planned. "

"Yes, my man, you're right. I presume you've told the men about what we found in his flat? All those military trinkets? Let's not rule out him hiding in one of those bushes or over at the garage. He might be trying to be a clever bastard. Tread careful."

"Yes, Mr Stark. What about the wife? Do we need to worry about her?"

"Christ, no. We saw her leave. No – he's on his own. He's got no friends here. The only ones he had are...unavailable. It's just him. And all of us. I think we can take some time over this."

"I think you know me well enough to know that I have a strong stomach, Mr Stark."

"That I do, Son. That I do," Stark said, as he handed the phone back to the Red Pope.

The Red Pope scanned the area, ensuring he made eye contact with as many of the men as he could. Be on your guard, it said. Don't fuck up, it said. Mr Stark is here, it said. Nods were returned, and the ring of men closed around the building as the Red Pope stood and observed, with Stark a few feet behind in his car.

One of the men stopped his steady pace towards the building, holding a hand up. A brief, shrill whistle informed the entire circle that something was up.

There, on the scaffolding, having stepped through the plastic sheeting was Tony Grace, a beer in one hand, and the bright screen of a phone in the other, hands up. Tony took his time observing the scene, draining the bottle of beer, still displaying the phone, before crouching down and setting the bottle on the wooden plank of the scaffold he was standing on. He stood up again, turned until he saw the Red Pope, and pointed at the screen of the phone, before stepping back inside the building, pulling the sheet aside, and over the windowsill.

The Red Pope's mouth was open, shocked at the confidence of the man, surrounded by stone killers, and no escape. But image was everything, and the Red Pope had long since learned how to quash any expression other than implacable. He was in control here. He turned to Stark, still sat in his car, who nodded.

Permission given, and safety in delegated responsibility, the Red Pope took out Cold Cut's phone. This was the phone that he had sent a volley of increasingly graphic and detailed texts to Grace previously. The phone that eventually received that incendiary, and despite everything, somewhat unexpected invitation yesterday, passed to him like treasure by the little rodent cowering in the other car behind him. He pulled up the text on the display, and clicked through to "call". It rang and Grace answered.

"Look, you've come mob-handed, and you can see it's just me. I just want to settle this. Talk this out, and then you'll never see me again. No need for anything messy. We just want to be left alone," Grace said.

"Yeah, sure. We can talk. But we're certainly not stupid enough to walk into a building with you skulking around in it. Army man on manoeuvres shit, or something."

"You've watched too many films, mate. Not a good spot, is it? It's just me, and what? Six? More of you?" Grace seemed confident, and that concerned the Red Pope, unsettled him. Despite the men who surrounded that building, he couldn't shake the feeling that something was not quite right. Not as it should be. But he couldn't show weakness or doubt. Not with Stark here.

"Pays to be careful. We can wait this out. Get some more men over," the Red Pope said.

"True. Bet the boss doesn't like to be kept hanging about though, eh? Tell you what. Send someone in. I'll stand by the window so you can see where I am, and then he can call you back on this phone when he's seen I'm on my own, and unarmed. Seem like a fair solution?"

The Red Pope hung up, and walked back to Stark, to relay the conversation.

"He says to send someone in. To check it's clear. What do you want to do?"

Stark was not a patient man. He was a shark. Always moving, always aggressive, and finding this whole situation unpalatable. He felt exposed, pulled from his suburban camouflage, uncomfortable to be out in the open in a situation that, if he had his way, would be concluded in ways that would see him in a cell for the rest of his life, if ever he was stupid enough, or careless enough, to actually be caught. Cold logic had heated up to boiling, and he'd lost his self-control.

"Get it done," he barked.

The Red Pope didn't dawdle. He marched to the ring of his men, and simply by dint of proximity, selected the man who'd noticed Grace on the scaffold. He beckoned him over.

"Go inside. Check he is unarmed and alone. Call me back on the phone he gives you."

The man looked up at the Red Pope, wide-eyed with "why me?" before making a split-second assessment of his future employment, and existence, prospects, and grasping subservience like a life-jacket, he walked towards the door of the building.

The Red Pope was bad at waiting. He shuffled his weight from foot to foot, gnawing at an imaginary hang-nail on his thumb, staring at the place on the scaffold where he had last seen Grace. His imagination was conjuring up his adversary and binding him to the metal poles with the power of his hate. Minutes passed. He surveyed the scene, checking and double-checking, as best he could, to see if there was anything he could see, or better, shout at, that would make the situation move along faster. Nothing. The minutes passed. The quiet rumble of faraway tyre-on-tarmac, and the heave and sway of the river, was all that could be heard.

The phone rang.

"He's clear. Just him. I've checked all the rooms. He's just up here, with a couple of chairs in the middle of the room. Says he just wants to talk – you and Stark..."

"*Mister* Stark."

"Mr Stark," parroted the underling, chastened.

"Come to the window."

The plastic sheeting moved, and the man's face appeared, waving the phone like a trophy, before putting it back to his ear.

"OK. Meet us at the door. Tell Grace to stay put."

The Red Pope hung up, putting the phone in his inside pocket again, before signalling to Stark that it was safe for him to step out of the car. The door opened, and Stark strode across the forecourt towards the Red Pope, like he owned the place. He owned the place. Stark reached the Red Pope and kept walking, confident and comfortable in the security of the situation. He was in control, and he relished it. The Red Pope took a couple of quick steps to catch up, then matched Stark as they both walked to the front of the building.

As they reached the door, the Red Pope saw the first man

had walked back down to the reception, holding the door open for Stark as he approached. The Red Pope turned back to his men, and by hand signal, ordered them to stay where they were, to prevent any escape from inside. The Red Pope pointed to the perimeter, and the blackshirt nodded then waited until Stark and the Red Pope had passed before hurrying off to replace the Red Pope's position in the perimeter circle as the door closed behind them.

Downstairs was dark. Shapes could be ascertained, but no more than that. Not much had changed, since the last time the Red Pope had been here, and there was no fear that the dark hid any dangers, not now. He was the Red Pope. No man who felt he had to hide behind desks or in dark corners was going to be a danger to him, and he had the reassurance that the building had been checked. And there, like a beacon shining a godly path to salvation, the light from upstairs shone through the glass in the door opposite, showing the stairs to the first floor, and, he knew, now so certain that it made his guts knot, Tony fucking Grace.

The Red Pope took the lead. Stark was angry no doubt, and lethal with it, with Caligulan whims, but his power came from his demands from others, and despite every-thing, and all the people that he scared, and intimidated, the Red Pope knew his place. And his place was the sharp end. He walked up the stairs steadily, and opened the fire door at the top of the stairs, into the wider office room.

The room was, again, set up with furniture pushed to the walls, this time away from the side of the building where the most extensive building work had begun. The last time he was here, the Red Pope felt it was his crucible, or one of those Victorian operating theatres, arranged so an audience, even an audience of one, could do nothing but focus on the matter in hand – that time it was Grace being given one chance to prove himself to them, with a sharp knife and a traitor. This time, though, it didn't feel like that. Walking through that door, ahead of Stark, it felt like a place of reckoning – an uncomfortable atmosphere where he couldn't be completely sure he was in control, despite the weight of numbers and the confidence of past actions.

There were two chairs in the middle of the room, one facing the other. And sat in one of them, facing the door, was Tony Grace.

"I hope you can see I've come here in good faith. It's just me. No tricks. I just want to end this," Grace said.

He held his hand out and invited Stark to sit.

Stark chewed down on his anger and irritation and managed to retain the salesman patter that had been so practised for the decades he had spent hiding in plain sight. He managed a smile, walked across the room, Red Pope following behind him, and sat down. Tony Grace started talking.

"Mr Stark. We just wanted to get away. I'm not a killer. I've never killed anyone and I wasn't going to kill for you, or anyone. I wish you hadn't killed Ringo, but we weren't going to come back at you over it. That would've been stupid."

Stark listened to this, not making a sound, not even blinking. When Grace had stopped, he waited a few seconds, letting time pass like poured molasses, before speaking.

"You don't say no to me, Grace. No-one says no to me. Ever. You had one chance and you chose not to take it. Surely a man of your background must appreciate there would be consequences when you say no about a thing like that."

"We are no threat to you, Mr Stark. We just want a quiet life."

"You should've chosen your friends a little better then, Grace."

Grace looked away. Was it fear? Frustration? Anger? Whatever it was, he reset, and then turned back to Stark, whatever emotion it was that bubbled up in him receded back.

"So what happens now, then? How do we move on from here? I just want me and my wife to live our lives without worrying about you lot turning up. I don't want any more of my friends to die over this."

Stark smiled. A Great White grin. Perhaps he should've felt insulted, that this man seriously thought he could reason with him. The naivety was astonishing, especially for a man forged in the fire of military life. A killer, judging by those medals, despite the words coming from his mouth. Stark furrowed his brow for a moment, kneading a worry into a better shape – perhaps he meant he hadn't killed anyone away from the battlefield? These soldiers and their sentiments. It was all death and glory, wherever it happened.

"What happens is this. I'm going to walk away now, and my associate here, is not going to worry about his fists. He's just going to pull out that gun he's got inside his jacket, and he's going to shoot you in the head."

Stark made to stand up, making it halfway to his full height before Grace held his hand up, as if asking for permission to speak. Stark took his seat again. This was unusual. Was he going to beg?

"You didn't have to do any of this. You never did. Not one bit of it," Grace said, his calmness at odds with the situation.

Stark leaned forwards, subtly but definitely.

"I know. But I do what I fucking want. When I want. This. City. Is. Mine."

Stark flicked a beckoning finger to the Red Pope, who took a couple of steps forward, pulling out the same gun he'd used on the beach, and aiming it at Grace's head.

"Don't move. It's done now, son," the Red Pope said. He'd done this before.

Grace sighed, sounding disappointed rather than terrified. This was not how someone should react when on the wrong end of a gun. The Red Pope felt uneasy. This wasn't right.

"Jesus. For once. I'm not your fucking son," Grace said.

"Ha!" The Red Pope's laugh was humourless. Sarcasm and no warmth. "True. You've got a point." Arms wide open, and a mock bow. "Please forgive me."

"I don't fucking care, you know. Don't bore me with some pithy little speech, either one of you. You asked me to make a choice, and I did. I don't regret it, but you will," Grace said, in a steady voice, sounding more irritated than anything else.

"Good man! This is new. They usually start crying. Or talking to Jesus. Good Catholic lot round here, you know," The Red Pope said as he scratched an itch at the side of his head with the barrel of the gun.

"Fascinating," Tony said.

"But, don't you want to know how I got my name? I like to tell people...in your position."

"Dear god. Just fucking kill me already."

The Red Pope continued, undaunted. "See, the Red Pope. Red is easy, isn't it? Koppite, aren't I? But it sounds kinda cool, I think. And Pope? It's because" – he bent down, towards Tony – "one way or the other, you're either going to kiss the ring, or go to Jesus, and that's..."

"Oh, for fuck's sake. Don't you hear yourself? Don't you know?" Grace said. The Red Pope had stopped talking, and stared at Tony, a mix of incredulity and anger playing on his face. Stark too had lost the smug command of this room. He'd stared down thieves and killers, dealers and scum. None of them had ever behaved like this, with a gun at their head.

"You stupid fucking child. With your silly little name, and your pathetic...uniform, and your scar – I bet you even carved that in yourself, didn't you? Are you a bit unhinged? A bit of a loose cannon? Do you give little speeches before you get your knife wet? Do you dole out beatings because someone splashed water on your shoes? Build that rep. Get them talking. Do the dirty work with a grin and a joke? Do you think that makes you a hard man? A bad man? Like fuck it does. Hard men keep their mouths shut, and just get on with it. They don't have stupid names they shout about. They just do it. Bang, dead, and move on." The words poured out of Tony, a fury he couldn't dam any more.

The Red Pope knew never to show the slightest sign of weakness or confusion, but this was unlike any situation he had ever been in before. Instead he tried to mask his uneasiness with laughter. He had the gun. Mr Stark was here, watching. He had five men outside, in a quiet part of the city. He was in control. He was in control.

"Finished? Said your piece?" He lowered his voice, "I'd hoped to do you and your missus at the same time, but we'll find her. I mean, we found you before, didn't we?"

Tony glared up at the Red Pope, refusing to flinch. Daring him.

The Red Pope smiled, one more time, "Are you ready, soldier? Decorated man like you must've been ready for the end of a gun once upon a time."

Tony sighed again. He looked up at the Red Pope, the gun, and then to Stark.

"Can I tell you something? One last thing?" Tony was glowering at the Red Pope, driving his forehead into the barrel of the gun, almost challenging it to fire and interrupt what he had to say. "The problem with people like you is that it's been too easy. You've never had to work for something. You've just taken it, all nice and simple. So you don't do much thinking anymore. You break into my place, and you see all those photos and all those medals but you don't look at them. Not really. You just presume. Because, you stupid fuck, then you might have noticed something important. All those medals, all those photos? They're not mine."

Tony raised his hands, in surrender, then slowly interlocked his fingers behind his head, and bowed his head. The Red Pope still had the same confused expression on his face when the first bullet hit him.

A muffled crack rang out. The Red Pope staggered backwards, a gout of blood bursting up from his neck. Like a boxer trying to find his feet after a knockout punch, he staggered backwards, a gurgle coming from deep within his ruined throat. As he floundered, clamping a hand to the hole in his neck, the Red Pope saw everything with the clarity of the dying. Tony had pulled himself to his feet, reaching down to take the Red Pope's pistol from where it had fallen. Colours were fading now, as his life poured from him. He fumbled for Cold Cut's phone, from his inside pocket, but his hands were slick with his blood, and the phone squirted out, onto the floor, like a bar of soap. Stark was still sat in the chair, eyes wide, the purest terror on his face as he realised that his house of cards had fallen down around him, and he had lost his grip on anything that resembled control, set adrift in his own panic.

"It was my fault, really. I got sloppy," Tony said.

The Red Pope, confused, lost, dying, could do nothing

but listen as Grace's voice faded out. "One little mistake, and you found us. But one mistake doesn't mean that I'm an idiot. Or maybe I might be, but my wife certainly isn't." He waved the gun over his shoulder, indicating vaguely to something through one of the glass windows now spider-webbed with a bullet-hole. "We still keep some things hidden away for a rainy day. Still have a few friends who'll hold things safe for us. My wife's rifle, for one. Just in case."

As if on cue, more shots echoed around the riverside. An unstoppable rhythm as Eleanor, from her perfect position on the cab roof of the small crane in the car garage in the adjoining plot, took down every single one of the Stark crew with ruthless efficiency. The Red Pope was dead – the light gone from him, finally – Grace turned his attention to Stark.

"You killed two friends of mine. Daft twats, but still, my friends. My friends. Then you came to kill me and my wife."

Stark gripped the side of his chair with both hands, a white-knuckle ride he didn't know how to escape. His mouth was flapping like a beached fish, eyes wide and white, and his head shaking as if he could deny everything and find his balance again. It was too late for that. Stark's mind was overloading.

ELEANOR GRACE WALKED into the room.

She found her old self still fit her perfectly. She loved the new life she'd built with Tony, and had put this old her in a closet at the very back of her mind, keen to put as much distance between *then* and *now*. But it was still there. It was and always would be there. And now, at the sharp end, these men forced her to find it again. She had gone to see her old family. The family she knew she could always rely on, no questions asked. When she asked her old squad commander, he handed a bag of supplies over with a nod. If she wanted it, she needed it.

She was a soldier again. Boots, camo and face paint, hair pulled back into a ponytail. Her sniper rifle slung over her shoulder. Even without a spotter, she was lethal. There were five men face down outside and the Red Pope staring with dead eyes at her who were proof of that.

Eleanor took the gun from Tony's hand. Then she knelt down, so she was the same height as Jim Stark, who had collapsed to his knees, and spoke softly to him.

"You came after me and mine. When you're found, maybe someone else will learn something."

Then she fired.

42

The Graces walked out of the building free at last. But their night wasn't over yet. The highest hurdles were cleared, but now, they just needed to drift away becoming smoke in the wind once more. They had to leave this city forever.

The road was quiet. They were in a part of town that shut down once six'o'clock struck – even the houses on the estate on the other side of the road had long since learned that there was nothing to see down here after dark, and instead closed their curtains to their gardens, and fell into the arms of the plasma screen. The Graces were meticulous in their preparation. Cameras were spotted and avoided, and they'd planned for changes of appearance, and of transport, on their way out of the city. A gangland hit would be the story. Not a middle-aged couple that no-one had ever heard of.

Bodies littered the forecourt. Not one wasted shot. Sightlines perfect for two-thirds of that perimeter, and the other third behaved exactly as Eleanor had hoped, loyalties jettisoned as the bodies started falling, and escape the hope they ran towards. And as they ran, they ran into her sights, and she didn't miss once.

They didn't look back. Shoulder to shoulder, walking across the forecourt towards the gate, and the two cars doing their best to blockade it. Eleanor pulled at her zipped camouflage jacket, shaking herself free of it, before casting it aside like a shed skin without breaking her stride.

They reached the car. Cold Cut was still inside, paralysed with fear, too scared to run *then* and too scared to run *now*, knowing he had bet on the wrong side by staying, when he should've run as soon as the men started falling. Tony Grace paused as he reached the car, and tapped on the window.

Cold Cut pressed the button, despite his instincts, finding it easier to just obey than attempt any other lateral thoughts, and the window wound down with a whirr.

"You can have this back," said Tony Grace.

Tony tossed Cold Cut his phone, through the window, it landing on his lap like a live grenade. Eleanor put her hand on Tony's back, and looked down at Cold Cut. She smiled so warm and friendly that it would haunt Cold Cut's thoughts for the rest of his life.

Then they were gone. Into the dark, and away from this city forever.

EPILOGUE

Cold Cut found his thoughts ricocheting in his skull, a harsh static of information all fighting for superiority. One thought loomed large. Time. He had no time. Someone would be here soon. More of Stark's men, who would find this massacre and put Cold Cut in a little room again, until they decided to make him disappear forever. Or the police, who would leave him in a cell until he felt a hot blade in his guts next week, next month, next year sometime. He had no time.

He concentrated on just the simple operation of his limbs. His hand slipped on the door handle a few times until it found purchase, and the door swung open. He climbed out of the car, stood up straight, and looked up and down the road. He couldn't see the Graces but he knew which way they had gone. He looked back at the forecourt, slowly, hoping that he'd see no sign of the carnage, as if it hadn't actually happened, but the bodies were still there, unmoving. It was the jolt of reality that he needed. A shiver of energy, of electricity, of fear particularly, ran down his spine, a hot-wire impulse that demanded movement.

He had one last look at the forecourt, then, with tears streaming down his face, ran as fast as he could, as if the wild hunt itself was at his heels.

"Hello, Mum," Cold Cut said.

He'd inched into the common room as if he was expecting booby-traps. Half of the large room was dominated by a hotchpotch of high-backed chairs that were set up in a semi-circle in front of a large TV screen, loudly blasting out antique show banter with the subtitles five seconds behind. The other half had a large dining table, clear of any crockery now, and eight matching chairs pushed in underneath.

A nurse ushered him in, gently, with a warm hand on his shoulder. She'd seen this before, almost every other day, with some lost relative motivated to visit by duty, or guilt, or simply because they'd run out of excuses. Cold Cut had a different motivation. He'd seen dead bodies on the floor, his neck had been in a noose. But he'd been given new life and a blank slate, scared straight by mortality that was almost unavoidable. His way was the wrong way. He needed to be better, and safer, and maybe, happier. And he needed to find comfort again, and go back to where he was truly happiest – a boy safe in his family, surrounded by a million potential roads forward, and the only worries left to him were the words he would have thrown at him if he ran mud through the house. He needed his mum.

The chairs were all occupied, though for some, it was barely, cut adrift from a solid reality by failing minds, or failing bodies, moans and snores the soundtrack as the TV voiceover boomed perpetually. Bones were warped, old men and women hunched, hands clutched at nothing. Living, breathing souls sat calcifying becoming statues of their younger selves. Nurses busied in and out, checking residents like bees checking honeycomb, then off again, called to a far off part of the home by a ringing bell, or an insistent duty.

The nurse left Cold Cut stood by the door, as she too was called away. He inched forward, cap in hand, wrangling it absentmindedly as he moved towards the henge of chairs, looking like a Dickensian orphan, ready to ask for favour from some overbearing matron.

There she was. Undeniably. He hadn't seen her in years. Long, long years. But despite the rigours time had laden on her, there was still enough of her – the real her - in her face, and in her mannerisms, that he knew he was with his mother.

Her eyes were wandering, not settling on anything in particular, and her hands were scratching at the fabric on the chair she was sat in. Next to her was a small table, with a plastic cup filled with weak tea, and a small plate next to it. Every so often, she stopped scratching at the chair, and reached for a biscuit from the plate, but never quite managing to find one to grip and put in her mouth, instead just shunting the plate a few centimetres away from her on the table.

He stood next to her, looking left and right at the other occupants of those chairs to see if he'd been noticed, or was going to cause upset somehow. All but one of the old people there were ignoring him, with just one lone pair of eyes from a sharp-faced old lady with dyed-black hair, staring at him hawkishly. He smiled at her, but her expression didn't shift. He wasn't sure she really saw him at all.

Cold Cut knelt down next to his mum.

"Hi, Mum. It's me. It's Graham."

"Graham..? Have you seen him?" She shook herself to life, eyes finding some focus with Cold Cut close to her.

"It's me, Mum. I'm Graham. I've come to see you."

"My Graham. My Graham. Have you seen him?"

Cold Cut sighed, and his eyes started to mist and sting. She had gone. He was too late. Much too late.

"Son? Is that you? Where have you been?"

She was staring at him now with clear eyes. A cold, knotty hand had curled around his fingers.

"I've been lost, Mum. I've been lost." He sniffed loudly as the tears started to fall. "I've come to see you. I've come to tell you I'm going to change. I'm going to be better."

"Is that my son? Have you seen him?"

He sobbed quietly, bending his head and finding himself staring at the weave and pattern of the chair his mother was sitting in. His head was spinning – too many emotions were flooding in, for so long emotions that he had waved away, or smothered, the moment they showed any sign of bloom.

"Is it dinner-time yet?" her faded voice said, confused eyes looking up at him.

He found a solid ground. His eyes had cleared. His cheeks cooled. He stood up.

"Ok, Mum. See you sometime." He reached down and picked up the plate of biscuits. Just one left, iced and choco-late. Her hand swung up searching for them, eyes only on the plate. Cold Cut picked the biscuit from the plate, put the plate back on the table, and stuffed the biscuit into his mouth in one mouthful.

"Bye, mum," he said, through a mouthful of crumbs and icing, and walked out of the room.

ABOUT THE AUTHOR

More information about Craig Dawson can be found at his website: craigdawsonwrites.com

Please visit to sign up to the mailing list for updates. If you enjoyed this book, please consider leaving a review.

Printed in Great Britain
by Amazon

**Tony Grace is
running for his life.**

His peaceful existence is shattered when a past
he thought he'd put behind him comes crashing back
into his world. Old acquaintances unhappy that he left
them for a new life in a sleepy seaside town,
now want their revenge.

With his hopes and dreams in flames, the only
road left leads back to his past. Back to the gang
that wants him dead.

Tony can only do one thing - fight back or die trying.

NO SAFE PLACE is the debut novel from
a new, exciting voice in crime fiction.

ISBN 9798617632653

9 798617 632653